A FALL KILL

THE KILLING SEASONS
BOOK 4

JK ELLEM

D1519957

"In my hand, I hold an ax, warm, slippery, and wrapped in blood. Let the bloodletting begin."

—Carolyn Ryder

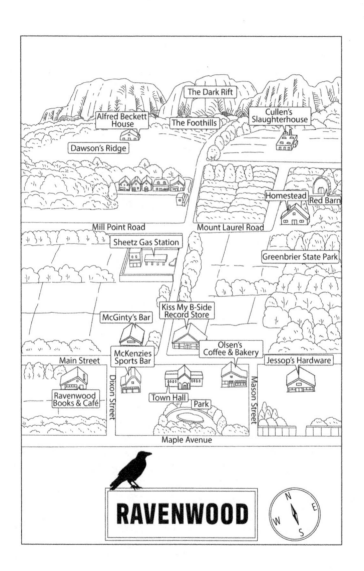

A FALL KILL

1

BEAU

I pass endless fields of swaying corn, tall, ripe, drooping with plump golden cobs ready for harvesting in the next few weeks.

The last time I was here, the landscape was cold and desolate. Stripped bare, dry, and glassy with sheets of ice, the ground was just yellow scrub and crop stubble.

Reaching the intersection, I turn and head east. Low foothills covered with forest rise in the distance. Hard maples flame in fiery oranges and rust reds while cottonwood, elm, and hackberry drip with deep, buttery yellow. The prairie grasses have lost their greens and now have soft purple hues. Beyond, low jagged peaks, bare of snow this time of year, cut the morning sky that rises in shades of smoky orange, then pale eggshell blue until reaching aqua blue.

Fall. My eyes, glassy with tears, take in the beauty of God's grandeur. I didn't think I'd see it anywhere—fall, except in my dark, dying dreams, let alone late October in Iowa.

A mile later, the entrance to the property comes into view, and a lump swells in my throat. He saved my life—carried me two miles through the snow and darkness to safety, leaving a third of his own body's blood in his wake.

The main house, surrounded by a scatter of smaller outbuildings, is as I remember. It is large and well maintained, built from a mix of brick, stone, wood, and steel sheeting, fashioned by one who has an eye for practical design, measured angles, and loving workmanship. There's no twist of woodsmoke rising from the large stone chimney built into the side of the main house.

Away from the main house sits a large red shed made from corrugated iron sheeting. The bear of a man who lives here is not a farmer. Inside the red shed, he spends his days shaping, bending, and folding sheet metal and tubes with his paw-like hands. He also hunts.

A massive pickup is parked next to the red shed. It's a battle tank of a beast, painted olive drab, with a huge front bull bar, a row of large spotlights, jacked-up suspension, and big deep tread tires—a true chariot of the apocalypse. And the end is coming. The circle is almost complete.

I park next to the pickup and get out.

The large outdoor cages made of tubular steel nearby are now empty and silent, thanks to Dr. Michael Ritter. Robin Hood. But in my mind's eye, I see ghostly dark shapes roaming restlessly back and forth behind the thick gauge mesh and hear their deep, guttural growls. My heart feels as empty as the dog cages. I'm still sad for the dogs, the man who loved them, and the fierce loyalty and love they gave him in return.

Inside the barn, arc light strobes across the walls, and the air is thick with the smell of ozone and burning metal. A man hunches over a small exploding sun of pure white light that, even at this distance, paints a moving ball of white on the back of my retinas.

Cautiously, I step closer, and there's a pause in the welding. The ball of pure white vanishes and his head swivels toward me as he rises to full height. His face is shielded by a thick helmet-like mask with a rectangular window. Like Gort, the fictional humanoid robot, he lumbers toward me, growing bigger with each step until he towers over me. With a simple flick of his head, the mask flips up, revealing his face.

Beau Hodges.

He's wearing heavy coveralls smudged with metal, grime, and grease and has on his heavy work boots—six feet tall, three hundred pounds of solid muscle and bare-handed neck-twisting menace. Shoulders like the wingspan of an albatross tapered to a sprint swimmer's waist. And the eyes. Oh... those calm, dark, infinite seas of hope and despair. Beau Hodges is quiet, unassuming, Rodin's *The Thinker*. Not a shy person but someone who ponders and is not prone to rash actions. Someone who prefers to think things through. He is a patient man, yet he has no paralysis by over-analysis. Qualities people often misjudge for being slow or simple —a deadly mistake. For when he moves in rage, the planet shifts a few degrees off its axis.

There is a Black Angel statue in Iowa. It stands many miles east of me in a small park with a brass plaque, almost hidden among the shrubbery. It is a monument to Ruth Anne Dodge, who was also dying of cancer when her angel visited her three times in her dreams before she finally died. I haven't died, but my black angel is now standing in front of me, not an apparition, but a mighty and powerful sculpture, nonetheless, made of flesh, blood, and bone, not bronze. And he's my Black Angel. Beau Hodges is my Gabriel to face Hell's Lucifer.

"Yes," he says.

I'm confused. Is it a question or an answer to a question I have not yet asked?

"Yes?"

Hodges shrugs. "You didn't come all this way to talk about the weather." He smiles, and my heart brightens to see it. "And you're not the sentimental type, Carolyn."

I must admit, no postcard, not even a phone call since we last saw each other in the hospital almost a year ago. I don't do friendly catch-up chats. My life doesn't allow for it. "How do you know how far I've come?" I ask.

He steps closer, and it's like I'm standing on West Thirty-Fourth

Street, looking up at the Empire State Building. He gives me an appraising look. "It's been a year. Last winter, but you look like you've traveled to Hell and back—some distance since I last saw you."

If only he knew, and he will, given time.

"How's the right shoulder?" he asks.

"Perfect," I lie. There's still that clicking noise if I move my arm a certain way.

"And your chest?" he inquires.

Thank God for body armor. "The ribs have healed." But what they encase and protect hasn't. My eyes shift first to his arm, then his thigh, and finally his torso. I am almost expecting to see a crossbow bolt buried in each. I was told it took six hours of surgery to remove all of them. "And you?"

That smile again. "Can't complain." He sighs. "But we got him. Ritter. We got him."

Ritter. It seems like eons ago. "You got him," I reply. "I just—"

"We both got him," Hodges repeats, his expression innocent but firm. He pulls off his welding helmet, tosses it onto a workbench, and then faces me again. "Like I said, yes."

"You don't know why I'm here. I haven't asked you anything yet."

He gives me a knowing grin. "You've found another."

"Another what?"

"A monster like Ritter, and you want my help, Carolyn." There's a glint, a spark of excitement in those dark eyes—hunter's eyes—like whenever prey is nearby. "And I'm in."

Now, it's my turn to smile. *Yes!*

2

BETH

Frank had taken an early retirement package from his job. It was a decent amount that added to the 401K money they had saved. In total, it was more than enough to retire comfortably in the nice, proper community in Florida where they had lived. Then, life took a wrong turn, and they ended up at a dead end.

The stock market fell, and their retirement savings took a hit. Beth Rimes, Frank's wife and a police officer nearly all her life, was three years shy of retirement and didn't count on her husband gambling away the rest of their retirement savings either. By the time she had discovered the cell phone Frank kept hidden from her and the five online casino accounts he had running, it was too late. She had almost pulled her gun out that fateful day and shot him herself.

It was all gone. All of it. More than forty years of hard work, sweat, and savings. Frank had even gotten into their home equity account and drawn money against it, maxing out the debt and gambling that away, too. They had to sell their home in Florida, a home Beth had planned to be their retirement home, where the grandkids could visit and play in their pool, where they would throw dinner parties overlooking the canal their house backed onto. The bank said it was either a sale or foreclosure. Take your pick.

Selling in a real estate downturn meant they had lost money. After paying off the fully drawn loan, Beth had placed what little cash was left into a separate account that Frank couldn't touch. She still loved him but hated how he had destroyed their later years.

They moved to a place where they could afford to live—Three Pines, Utah—in a trailer park that served as a daily reminder to Beth of how far they had fallen. It was a double-wide block even though it was about an eighth of the size of their ranch-style home on the water in Florida.

To keep her mind off their financial woes, Beth threw herself deeply into her job, into one case in particular. She had spent years searching for The Highway Killer, an elusive, cunning serial killer who had left a murderous trail of young women in his wake and a pile of unsolved disappearances that matched his MO—women whose bodies had yet to be found.

At the time, Beth didn't know his name was Samuel Pritchard— a man who drove trucks back and forth across the country, picking up women, then killing them. For Beth, finding him became her obsession, and she amassed a private catalog of police reports, victi- mology, and crime scene information that rivaled even what the FBI had on him. She had come close, really close, to apprehending him, only for him to slip away like a ghost in the night.

After that encounter, she finally left Frank, retired, and was now living off what meager savings she had at the inaptly named Seabreeze Mobile Home Park, Southeast Arcadia, Florida, where the closest sea breeze was a one-hour drive west to Venice Beach on Florida's Gulf Coast.

Beth stood in her tiny kitchen and stared down at her chicken and mushroom pot noodles. This was the third time she had eaten the gluggy, yellow mixture this week.

Car headlights flashed through the window, and a car pulled into her empty carport. She kept her .38 in the nightstand drawer and wasn't expecting any visitors. Pride ensured that no one visited her.

Then, a knock on the door, not a bang, just a courteous rap. There were forty-eight cabins in the trailer park, packed so close together on the dusty patch of land that neighbors would come rushing if anything untoward were to happen. It was that kind of community. Money was in short supply, but care and concern were in abundance.

Beth opened the door and momentarily thought she was staring at an apparition. "My God! C...Carolyn?"

Carolyn Ryder stood in the doorway. She was thin and wiry compared to when Beth had last seen her when they had sat in a bar in Utah, toasting each other with Tequila shots.

After the initial shock, Beth opened the door fully. "Come in." But first, they hugged on the stoop, and immediately Beth could tell the woman she was embracing was a pale shadow of her former self.

They sat on a tattered sofa, and Beth couldn't help but stare at Carolyn.

"I had cancer, Beth—a brain tumor. But it's gone now. I'm better."

Tears pushed into Beth's eyes, and she felt hollow in her chest. There was a deep bond between them, forged through shared pain, adversity, and personal, physical, and mental injury suffered together on the open road and deep within mine tunnels under mountains, chasing a villain who had gotten away with countless blood spilled in the aftermath.

"How did you find me?" Beth asked. Shame had made Beth not want to be found. Yet she knew this wasn't a social visit by her friend. Carolyn's face was a thin-smiled veneer, hiding something darker and disturbing.

"I called in a few favors," Carolyn replied. "I hope you don't mind."

Carolyn's next words struck both anguish and excitement in Beth. "I think I've found him, Beth. I think I know where he is."

Beth's mind stumbled as new questions, bad memories, gruesome autopsies, pictures of young women, bones and withered torn flesh in shallow graves, bodies, bloated and putrefying in the harsh sun, all came tumbling back. She swallowed hard, her throat dry. "Where? Where is he?"

"Maryland. A town called Ravenwood. I don't have eyes on him, but I'm certain he's there."

Disappointment came, and Beth said nothing for a moment. If anything, Carolyn was just as determined, resourceful, and relentless as she had been in pursuing Sam Pritchard. *Had been,* being the operative words. Speculation wasn't good enough. Beth had wasted and watched herself age all these years, speculating where Pritchard could be. Yet, Carolyn had tracked her down—found her to tell her she knew where he was.

"I know certain things about him," Carolyn continued. "Things that the authorities don't."

"I heard about Robin Hood," Beth said. "I saw it in the news. They said it was an unnamed female FBI agent who had caught him. I wondered if that was you. Willow Falls, Iowa? That's where your family comes from."

"That's where I buried my mother last winter—in Willow Falls, my hometown. Yes, that was me. Michael Ritter. Robin Hood. But I didn't kill him. He almost killed me."

Beth bristled. "Then who killed him? In the news, they didn't say much other than he had died trying to escape the police." After the news about Ritter hit, Beth spent the following months researching Ritter as much as she could. He was a brilliant cardiothoracic surgeon at one of Chicago's top hospitals, who hunted women with a crossbow for sport during his winter vacations, like Pritchard, a true monster. And Carolyn had caught him.

"Someone else killed him," Carolyn replied.

"I had a feeling that was you," Beth said. "In Iowa. You were the unnamed female agent." What Carolyn had said before about knowing where Pritchard was felt less speculative now—more factual. "How do you know for sure he's there and this is not just some wild goose chase?" Beth questioned.

"I can't be certain. But you must trust me. Something happened in the last few months—another case. A direct connection from that case led me straight to Pritchard and Ravenwood."

"Pritchard is nomadic," Beth countered. "He craves the open roads and highways. They provide him with endless possibilities for endless prey. Not to mention endless choices of escape. I dismissed him from settling down in any one place. He won't back himself into a corner in some town."

"He never had a reason to," Carolyn said, "until now."

"Why? What happened? What do you know?"

"Georgia."

Beth felt a surge of excitement run through her body. "That was you too?"

Carolyn nodded. "But he got away—again. I had to choose in the moment: kill him or save another."

"Kill him?"

Carolyn looked grim-faced. "No prisoners this time, Beth. He dies. No jury. No judge. No loophole or insanity plea. He's already been judged and found guilty by you and me. Carrying out the sentence is all that remains."

"Death," Beth whispered. As though shrouded in its billowing black cloak like it had just touched her shoulder from behind with its cold, bony finger. An unwelcome visitor if there ever was. Not for Pritchard, though. Since trying to shoot him in that hellish mine tunnel in Utah—and failing—Beth had wished nothing less on Pritchard but death, and not a quick and painless one at that.

"I made that same choice, Carolyn. Remember? Saving you and letting Pritchard go free, or going after him and letting you bleed out and die. It's the choices we make, not the mistakes, which define us."

9

Carolyn glanced at the small dining table, its surface buried under neat stacks of paper, open textbooks, folders bursting with newspaper clippings and scattered legal pads, the penmanship so determined that the pages curled into wrinkled, yellow scrolls. A row of bankers' boxes lined one of the fake wood walls.

She turned back to Beth. "You haven't stopped looking, have you?"

"No," Beth sighed. Surrounding herself every day with him was her lifetime's penance for not catching him.

"Then let me tell you how we can, together." And for the next half hour, Carolyn told Beth everything that happened in Erin's Bay —about Joel Renner, Dylan Cobb, and a brave young woman named Ellie Sutton, who had once been Emma Block.

And when she was done, Beth sat in silence for a moment.

"So, Renner was helping Pritchard and had suggested Ravenwood as a possible safe haven?"

"That's correct."

"And Renner discovered this from Dylan Cobb?" Beth had read about Renner and Cobb but never knew they were communicating with each other, let alone that Renner, AKA The Thriller Killer, was in cahoots with Pritchard.

"Yes."

"What do you want from me, Carolyn?"

"I want your help. I want you to come with me to Ravenwood."

"If he's there, won't he recognize us?"

"We're flying under the radar, Beth."

"Just the two of us?" Beth's skepticism began to grow. She wasn't getting any younger, and Carolyn had been badly injured before.

"I've got some help this time. And one of them is already on the ground in Ravenwood, keeping an eye out for him."

"How's the leg, by the way?" Beth said, scolding herself for not asking sooner.

"No problem. But I still need your help. I can't do it on my own."

"What about the crossbow bolt in your shoulder?"

"All healed. Just a scar."

Beth smiled. "You're like the walking wounded."

Carolyn didn't return the smile. Instead, she leaned closer, her voice low and menacing. "We both are, Beth. Scars on the inside. Scars on the outside. They're all the same. Now, it's time to end this. I don't want to go to my grave wondering *if only*."

Beth understood—deathbed regrets. "I know it's unfinished business for both of us. I don't want to die wondering, either. I would rather put a gun to my head and—"

A look of concern flashed across Carolyn's face, and tears welled up in her eyes. "Oh, Beth!" She took her hand in hers and squeezed it. "Please don't say it's come to that."

Beth looked away and wiped her eyes. "Just give me a moment," she said in a hushed voice. The pain was too much. It had to end.

"Take all the time you need, Beth. I'm sorry for the intrusion. I've upset you."

Beth turned back. "No. I meant give me a moment to pack my stuff."

3

HOMESTEAD

The property was along Mount Laurel Road, a two-minute drive east of Ravenwood.

It was a quarter-acre block backing onto Greenbrier State Park, along with a farmhouse and barn. The house had a large wraparound porch with wooden siding, sash windows, and a tin roof. It was a large, airy house but in desperate need of attention. A worn brickwork chimney ran up one side of the house. In its prime, the grand farmhouse would have been spectacular, but neglect, scorching summers, and brittle-cold Maryland winters had taken their toll. Someone had made recent improvements, though.

From the main road, a simple dirt track led to the property and split into two smaller, narrow tracks, one curving past the front steps of the porch, forming a circular driveway around a large cottonwood tree before rejoining the main dirt track while a second track angled to the right and led directly to the red barn.

Ellie Sutton thought the location was isolated, secluded, and perfect for the new occupants as she stood under the cottonwood, surveying everything. Admittedly, the place needed some work, but it was very livable. And the red barn was an added bonus. Already, she imagined that was where they would have their meetings to strategize their plan of attack.

She wrenched out the *For Lease* sign from under the cottonwood and made her way to the barn, where she tossed the sign into a large, hinged trash bin. A cold shimmer ran up both her arms. Looking up, Ellie saw a raven perched high on the peak of the front gable of the barn, an inky dark blemish on an otherwise flawless sky like a small tear on a light blue canvas. The raven craned its neck, one black eye looking down at her. The bird gave a shake of its head, ruffling its thick throat hackles before leaping and taking flight.

A thick chain had been tightly wrapped through the handles of the barn doors and secured in place with a brutish-looking padlock, preventing her from even slipping her hand through. There was one small sliding window on the west side, which she reached up and tried. A catch locked it on the inside, the glass coated with a grimy film of neglect, and the inside corners of the panes were laced with dusty cobwebs. She doubted the window would budge even if it weren't locked.

Moving to the rear of the barn, she noticed some of the wooden planks were rotted, warped, and crooked, like hillbilly teeth. Then she noticed three vertical planks stacked on the ground, leaving a hole where they had once been nailed to the rear wall—a hole large enough to crawl under the rail and between the wooden studs and into the barn. Ellie drew her gun from under her shirt, knelt, and then peered into the milky darkness of the hole. She couldn't see anything. Maybe kids had been inside.

She had the key to the padlock but had a better idea. If anyone were still inside, this would be their only means of escape.

With her gun pointing ahead, she dropped to her belly and, using her elbows, dragged herself through. Inside the barn, she stood up, dusted herself off one-handed, and looked around, aiming her gun wherever her eyes went. Narrow slits of light spilled through gaps in the wooden walls and through holes in the tin roof, bathing small sections in an ethereal, dusty glow. The air smelled of oil, grease, wood shavings, and human sweat. Workbenches with plywood tops ran along one wall. A wide assortment of saws, hammers, planes, and other carpentry tools hung neatly on a long pegboard above the benches, and above these were shelves made from rough, recycled planks that held a collection of glass jars and old rusty cans full of screws, nuts, bolts, and every fastener imaginable. Leftover boards were neatly stacked according to size and purpose. Paint cans meticulously sealed and labeled were stored in rows. Order and efficiency were everywhere—a place for everything and everything in its place.

The floor was dirt in some places, plain concrete in others, poured roughly and stained with a lifetime of hard work, dedication, and the unbridled satisfaction you get from making things with your hands. Patterns of oil, grease, paint, and maybe even blood stained the concrete, and weeds sprouted up from cracks, trying to reach the shafts of sunlight raking through the ceiling above. There was no large machinery. Ellie noticed a thick chain hanging from one of the exposed beams in the middle of the barn where the dirt floor beneath was plowed with the churn and skid of footprints.

It took her less than sixty seconds to search the interior. The barn was empty.

Taking a hammer and a box of nails, she crawled back through the hole in the barn wall and set about reattaching the planks. When she was done, she returned to the front of the barn, and using the key the estate agent had given her, she unlocked the barn doors and threw them wide open.

She then searched it a second time just to make sure no one had been occupying the place.

Ellie slid her gun away and then checked her watch.

After locking the barn up securely, she made her way over to the homestead. They would be arriving soon, and she had to get everything ready.

4

RAVENWOOD

Ravenwood was located eleven miles south of Hagerstown in Washington County, Maryland.

Set among rolling farmlands, narrow country lanes, and picturesque farmhouses, the town had a population of just over thirty-five hundred, according to the last census taken in 2010. It was also surrounded by numerous American Civil War battle sites and was steeped in history. The town itself was just off State Highway 66.

His first and only visit to Ravenwood was more than three years ago. A lot had happened to him since then. As he walked down the main street, the place seemed not to have changed during that time. On the surface, small towns rarely do, he thought to himself. The same quaint stores lined both sides as he remembered—practical establishments selling practical goods with an appreciative smile, not a bored smirk.

During the last few years, he had traveled through many small towns, yet Ravenwood was different. It had a homey vibe, the kind of place he could see himself—God forbid—settling down, planting roots. While he enjoyed his nomadic lifestyle, traveling the desolate highways and small back roads, a new discovery around each bend, and trouble, too, maybe it was time to stop for a while.

He walked past cafés, a farm produce store, and various grocery stores with fresh local produce stacked on the footpath in rough wooden crates. He could get used to being here, he thought as he walked under the Stars and Stripes hung proudly over doorways. The sidewalk was covered with a light scattering of fall's leaves, and a few stores had pumpkins clustered in the windows as decorations.

A friendly smile, a polite morning greeting, a welcoming nod, small-town politeness that felt genuine, warm, friendly, as though they had seen him just yesterday, walking the same route through town.

Yet, as he had felt during his last visit, something seemed odd about the place. It was like he was watching an old movie on cable, and the voices and mouths moving were slightly out of sync—not poorly dubbed—just a misaligned soundtrack of everyday small-town life.

Right on cue, Jessop's Hardware appeared across the street.

Whoa! Ben Shaw stopped and looked into the deep, dark, charred hole between buildings where a coffee store and bakery had once stood.

Olsen's, he thought. That was the name. He remembered the rendered brick exterior, brown and beige, contemporary stone edging, and dark green awnings like giant hooded eyelids over huge bay windows. Last time, it seemed like everyone in the entire town was inside, lining up for coffee. Through the bay windows and brightly lit interior, he had seen the dark wood veneer, rustic brickwork, and chalkboard menus that hung from the ceiling. A long, brightly lit glass display cabinet dominated the front counter and was filled with neatly stacked white plastic trays of cookies, brownies, muffins, bagels, and pastries. Now, all that remained was a charred, gutted carcass of twisted wooden ribs, blackened sheet metal, and a huge pile of ash. The roof was completely gone, and only one soot-smudged side wall remained.

He continued, passing McGinty's, a bar where he had shared drinks with a friend.

Much to his relief, a familiar sight came into view across the street.

Ravenwood Books & Café. Thrilling books and sinister coffee!

The store was warm and cozy, just as he remembered. Shaw felt instantly at home among the polished wooden floors, exposed brickwork, and piano-black floor-to-ceiling bookcases crammed with hardcovers and paperbacks. In a place like this, he could easily whittle away the hours just drinking coffee, reading, and watching the world pass by the large front window with cobwebs draped in each corner, complete with a few impossibly large black spiders.

However, unlike last time, when he was the only customer, the place was packed. Business had certainly picked up since he was last here. Thankfully, a table by the front window with a clear view of the street and the sidewalk on both sides was empty, so he dumped his backpack on the chair.

On the way to the counter, he paused at the same round table he remembered that sat in the middle of the store. This time, however, instead of the latest releases forming the spiral staircase centerpiece, ghost stories and horror books corkscrewed upward with neatly stacked paranormal paperbacks ringed around the outside.

Shaw picked up a copy of Mary Shelley's *Frankenstein* with the monster, its hideous face warped and disfigured, on the cover. Fiendish black eyes seemed to drill into his soul.

Working a gleaming stainless steel espresso machine, a woman with a dishcloth draped over one shoulder turned from behind the counter and smiled at Shaw.

"Hello, there!" she said cheerfully while the coffee maker made hissing and spattering sounds. She took one look at Shaw, and then her eyes popped. "Or should I say welcome back?" The woman's smile grew wider. "You were in here...." She made an expression of thinking. "My, it must have been three years ago."

She was petite, with dark hair fashioned in a short bob, dark brown eyes, pretty, mid-forties, with the physique of a twenty-year-old.

The woman had the same genuine smile and bright, attentive eyes that had greeted him before.

"Jenny?" Shaw queried, pointing a finger at her.

"Ben," she replied, mirroring his finger pointing with a chuckle. "You remembered."

"So did you."

"It wasn't hard. That Ben & Jerry's joke I made last time about our two names. You know. *Ben and Jenny's.* That we should start a rival ice cream company."

Shaw smiled. She did have a good memory.

"Double shot espresso?"

"That's right." Shaw was impressed. *Three years. Wow.*

"Coming right up. Take a seat."

Shaw turned to see that while he had been talking, the morning patronage had now thinned to just an older guy with dark hair at a table against the wall, typing away on a MacBook in a bright orange case, and an elderly couple seated near a corner bookcase labeled *Thrillers.*

Jenny came with his coffee and carried a small plate. "Poison pumpkin muffin," Jenny said proudly with a gleam in her eyes. "On the house."

Glancing down, Shaw noticed she wore the same bright red quilted sneakers she had on last time.

"Business must be booming," he said, watching as a teenage kid carrying a large plastic tub began clearing away cups and plates that were stacked on several tables.

Jenny blew her bangs with an upturned lip, then sat on a spare chair. "You just caught the tail of the morning rush. It's the first moment I've had a chance to take a load off all day. It's been crazy and all, especially this time of year." Her eyes darted to the muffin on the plate. "Baked them myself this morning, and they're damn good if I do say so!"

She touched Shaw gently on his hand and lowered her tone as though they were the only ones in the place. "I'll let you in on another little secret. It's not really poison," she whispered. "Just a dark chocolate sauce in the center."

"That's a relief. In that case, I'll buy a dozen to go."

Jenny's eyes lit up. "You will?"

"Yep. If you can box them up."

"No problem."

"So, tell me," Shaw said, "what happened to Olsen's, the bakery and coffee store a block away?"

"Well, it was the darndest thing," she said with a theatrical lilt in her voice and a tilt of her head. "About a month ago, Olsen's just burned to the ground one night—no rhyme or reason. It went up like a bonfire. No one was inside, thank God!"

Shaw took a bite of the muffin. It was warm and spicy with a delicious gooey sauce that just oozed out. "This tastes amazing," he said.

Jenny beamed at him, then gave him another wink. "I knew you would enjoy eating my muffin," she said.

A piece suddenly caught in his throat, and he coughed, then sipped his coffee.

"The fire department said it was like spontaneous combustion," Jenny continued. "The investigation was inconclusive."

"Someone else's bad luck is another person's good fortune," Shaw said as he studied her closely.

"Sure was," she said with another wink. "You staying for a while this time?"

"Maybe. I'm looking for someone."

"Oh. And who might that be?"

The door opened, and a young woman entered. She was lean, with short brown hair. She wore a Baltimore Ravens ball cap and dark sunglasses, and a fabric face mask covered most of her face. As

Shaw watched, her head moved ever so slightly to him, then to the man working away on the MacBook, then to the elderly couple near the Thriller section before returning to Shaw. She slipped off her sunglasses, then peeled away one loop of her mask from her ear, leaving the other loop in place so the mask was left dangling from her other ear.

"Hey, Allie," Jenny said.

"Hi, Jenny. Just my usual, thanks." The woman then moved away and began browsing the round table of books, running her fingers across the covers thoughtfully.

Jenny got up. "No rest for the wicked." She gave Shaw a mischievous grin. "Just make sure you come back and say goodbye before you leave this time."

"I will."

Jenny walked back to behind the counter to serve the young woman.

Ellie Sutton took a mental snapshot of the man seated at the window: lean, late twenties, dark hair and eyes, sharp features, faded blue jeans, white T-shirt under a weathered brown leather jacket, and sensible boots capable of getting the wearer out of most sticky situations.

An aura—suppressed menace mixed with boyish good looks—seemed to surround the man like an invisible but dangerous force field. While she hadn't seen him in here before, she figured he wasn't a threat—and definitely not Pritchard.

A worn backpack sat parked on a seat next to him. A tattered, well-thumbed book lay open on the table in front of him, various pages crammed full of what looked like bus tickets, train tickets, and traveling paraphernalia repurposed as bookmarks.

"Here you go, Allie," Jenny said, sliding a takeout cup across the counter.

"Thanks." Ellie paid for the drink.

"How are you settling in?" Jenny asked.

"All good," Ellie replied, taking a sip.

"And those articles you're writing about small-town history for that magazine you work for? How are they going?"

"They're coming along. I might need to come back and pick your brain about any interesting locals you have here I could interview." She looped on her face mask and slid her sunglasses back on.

"No problem. See you around."

As Ellie headed to the door, she shot the guy another glance, almost expecting to catch him looking at her. But he was disinterested, staring intently out the window at something across the street.

Shaw gazed out the window, wondering if this was the right town. Could he really be here? Shaw had left a message on Haley Perez's cell phone. He had run out of ideas and needed her help finding him. Six long months of searching had resulted in nothing. Yet, the man's face was burned into Shaw's memory. He finished his muffin and drank the last of his coffee. Maybe this was the wrong town. Maybe he wasn't here. Now, he began to doubt if he would ever find him. He glanced out the window again—and jolted in his chair.

Just like the other time when he had sat in this exact spot, she was again standing on the opposite sidewalk, rigid like a statue, people milling around her like a school of fish swimming around an obstacle. She was looking directly at him from across the street, her piercing eyes boring deep into his head. She had reverted back to her natural blonde hair, not the unruly nest of raven black he had last seen. And the thick, heavy-looking burial shroud she had worn last time was replaced by the light and airy cornflower blue dress he'd seen in the photo her heartbroken parents had shown him.

Shaw blinked hard, but Lettie Harrison, the eight-year-old dead girl from Ghost Crossing, Nebraska, didn't vanish. She remained standing across the street, watching him.

Then she smiled and waved—a small wave just meant for him. Then she began nodding at Shaw. The answer meant for no one else but him to his question no one else heard but her.

Yes.

5

HALEY

"Haley, it's Ben. Ben Shaw. Look, don't call me back. I'm at a gas station just outside Harrisburg. I'm coming to Ravenwood, and I really need your help. I need to find someone. Thinking about it now, I should have contacted you sooner. I'll explain everything when I get there. See you soon."

Detective Haley Perez stared at her cell phone, then played the message again.

Harrisburg? That was about eighty miles north of here along I-81. The message was left around eight this morning. It was now almost midday. Was he here now, in Ravenwood? Eighty miles wasn't far, and Ben wasn't the type of person to loiter around when his mind was made up. Mind you, it had taken three years to hear from him again.

Calling from a payphone? He had no cell phone, so Perez couldn't call him back.

Haley Perez, twenty-five years old now, had started as a rookie police officer in the Uniform Patrol Division of the Hagerstown

Police Department three years ago when she had first met Ben Shaw. With an associate degree in law enforcement, she topped her class at the academy, the only female in the entire cohort. She was a loner, introverted, and sometimes socially awkward—according to her superiors. She was half Puerto Rican, half Colombian. Perez wore her pitch-black hair in a tight ponytail. Her striking hazel eyes had a mysterious quality to them.

The Hagerstown Police Department was housed in an old brick building that was once the Western Maryland Railway Station, and she was just one of eight detectives in the criminal investigation division. They hadn't yet replaced Nate Garland after his horrific demise.

"I ain't got all day," Kershaw bellowed through his open office door at Perez.

Snapping back to the present, Perez slipped her phone away, entered Kershaw's office, and closed the door behind her.

Brandon Kershaw, Perez's sergeant, didn't look happy. He sat with his thick arms resting on his desk, glaring at Perez, who stood opposite him.

Brandon "Fred" Kershaw was one of only two sergeants in the Criminal Investigative Division of Hagerstown PD who supervised the detective pool. Perez was the youngest and, according to most of her more seasoned colleagues, the least experienced. Females were in short supply in the Hagerstown PD, with Perez being the only female detective on the roster. Kershaw and Perez's mentor, the now-retired Detective Marvin Richards, were instrumental in fast-tracking her to junior detective in the CID after the Eden Killer case had concluded. Now, she had been promoted to full detective.

On Kershaw's desk sat an open box from Ravenwood Books & Café, and inside were what looked like twelve orange muffins drizzled with thick icing. Someone—Perez guessed it was Jenny Langdon, the owner—had also placed a fake plastic spider inside the box.

"These arrived for you at the front desk," Kershaw grumbled. "Damn spider scared the bejesus out of me!"

They called him Fred after Fred Flintstone because, like Fred Flintstone, Kershaw was short, squat, barrel-chested with thick arms and neck, and had an unruly mop of dark hair. And like his cartoon namesake, Kershaw could often be heard hollering from one end of the detective's squad room to the other. Kershaw was hard but fair, wanting the best from his cohort of detectives.

"They're pumpkin, not orange," Kershaw explained. "And I didn't taste one if that's what you're thinking."

He slid the box toward Perez. "There's also a note."

She picked up a small envelope taped to the box and read the front. *Detective Perez.* She didn't recognize the handwriting. Inside was a note. *McGinty's. 6:00 p.m.*

No name, but she knew who it was from. She came off her shift at five, which meant she had enough time to get home, shower, and change.

"Seems like you have a secret admirer," Kershaw smirked, looking at Perez as though she would elaborate.

Had Kershaw read the note? Without saying a word, Perez pocketed the note. Maybe not so secret after all, she thought to herself.

"Anyway, that's beside the point." Kershaw gave a dismissive wave. "That's not why I called you in."

He shoved a police incident report at Perez like he wanted to stab her with it. "This statement was taken around 2:00 a.m. by Patrol Officer Daniels. Just like the others, no crime was committed. The woman, Denise Glover, reported seeing someone looking through her bedroom window."

Perez scanned the report. It seemed like the others. Late-night disturbance. Hooded figure, most likely a male, looking through a bedroom window. Reports of trash cans being knocked over in the middle of the night. Footprints—possibly a hiking boot—found in surrounding garden beds. No actual breaking and entering. However, the insect screen at two locations had been partially slit with a knife, not ripped, leaving enough gap for a hand to slide in and force open the window. Again, the perpetrator hadn't entered the home.

They had dubbed him the Peeping Prowler inside the department simply because that was all he had done so far—peeped into women's bedroom windows at night. Nothing more. Yet there was a clear pattern here: young women living alone, in single-story dwellings, with no pets, no forced entry or otherwise, at night, and all within a mile radius of each other.

There were no leads so far. What concerned Perez and Kershaw was that it might be only a matter of time before the *Peeping Prowler* escalated his nocturnal peeping and broke in and sexually assaulted a woman, or God forbid, something worse.

"I need a progress report on this, Perez." Kershaw eyed her impatiently. "I want women to be safe in their homes and safe out on the streets in Ravenwood, day or night. Word of this prowler is spreading. And the mayor"—Kershaw twisted his face, as though under the desk he was having a rectal examination by someone with really big fingers—"was on the phone this morning, up my ass, wanting to know if we've made an arrest."

The Peeping Prowler Case file on Perez's desk was anorexic. Five other incident reports were sitting inside, all similar to this one and very little else—a few photos of footprint impressions taken from garden beds and a map of the area.

At all the scenes, windowsills, sliding doors, front doors, back doors, and any likely external surface the prowler could have touched had been dusted for prints. Nothing. They had worn gloves each time, Perez had concluded.

Patrol officers had door-knocked the neighborhood, yet no one had seen or heard a thing. Perez had also conducted some demographic research. The neighborhoods in question had a high population of dog owners, as well as several legally registered gun owners—mainly women.

It was as though the *Peeping Prowler* didn't care. He was either a risk-taker, confident, or just stupid. Perez didn't think it was the latter.

"What progress have you made?" Kershaw asked, eyeing the muffins in the box.

Perez decided that the best form of defense was being bluntly honest. "I've made no further progress." She glanced at the incident report again. "But I will personally call on Denise Glover at home this afternoon and talk to her. I'll also make it a priority to go back and visit the other women tomorrow." Perez knew that, while patrol officers took detailed reports and were thorough in their questioning, sometimes having a detective right in front of the person who made the call seemed to open up their memory door slightly more, recalling details that they had either forgotten or simply didn't think were relevant at the time.

Perez's response seemed to appease Kershaw—for the moment.

"Well, keep me in the loop," Kershaw said, the scowl on his face fading slightly. "I need some solid progress on this case by the end of the week. Otherwise, the mayor is going to chew me a new one." He gestured regretfully toward the box of muffins. "Don't forget your muffins."

Perez slid the box back toward Kershaw. "I'm on a diet. Knock yourself out. Let the other detectives have some, too."

"Free muffins in Kershaw's office," Perez called out, heading back to her cubicle, then stepped aside to avoid the stampede. Sitting at her desk, she placed the latest incident report into the file. Then, leaning out, she glanced over her shoulder at the photo on the noticeboard and the words beneath *#1 Most Wanted*. Dark, fathomless eyes stared back at her as she thought for a moment.

She shook her head. No chance. If it were him, then all six women would be well and truly dead by now.

6

REVENGE

They sat in McGinty's bar, and Shaw bought the first round.

"It's hard to believe we sat in almost this exact spot just over three years ago," Perez said. "And your arm was bandaged back then."

"No thanks to Malcom Rodney Boyd."

Shaw had been passing through Ravenwood, heading east, when he became embroiled in the case of a young woman named Bridget Wilson, whom Boyd had abducted. At first glance, Perez took a real dislike to Shaw's abruptness and disregard for authority, yet begrudgingly teamed up with him to locate where Bridget was hidden.

"And you had just caught the Eden Killer and were made junior detective," Shaw added.

"For my sins, yes." Perez sighed. "A lot has happened since then." She wanted to know what Shaw had been up to since then.

"For both of us," Shaw replied.

"The guys back at the station said thanks for the muffins."

"No problem."

"I often drop by Jenny's place when I can. She can be a hive of information about the town—fact, not gossip." Perez noticed a touch of darkness had crept in behind his eyes, his smile not so authentic as when they had first arrived. After they had caught Malcom Boyd and rescued Bridget Wilson, Perez's opinion of Shaw changed dramatically. She found herself drawn to him as a fellow law enforcement colleague. He was... unusual—brash and determined to do good, even if it meant bending or breaking the rules. He'd told her about his past, how he used to work for the U.S. Secret Service until he got fired for punching the vice president—an act in itself that pretty much summed up his persona.

She was also physically drawn to him. On more than one occasion during the last three years, her thoughts had drifted back to him, wondering where he was and if he was thinking about her too.

Perez took a swig of her beer and then spoke again. "I remember what you told me about small towns and how things—bad things—tend to be hidden in places just like this."

"I remember. The worst kind of villains hide in plain sight." Shaw gestured around with his bottle; then, his eyes settled back on Perez. "Why? What happened after I left?"

Perez leaned forward. "What you said that time when we were sitting here. About James Moriarty. The arch nemesis of Sherlock Holmes. You suggested that perhaps there was someone similar to Moriarty who plagued Holmes—always there in the background if you just looked hard enough."

"Did it help?"

Perez reached into her pocket and placed the worn, crumpled napkin on the table.

"You're kidding me," Shaw said, picking it up in disbelief. "You kept it?"

"It's a daily reminder of what you said. And it helped me catch —well, stop a true monster who was hiding right under my nose in this very town." The name Perez had written on the napkin was faded but still legible.

James Moriarty.

"I even bought all the books from the Ravenwood Books & Café and read them," Perez added.

"I'm impressed," Shaw replied, handing back the napkin. "But I really did nothing. You're a terrific detective, Haley. I knew you would figure it out. You deserve all the credit. Let no one tell you otherwise."

"So, where did you go after here?" Perez asked, her cheeks a little hot from the compliment. Or was it the beer? Or was it Shaw? "What have you been doing for more than three years?" After over three years of silence, she wanted to get to the reason for his call.

"I spent three of those years just traveling around, taking odd jobs when I needed the money, and didn't really settle down in any one place for too long. Saw some of Alaska too. Then I ended up in a small town called Bright Water in New Hampshire. Stayed in a log cabin up in the mountains."

His eyes grew darker. "But before that...." His expression altered. The look you get when bad memories, black and oily, start seeping to the surface, like how bad memories surfaced for Perez about her mother and father and what she had done as a child.

He continued. "But before all that, and after we met here in Ravenwood, I traveled to Long Island first and spent awhile in a beachside town called Erin's Bay."

Perez felt a tingling sensation in the back of her throat. Erin's Bay? Why did the name sound so familiar? Then, it hit her like a landslide.

"Go on," she said. It was like she was standing at a door she didn't want to open, for behind it lurked one of the darkest demons she had ever crossed paths with—Dylan Cobb.

For the next twenty minutes, he gave Perez an intricate, first-hand account of what had unfolded in the town of Erin's Bay while he was there. When he was done, he looked wrung out from describing the unimaginable horrors that were obviously still preoccupying his mind.

"Dylan Cobb?" she said in disbelief. "It was you who caught him in Erin's Bay? You were involved with the Brenner Case, too?"

"I left before the police could question me. Let's just say I value my anonymity, and I'm glad he was caught and thrown in prison. He deserves to spend the rest of his life behind bars," Shaw said in a seething tone.

Perez regarded Shaw for a moment. Did he not know about what happened to Cobb *after* he was sent to prison for his sins in Erin's Bay?

Shaw looked up. "What?" He tilted his head. "Do you know Dylan Cobb?"

"Not as intimately as you, apparently," she replied.

"What do you mean? What happened? He's still in prison, right?"

Perez nodded. "But he came here, to Ravenwood." Perez knew she had to explain to Shaw what had happened. "You didn't know?"

"Know what?"

"Wow! You really have been off the grid all these years, haven't you? Since you left Erin's Bay."

"Like I said, I was on the road for years. I kept to myself. I wasn't really interested in Dylan Cobb after he was arrested. Why? Tell me."

"Dylan Cobb served only three years of his sentence for what he had done," Perez said.

Shaw's eyes went wide. "You're kidding me."

"I wish I were," Perez replied. "He did a plea deal."

Shaw sat back, shaking his head.

"And when he got out, he came here to Ravenwood and killed a young woman."

Shaw's face twisted, not in pain but in anger—visible, raw anger. "But he's back in prison? You caught him again? Here in Ravenwood?"

"I did. I put three rounds into the bastard."

"And he survived?"

"Monsters like that are hard to kill."

"You should've put the three rounds into his head," Shaw said, his voice a low, seething growl. "And there's no chance he can get out?"

"He's in maximum security again. Multiple life sentences. No chance of parole ever. He ain't getting out."

Perez wanted to change the subject. Thinking about Dylan Cobb was making her feel... dirty and stained. Apart from being a total psychopathic multiple murderer, he was a master psychological manipulator who screwed with people's minds long after they lost sight of him.

"Why did you call me, Ben? Why the cryptic message you left on my cell phone?"

Shaw reached into his leather jacket pocket and slipped out a piece of paper without saying a word. He unfolded it and then slid it across the table toward Perez. "I'm looking for this person."

Perez looked down. It was a sketch, two sketches of the same man. A cold, bony hand suddenly gripped her heart, slowing its rhythm. She looked up at Shaw. "You're kidding me, right? You're looking for *him*?"

"Him?" Shaw replied. He sat up and leaned closer, his voice anxious. "You know him?"

Two heart-stopping revelations in one night. Perez couldn't believe her bad luck. "You really have been living under a rock for the last three years, haven't you?" She rotated the sheet toward Shaw and then tapped it with her finger. "This guy's picture is plastered in every law-enforcement office from LA to New York. From Alaska to Hawaii. Interpol, too."

"Well, for the last six months, I've been looking for him as well," Shaw replied.

"You and everyone else. Why are you looking for him? Have you suddenly become a bounty hunter? A vigilante that needs to track down the worst of the worst?"

"No," Shaw replied. "That's your job."

"So why the sudden interest in this person? He's the most wanted man in all of America."

Shaw's eyes narrowed, then he rolled up the sleeve of his right arm, all the way up to his elbow, and turned his forearm toward Perez. "That's why."

From the wrist up to the bend of the elbow, the skin was warped and blistered. He had suffered an excruciatingly painful burn all the way along his forearm. "Christ," she whispered. She looked up, and their eyes met. "What happened?"

Without replying, he rolled down his sleeve, gestured to a passing waitress, and ordered two more beers.

Now, there was a deathly look in his eyes that Perez had only seen in the most ruthless of killers.

"Let me tell you why I want to find him," he said.

7

DEADLINE

Beth was the first to arrive, preferring to drive herself from Florida rather than hitch a ride with me, and both Ellie and I greeted her at the homestead.

An hour later, Beau Hodges arrived from Iowa. Thankfully, he hadn't brought his Mad Max end-of-the-world pickup truck. Instead, he settled on a smaller, less obtrusive pickup truck.

I had arrived a full day before and was delighted to see Ellie and the work she had done on the homestead to get it ready. The fridge was well stocked, and there was enough bed linen and towels for everyone, thanks to Ellie.

After introductions were made and sleeping arrangements sorted out—the homestead is large enough that everyone has a separate bedroom, and there are three bathrooms to share—Ellie gave the others a quick tour. We then decided that the red barn would be our "war room" to strategize and plan our attack.

Under the guise of a journalist/blogger, traveling through the Northeast, visiting places just like Ravenwood for a book she was writing on small-town America, Ellie had already scoped out the town and surrounding area and had spoken to a few locals. I liked her change of appearance; it was less severe than her previous look. It's all about blending in and not standing out.

Around town, she said her name was Allie, not Ellie, a name she deliberately chose so that if she accidentally introduced herself as Ellie—the name she had made her own—she could quickly and easily put it down to someone not hearing her correctly. Clever.

Before I knew it, it was dusk. The vehicles were parked around the back to avoid prying eyes, and we were all at the rear of the homestead, sitting under a starry fall sky in front of a log fire on Adirondack chairs Beau had found inside the barn.

I then began explaining some basic ground rules. Ellie, as Allie, was the only one to go into Ravenwood for supplies while doing reconnaissance, staying well away from the local cops. For exploration farther afield, the rest of us would go as a group without her. I didn't want too many new faces in town.

With my police scanner, I would monitor local chatter. At the same time, Ellie would keep an eye on any goings-on in the town, continue talking to locals, pretending she was doing research on Ravenwood for her book while quietly inquiring if there had been any recent incidents of missing women, reported stalkings, a spike of break-and-enters, or anything out of the ordinary. Unlike Erin's Bay, I pray that if Pritchard is really here, then the first true indication isn't a body suddenly turning up. Ellie had also struck up a casual relationship with the local bookstore and café owner Jenny Langdon. According to Ellie, Jenny seems to be plugged into everything in the town and the surrounding area.

"What about Dylan Cobb?" Beth asked.

It's fully dark, and there's a cool fall chill in the air. I glance at Ellie. We, including Beatriz Vega, had discussed paying Dylan Cobb a visit in prison. But I can't risk that Cobb might immediately notify Pritchard of our presence.

Ellie speaks. "We have to assume that if Joel Renner was in contact with Pritchard, as well as Dylan Cobb, then Cobb and Pritchard are now also in direct contact with each other, given that

Renner is dead." She hands around photos of Renner, Cobb, and Pritchard for all of us to see.

"The axis of evil," Beth says, flames glinting in her eyes.

"So, what is the plan of action?" Beau asks. He's been characteristically silent up until now, listening and watching the fire. He brought two hunting rifles, his best, he told me, together with both day and night scopes. Somehow, I get the feeling we won't be killing Pritchard from a distance, like an unsuspecting deer grazing in a field. It will be up close, brutal, and bloody. And some of us may not make it to the winter.

"That's what we need to figure out together," I say. "That's why you're all here."

"Do you really think he's here?" Beth asks.

"I have to trust my instincts. We know for a fact that Renner told Sam Pritchard about Ravenwood, describing it as a safe haven for murderers like them. Renner found out about this by contacting Dylan Cobb, who was again caught here. In this very town."

"The same town that was home to the notorious Eden Killer," Ellie adds. "Caught by Haley Perez."

I nod. Ellie has been busy researching online what she can about Ravenwood.

Ellie goes on. "She's now a detective in the Hagerstown Police Department. Perez apprehended the Eden Killer a few years back while she was just a patrol officer—a rookie fresh out of the Academy. She then rocketed to prominence." She hands out a photo of Perez. "She was also responsible for apprehending Dylan Cobb a second time after he had been released from prison. He spent time inside for what he did in Erin's Bay three years ago."

"Pritchard is not going to be walking down the main street like everybody else," I say. "He won't want to be seen in public because of his injuries."

"He'll move around at night," Beau says, his voice flat and lonesome, like he's talking to himself. "Go hunting after dark."

"He might even wear a mask," Ellie says. "Like how I do in town until I definitely know he's not around. Plenty of people still do, and no one seems to care. There was no mask mandate here, so I can't imagine getting into a fight in Walmart or a 7-Eleven. If questioned, I just tell people I've got a cold, and they should appreciate the gesture."

I turn to Beth. "What are your thoughts, Beth? You've done more research into him than any of us. Will Pritchard ever stop?"

"Unlike the two of you," she says, referring to Ellie and me, "I've never really interacted with him up close—face-to-face like both of you. In that mine tunnel in Utah, it was just his silhouette. But my Spidey senses told me it was him."

Spidey senses? I smile.

"But that silhouette was like a black hole, sucking everything into it. It was pure, heartless evil. I felt it." Beth shivers, gets up, and then throws another log on the fire, sending a shower of orange cinders spiraling into the black heavens. Then she sits back down. "Will he stop? No. He never will. If anything, I imagine he'll speed up, escalate, especially after what you did to him in Georgia." She looks at each of us individually before speaking again. "He's not human, not of this world."

"Ritter was no different." Beau stirs like a giant coming awake. He looks at me. "And we killed him." He pokes the nearest burning log with the toe of his huge boot. "Pritchard is no different. He's not some mythical beast out of Greek mythology that can't be killed or can rise again from the dead. He's human. He will bleed. He will be killed."

"So, how do we hunt him?" I ask. "How do we lure him out into the open?"

Across the rippling air above the flames, I can feel Ellie's eyes burning into me. I know what she's thinking. A conversation we once had comes back to me—about her being bait to coax Pritchard out when we were just biding our time in Erin's Bay.

Beau looks at me. "You know how we do that. It's how Ritter hunted all his victims."

Christ. I'd almost forgotten. "A kill plot." Everything is coming full circle. "Except Pritchard is the hunted," Beau says.

Beth and Ellie exchange glances.

Hodges goes on to explain what he means. "It's like setting a trap. Clearing a narrow plot of land, then planting it with fresh young saplings to entice young deer to come out from their hiding places at dusk to feed."

"Like a crocodile hiding in the murky depths of a watering hole, waiting for a gazelle to come to the water's edge and drink," Ellie says, a hint of excitement in her voice.

"I like how you think." Beau nods thoughtfully at Ellie, his voice low and deep.

Ellie smiles, which is extremely rare these days. They seem to have become instant friends, and it troubles me.

Then comes the inevitable question from Ellie, nonetheless, accompanied by an unnerving smile. "So, what do we use as bait?" She shoots me a look, and I know what she's thinking. She wants to be the bait. *The girl that got away.* I've already explained to both Beth and Beau what happened to Ellie in Georgia—how Pritchard and Dolores Gruber abducted her.

Ellie looks around the group as though it is a foregone conclusion. "It has to be me."

Beth suddenly looks horrified. Beau rubs his chin, pondering—always a hunter.

"Without some kind of bait in the kill plot, you're just relying on pure luck that Pritchard will come stumbling out into our crosshairs." He then looks pointedly at me, and I know I've just been ambushed by the two of them. Beau and Ellie had already discussed this during one of their little huddled discussions I've seen them having away from the group despite only knowing each other for a few hours.

"And if you recall, Carolyn," Beau addresses me, "that's exactly what happened in Willow Falls with Ritter. You went to his cabin and rattled his cage. You made yourself the bait."

Ellie cocks her head like she's just check-mated me. I'm incensed. "And if *you* recall, when I went there, I had no idea who he was at the time. I didn't know he was Robin Hood. I was just accepting a dinner invitation."

"Nonetheless, you got his attention," he says. Beau doesn't back down, much to Ellie's glee, as she watches on. They seem to be aligned in their thinking of how to corner Pritchard.

"You made yourself bait, Carolyn, didn't you?" Ellie presses on with her argument. Courage is one thing; mindless bravado is another.

"I guess I did, in a way. But then Beau and I returned to his cabin. We went after Ritter together."

Ellie slides to the edge of her chair and slaps her thigh. "Exactly!" she declares. "You didn't wait around for Ritter to come hunting you. You turned the tables and went after him, and that was after you enticed him out of hiding. He had no choice but to reveal himself to you."

"It wasn't like that!" I protest.

"Look, we will never know what Ritter was thinking," Beau interrupts.

Ellie starts to look slightly unhinged, her eyes darting about.

Beau continues. "We must deal with the here and now. We have options. They are limited, but we have them, nonetheless."

"They're not the kind of options I want to consider." Beth throws her hat in the ring—on my side.

"We must," Beau replies. He turns to Beth. "Otherwise—as you said yourself, he will escalate, kill another woman."

Ellie sits back, her face defiant. "We can't wait around for a young woman to be murdered. I've said that before."

And with that, we're back to square one. All faces turn to me, the leader of this little rag-tag posse. What do we do? I need to make a decision.

"We'll give it forty-eight hours." I look at Beau as I speak. "Then, if there's nothing, we will then set up a kill plot for him—lure him out."

Some of the sting goes out of Ellie's eyes, and perhaps I see a slight smile there now. Not the kind of smile you expect from winning a small victory. It's more like I've just caught a glimpse of something sinister under her skin.

"But I'm going to be the bait," I hasten to add, making sure there is no misunderstanding. "No one else. Just me." I look poignantly at Ellie.

Her unnerving smile is still the same.

8

PERSONAL

"What makes you think he's here in Ravenwood?" Perez asked.

Shaw had spent the last twenty minutes explaining to Haley Perez how he had been abducted while hitchhiking along the road outside the town of Bright Water, New Hampshire, by Sam Pritchard in his truck. Pritchard had offered him a drink that had been drugged. Shaw estimated he'd spent three days in the company of Pritchard, swinging in and out of consciousness.

Perez knew he wasn't telling her all the details, other than he had seen an opportunity on the third day to escape and took it.

"It's just a feeling I get," Shaw said, looking around.

Perez noticed two women playing pool nearby who seemed to spend more time glancing in Shaw's direction than focusing on the game.

"I think he's here."

"But he didn't mention Ravenwood, did he?" Perez asked. To her, it seemed highly unlikely that Pritchard was here. He was a truck driver with the entire country at his disposal. There would have to be a good reason for him to come to Ravenwood. From what she had read about Pritchard on internal law-enforcement bulletins and updated reports, he, like Shaw, was a drifter who saw the open roads and highways as his domain—a whole backyard of lawlessness.

"What's the latest news you have on him?" Shaw asked. "That's why I'm here. For your help."

"There isn't much new information on him—no recent sightings, at least. Something happened in Georgia a few months back in a state forest there. He killed people and kidnapped a teenage woman, but she escaped. He slipped through the police cordon and vanished. The trail has gone cold ever since. I need more than a hunch, Ben, to think he's anywhere remotely close to this town."

"What about Dylan Cobb? Maybe they're in contact."

"What makes you think that?" Perez asked. It was something she had not considered. Had Cobb been following Pritchard's exploits? Admiring him as one would admire a peer? Cobb had a history of aligning himself with notorious murderers like himself. What had happened in Ravenwood was a testament to that.

"I'm just putting it out there," Shaw replied. "I've run out of options, and it's not unheard of for prisoners and killers who are running free on the outside to be secretly communicating with each other. How much freedom does Cobb get on the inside?"

"Cobb is locked up in a prison cell," Perez replied, "at a maximum-security facility."

Shaw shook his head. "That means nothing. You know that anyone on the inside, especially someone like Cobb, has reach and influence that can extend well beyond the prison walls."

Perez thought about it for a moment. If Cobb was communicating with Pritchard, and Perez seriously doubted it, would Cobb tell her if she asked? She had no intention of ever coming face-to-face with Dylan Cobb again. Cobb was a compulsive liar and psychological manipulator of the highest order. She had already lost her soul once to him, and she didn't intend on losing it again through his insidious machinations, cryptic games, and twisted mind.

"There's also a one-million-dollar reward on Sam Pritchard," Perez said. "You should leave it to the police."

"This is personal," Shaw replied, anger in his eyes. "I'll find him with or without your help."

"But in six months...." She didn't finish what she was going to say. What she meant to say was that Shaw had made no progress in six months. It was like he was wandering around lost. No plan. No direction. He was extremely capable, though. Finding Bridget Wilson and saving her had proven his abilities beyond a doubt. And if anyone could find Sam Pritchard, it would be Ben Shaw. He just needed a little help.

"So, where are you staying while you're here?" Perez asked. He looked like he desperately needed a shower and a shave.

His gaze softened. "I was thinking of crashing at your place—on your sofa if you have one."

Perez went to open her mouth, then closed it. It wasn't such a bad idea. While he was in Ravenwood, it would be easier for her to keep tabs on him if he did stay at her place. Especially if he was determined to continue with this vigilante crusade of his. Keeping Shaw close at hand, in sight, was much better than him disappearing into town and her constantly wondering when he was going to pop up and what mayhem would ensue.

"No problem," she replied.

Her answer seemed to surprise him.

"But you're not sleeping on the sofa. I have a spare bedroom. You're welcome to it while you're here in Ravenwood."

"You'll help me then?" His eyes brightened.

"Of course, I will help you. But I don't think you'll get anywhere here. I think you're wasting your time."

"We'll see," Shaw replied with a boyish grin on his face. "I might get lucky."

Perez got the double meaning and shook her head, even though she laughed. "Fat chance there, Freddie."

9

ROOMIES

Perez's two-bed apartment was cozy, functional, and where Perez called home.

It was an open plan with living and dining areas and a decent-sized kitchen. It also had a small balcony overlooking a street below lined with small grocery stores, a deli, and various cafés and convenience stores.

It was a busy, vibrant little neighborhood block, and after moving in a few years back, she soon became known as the "nice young lady cop from the block," a tag she didn't mind. Elderly people would nod and say hello to her in the street. Teenagers and kids would keep her up to date on local gossip as they congregated outside a deli or on street corners. They never saw her as a threat or feared her as a cop. She was nice, courteous, and, most of all, respectful. These little things allowed her to tap into the vibe of the local community and keep tabs on trouble before it escalated.

It was after 8:00 p.m. by the time Perez and Shaw walked through the front door.

After showing him the spare bedroom, she insisted he take a long shower before they ordered Thai food from her favorite local restaurant. While in the shower, she threw his clothes, minus the leather jacket, into the washing machine.

Ten minutes later, Shaw emerged from the bathroom and had changed into clean jeans and a fresh T-shirt he had packed in his backpack. "You're like a snail," she said, eyeing him. He was clean-shaven, and the white T-shirt clung to his skin like it was wet. Which it wasn't. She had to stop herself from staring.

"You said to take as long as I wanted," he said, drying his hair with the towel.

She pointed at his backpack, which lay in the corner of the small living room. "I meant it as though you seem to carry all your worldly possessions on your back. How long have you been living out of that backpack?"

"A while," he said sheepishly. "I travel light. It's got everything I need inside it."

"I'm sure it does," she said, shaking her head.

They walked a block, grabbed the takeout—which Shaw insisted on paying for—then returned, sat on the floor at the low coffee table, and ate.

She didn't want the complications of a man in her life right now, but it was nice not to eat alone for once. And she liked Shaw, trusted him.

Previously, Perez didn't care for men. It didn't worry her that she wasn't in a relationship like some of her friends, like Annabel Chandler, the chief of ER surgery at Ravenwood Hospital. Most men Perez had met on those rare social occasions ended up being Neanderthals, primitive oafs who did nothing but eat, sleep, drink, and watch television, or—on the other end of the male spectrum—were self-obsessed, groomed like poodles, usually had Mommy issues, or took selfies of their puckered faces and ranted about their softer, compassionate side.

At this stage of her life, she found nothing appealing about the male species. Maybe she just hadn't met the right type of man, not that she had met many men as it was. Most found her intimidating, abrupt, or just plain rude, which she wasn't.

Ben Shaw wasn't like either of these, as she watched him closely now. He was... just different. Attentive. Didn't try to talk over you with an inflated opinion and have this subdued menace about him. He was pragmatic and could make a decision fast, and when he did, he acted even faster. Most of the time, he was calm and considerate. Then there was that other side to him. A side she had only seen once when they were chasing after Malcom Rodney Boyd in the drainage tunnels under the town. It was like a switch had been flipped inside his brain, and he went into a torrent of ruthless determination, throwing aside his own safety to save Bridget Wilson. *God help anything or anyone who stands in his way.*

"So, what's the plan?" Shaw asked, helping himself to another pork dumpling.

Perez wiped her mouth on a napkin. "I'll do some more digging tomorrow on the LE databases on Pritchard and scan the recent updates. But I can tell you now, Ben, don't get your hopes up. He's not here."

"Any local missing persons?" Shaw asked.

"None that fits his target profile. Young women under twenty, typically blonde. Beauty pageant or college cutie look."

"He took me."

Perez paused. That was true. "And you didn't report it?" Perez imagined Shaw would enact his own form of justice if someone wronged him or those who couldn't take care of it themselves.

"No. That's not my style." He let out a long breath, the frustration evident on his face.

"Oh, damn!" Perez cursed. She had totally forgotten.

"What? You know something?"

"No—I mean yes. Damn!" Perez dumped her plate onto the table, quickly got to her feet, and pulled out her phone. She checked the time on the screen. Not too late. She thumbed through her notebook and then dialed a number, covering the mouthpiece as she whispered to Shaw. "I was supposed to call in on a woman today. Denise Glover. We have had a recent spate of a reported peeping prowler."

Shaw got to his feet.

Denise answered, and Perez apologized, saying that she was leaving the station now, and if it's not too late, could she drop by and talk to her about her report? Denise agreed and ended the call.

"A prowler?" Shaw said, disappointment in his voice.

Perez grabbed her jacket off the sofa. "Come for the ride. Keep me company."

Shaw got to his feet. "Come with you to take a statement? I'm not a cop."

Perez threw him a smile. He certainly didn't look like one. But she'd think of something. "Who knows? You might learn something," she added, grabbing her keys and gun.

10

ALL DARKNESS

She had pruned the bushes outside the downstairs living room window just last week. But there it was again—that distinct, incessant scratching sound on the glass like fingernails slowly moving up and down the pane.

For the last hour, Stephanie Dance sat safely ensconced in her warm bed upstairs, perched up on plush pillows. Steph's evening had been peacefully quiet except for the murmur of the wind under the eaves and Sade's smooth voice drifting from her cell phone on the bed next to her. And just when she was getting to the good bit in the utterly boring and drawn-out thriller book that TikTok had made her buy, that damn scratching sound had started up again.

Dana's Dark Reads on TikTok was usually good with her book recommendations. But not this time.

Steph checked her watch. It was almost midnight, and she knew she should've gone to bed two hours ago. She needed to be up at six for her shift as a nurse at the Ravenwood Hospital. Eight hours of sleep—that was what you needed to function properly. And stupidly, like swiping through TikTok videos on thriller book recommendations, she had persisted with another few chapters of this shitty novel (that she should have DNFed yesterday), hoping and praying that it would get better. It miraculously just did. Finally, someone was about to be murdered!

Steph put the book down and listened again. Nothing now. Maybe it was her imagination, the sound downstairs. She rubbed her eyes and reached for the lamp on the nightstand—then the sound again.

Christ! It was definitely coming from downstairs. But how could it be those damn branches on the glass? She had cut them back. Right back.

Cursing, she threw off the covers. Barefoot and dressed just in her pajamas, she trotted into the hallway outside her bedroom and looked over the balcony.

Like twisted skeletons, thin shadows, tree branches swaying in the wind, played up the wall along the stairs leading down to the front door. Moonlight, ghostly blue, shone in through the front door glass. A shiver went up Steph's spine as she hesitated. The sound had gone. But she was certain she had heard it. She turned to go back to her bed when the scratching sound floated up again from downstairs. Steph paused and went to the top of the stairs. Except for the wedge of moonlight coming through the front door glass, the rest of the downstairs was draped in thick shadow.

The sound was definitely coming from the living room. *Those damn bushes!* Maybe she had missed one, and it was now scraping at the glass in the wind.

Feeling very pissed off, she trudged down the stairs, not bothering to turn on the light at the bottom, and stepped into the living room. More spindly shadows swayed across the walls and furniture as she looked around.

She felt it first before the sound came—a new sound. A creak on the floorboards—behind her.

Steph whirled around.

A figure was standing right behind her—all darkness. No face. No anything. Just an outline. A body drained of all light but filled with skin-prickling evil. Steph felt boneless as she stared at the person.

"Hello, Stephanie."

She backed away, her voice stuck in her gullet.

He followed her.

The back of her legs hit a side table. A vase toppled and smashed on the floor. Steph stumbled, and shards of glass stabbed into the soles of her feet. She gave a muffled cry of pain.

A powerful hand clamped over her mouth, and an arm wrapped like a serpent around her waist.

Breath, warm and moist, curled into her ear. "I've been waiting for you."

11

STENCH

There was a chest freezer in the garage.

He had seen it, opened it, looked inside. It was nearly empty and more than adequate. But no. He wanted her to be found, but not today. In a few days. Not next week. It was important. Special. In his mind, it was the beginning of the end. And all good things must come to an end.

When things come to an end in our lives, we typically slow down—ease back and play it safe. Not him. With the end in sight, he was going to sprint all the way to the finish line. Leave nothing. Leave no one.

In the darkness of the kitchen, he steadied himself against the counter as another blinding fissure of light cut through his skull. It was like one of those old magnesium powder flash bulbs detonating behind his eyes, blanching the world white. He closed his eyes, and for a moment, he could see all the blood vessels inside his retinas reflecting back.

The skull-splitting pain began to subside; then everything came back into focus in muted color. That was a bad one, lasting longer and cutting deeper than any of the previous episodes. They had started a few weeks ago. At first, one every few days, just a sharp pain up one side of his skull—no distinct pattern or warning to them. Then daily, usually at night. Then twice daily. Day or night. It didn't matter. Now, they come every few hours, escalating in duration and intensity. Longer. Deeper. More time was needed to recover. It would only be a matter of time before time ran out, and there would be no recovery. The fissure inside his head would split and stay open, letting out all the brightness that would consume him.

Going to a doctor or an ER wasn't an option. It would be a sure death sentence. Nevada. Utah. Kansas, Georgia. Lethal injection. And his deteriorating condition was enough of a death sentence. The end. *His* end. Better than at the hands of someone else with him strapped to a table and a needle in his arm.

Plans had to change, be brought forward, and sped up—cramming what he intended to accomplish in the next ten years into just a few days. While physically impossible, he was determined to do his best.

That was why, in two days, not tomorrow, it would be special. It wasn't his birthday. It was something better. He hadn't celebrated his birthday in decades. In two days' time, it would be the culmination of all his future Christmases at once—like getting all his presents for the next ten years in one go.

It was symbolic, meant to be. Fate. Destiny. The timing was so perfect. It was meant to be. His worsening condition was meant to be. His being here, in this place, was meant to be.

The door to the pantry was already open. With gloved hands, he lifted and carried her inside, then placed her propped up on the floor against the shelves. He didn't stage her. He never staged anyone.

When he was happy, he stepped back and looked at her. This was where she belonged. She looked like she was taking a nap in the pantry among the canned beans, vegetables, pickles, flour, pot noodles, rice, and herbs—a nap she would never wake up from. A nightmare that her family and friends and anyone whose lives she had touched during her short life would never wake up from either.

He looked around. Perfect. While the pantry was cooler than the other parts of the house, it wasn't cool enough to prevent the decay from starting immediately.

By morning, there would be a smell, faint at first, growing stronger by the hour. Then, in two days, a dry-retching stench would draw the attention of a nosy neighbor, a curious parcel delivery guy, or the drive-by thief who came to steal the package left on the porch by the same parcel delivery guy. The kind of smell that wouldn't make you gag when you opened the front door. Not even when you hesitantly stepped into the kitchen, wondering if someone had left a leg of pork out on the counter from last week's shopping. But when your brain led you eventually to the source, and you opened that pantry door... That was when you'd drop breakfast, lunch, dinner, and anything else you ate in the last twenty-four hours right there onto the kitchen tile.

He left the pantry door open so some of the smell would permeate throughout the rest of the house, then went back through the sliding patio door. In the darkness outside, he paused and looked across to the small security camera with the red blinking light under the eave. He had spotted the camera after he had scaled the back fence and had given it a wide berth. He didn't want it to spoil his fun.

Now, he approached the camera through watery moonlight and positioned himself right in its path. Then, he looked up directly, showing his face in full. He didn't pose. He didn't smile. He just stood there, looking up at the camera for a good ten seconds.

Satisfied, he turned and walked away, vanishing into the night.

12

PROWLER

Shaw sat upright in his seat and watched through the windshield as a dark shape stepped out between two parked cars about twenty yards away.

Ordinarily, he wouldn't have paid much attention. In the twenty or so minutes since Perez had gone inside the house to interview Denise Glover, Shaw, while sitting in her sedan, had seen three other people in the dark, lit street: the middle-aged woman walking her Labrador dog, a man in dark shorts and running shirt jogging and wearing a headlight band, and another person whom he couldn't tell was male or female, on a mountain bike.

This person was different, though. It was in how they moved—almost guiltily. Shaw was a master of observing people, in particular their body language. As Shaw continued to watch, the person's gait could best be described as cautiously quick, as though they were leaving the scene of the crime and carrying a slight limp, as though favoring their right side as they went, their head rotating left and right, scanning the street, seeing if anyone was watching them.

And Shaw was. Closely.

Perez had parked in the shadows, away from the nearest streetlamp, and while it was a clear night, it was not enough to illuminate the inside of her vehicle where he now sat.

There was also something odd about the person's shape. They were tall and heavy-set, but their head... seemed disproportionate, like overly large.

Reaching the other side, where no cars were parked, the person stepped onto the sidewalk, stopped, then turned back and looked in Shaw's direction.

Instinctively, Shaw slouched down in his seat. He could sense the person was looking straight at him.

Slowly, he undid his belt buckle with his left hand while his right hand reached for the door handle, his eyes still fixed on the person. Could they see him? He didn't know how. It was too dark. He shrugged off the seat belt, and with his eyes still focused on the person through the windshield, he reached his hand up, fumbled, then found the internal light cluster on the ceiling and flipped it to the off setting so it wouldn't come on when he opened the door.

The person began walking toward Perez's vehicle, stepping back onto the road, staying away from streetlamps, and making a direct line toward Shaw.

Shaw gently pulled on the door handle, and the door popped open silently. The internal light had, thankfully, remained off.

Next, he slipped his right leg out.

The person stopped in the middle of the street, maybe twenty yards away. It was just a featureless shape, a large box-shaped head.

Shaw stopped moving, his foot hovering inches above the sidewalk, one leg protruding from the car.

The person took another step forward and stopped again.

Shaw eased himself out some more so that he was half in, half out of the car.

Suddenly, the person turned away and ran.

Shaw leaped out, slamming the door behind him, and took off after the person.

They had seen him. But why run? Was it the prowler Perez had mentioned? The Peeping Prowler? He was going to find out.

The person was fast, but he was certain he was gaining on him as he sprinted down the middle of the road.

Cutting right, the person ducked between two parked cars, ran across the sidewalk, vaulted over a small hedge, and into the front garden of a house that was in darkness. Shaw followed, rounding the corner of the house, which opened into a narrow stone path with a tall hedge on one side between the homes. In the distance, a dog began barking, then another farther away.

Shaw tore down the side of the house, the person's hunched shape bobbing twenty yards in front of him. Shaw was closing the distance.

The person went up and over something, a low wooden fence.

Shaw followed moments later, landing in a flower bed between two spindly bushes on the other side. Crouching, he waited a few seconds to get his bearings. The moon painted another backyard in a ghostly twilight; a flat lawn with a scatter of shapes loomed into focus. A trampoline. Swing playset. Table and chairs under a pergola. A corner sensor light on the opposite side of the yard then triggered, dousing the backyard in yellow light just as a shape disappeared around the far edge of the house.

Shaw jumped up and began running, weaving through a mine-field of kids' toys lying haphazardly on the lawn.

Halfway across the backyard, Shaw picked up movement to his left; something dark, low, and fast, ears pinned back, was streaking toward him like a torpedo but bristled with fur. Then came a frothy, wet growl: feral, guttural, and, unfortunately for Shaw, ravenous sounding.

The dark torpedo took to the air and crashed into Shaw's side.

A dog, massive, squat, ass-face ugly, and with a skull full of gnashing teeth, dropped back down onto the ground on all fours before bouncing immediately again, snapping up at Shaw's face.

Twisting to his left, he swung his right arm across, his hand bunched into a tight fist, and delivered a blistering right hook that slammed into the muzzle of the dog just as it reached the top of its next leap. The dog's massive meathead bucked sideways; then it did a full pirouette in the air before collapsing to the ground unconscious.

Undeterred, Shaw kept going and sprinted toward the opposite corner of the backyard, where he'd seen the person disappear around the edge of the house.

Moments later, he burst into the front yard of yet another house and stumbled onto the street, looking up and down frantically. Then he saw movement, a shape bobbing between the trees on the opposite side, sprinting away from him.

Shaw took off again, running across the street, ducking past a parked motorhome, then across another front lawn toward a low chain wire fence he'd seen the person just jump over.

Reaching the fence, he went over in one leap—and was met with the full force of a fence picket across his chest. Shaw collapsed sideways but managed to stay on his feet.

The fence picket came again, this time vertically, aimed at his head.

Shaw stepped sideways, and the blow glanced off his shoulder. He staggered sideways and looked up. A dark shape loomed forward, wielding the piece of wood again like a Viking's battle ax. The person towered over him, broad-shouldered, their bulbous head just a dark outline against the moonlit sky.

They raised the wood again, ready to smash it onto Shaw's head.

Shaw ducked like a boxer, and the piece of wood struck the side of the house, then snapped in two.

Seizing the moment, Shaw rocketed his right hand forward and under the person's outstretched arms, punching his attacker deep in their midsection.

They gasped, recoiled, and dropped the piece of wood.

Shaw's vision then exploded with stars. His attacker had delivered a punch of their own that went crashing into the side of his head, just above his left temple.

Dazed, Shaw staggered back before collapsing into a row of rose bushes. He staggered to his feet and shambled around the side of the house and into the backyard. He looked around wildly.

A rear porch light flipped on behind him, and a screen door flew open. Then came the all-too-familiar sound of a shotgun being racked. "Don't move, mister, or I'll blow your brains out."

Raising both hands first, Shaw slowly turned around. He could make out the silhouette of a woman standing on the porch with a shotgun aimed at him. Her wispy nighty backlit by the porch light was almost translucent, her shapely figure like an x-ray.

"Sorry," he said. "I mean you no harm. I was actually chasing a prowler."

He went to step forward, and the woman spoke again. "One more step and I'll send you into the afterlife."

Fair enough, Shaw thought, standing his ground. "I'm not armed. But you can call the police. Ask for Detective Haley Perez. Get them to put you through to her cell phone. She's interviewing someone a few blocks from here. I'm with her. She knows who I am."

The barrel of the gun dipped a few inches. "You a cop?"

"No."

The shotgun barrel returned to its original position. "Then move again, and you won't see your next birthday."

13

SADDLE UP

After breakfast, I rounded everyone up back inside the barn, a map of the town and surrounding area on the wall. There are several red crosses marked on the map.

Now, all eyes are on me. Forty-eight hours. That's what I promised everyone yesterday, or I'll be used as bait for Pritchard if he's here.

"So, what's the plan?" Beau asks.

I don't have a plan. But I'm not going to tell them that. "Search and assess," I say. "Get the lay of the land. Ellie is our eyes and ears in the town, and we can search farther out."

"Anything on the police scanner from overnight?" Beth asks me.

I point to a street on the map. "Just a woman reporting a prowler in her backyard here. Apparently, it was nothing. Mistaken identity, the police called it."

I turn to Ellie. "I want you to go into town today. Keep up your inquiries."

Ellie nods.

I turn to Beth and Beau. "The three of us will check out a few of the out-of-town locations Ellie has marked on the map as possible locations where Pritchard could be hiding. I doubt he's going to be renting a place in town. He'd be too visible. We'll take your pickup, Beau. It has tinted windows dark enough for people not to be able to see us inside. Bring your rifle as well."

All of us are armed and have the required permits to carry.

I turn back to Ellie. It was she who bought the map a few weeks back and set it up in the barn, so she's familiar with the local landmarks and what had recently happened in Ravenwood. "Ellie, what can you tell us about the place?"

She moves to the map, and we all gather around.

"As you know," she says, "the Eden Killer was caught here over three years ago. So was Dylan Cobb after he was let out of prison."

Starting at the town's main street, Ellie works her way outward. Dawson's Ridge is the first marked location out of town. She explains there is only one house up there, and the rest is heavily wooded.

She points out an elementary school north of the ridge and a church. With her finger, she traces an arc behind the church's landmark over an expanse of green, marking the foothills and the start of the forest. A scatter of thin, spidery dashed lines mark trails, while thicker full lines mark back roads. "North of the church begins the foothills that lead to an expanse of forest," she continues. A few miles farther, the terrain peaks and is marked with one of her red crosses.

"What's that location?" I ask.

"It's called the Dark Rift," she replies.

"The Dark Rift?" Beth pulls a face. "Sounds ominous."

"And why did you pick there?" Beau asks.

"The foothills are riddled with mine shafts and boreholes from back in the day, dug out or blasted out with dynamite by wildcat miners."

"How do you know all this?" Beth asks. She shoots me a look, and I think back to that network of mine tunnels in Utah, where she and I had encountered Pritchard together.

"I spoke to a retired geologist who lives here named Alfred

Beckett. He is the town's oldest resident. It's his house that's up on Dawson's Ridge. Jenny from the bookstore café said I should pay him a visit. So, I did. I told him I was looking for interesting locations for the article I'm writing. Up there is an old borehole, one of the largest he had ever seen. It was drilled out by miners back in the sixties. According to him, the hills up there are littered with them, not as big as this particular one he mentioned. Some of the smaller ones were sealed off, but plenty weren't.

"Dynamite was then used to blast this particular massive hole shut. Instead, it sheared the surrounding hillside, wrenching a wide, jagged rent across the bore, turning it into a wide, deep rift. Hence the name, the Dark Rift. Beckett said the entire hillside is now a labyrinth of deep crevices, narrow trenches, bottomless sinkholes, and rocky fault lines. The original borehole now looks like a wide gaping, open wound."

Beth steps closer. "It could be the perfect spot for someone to hide. I also imagine it's popular with young kids—teenagers. A place where they go and do whatever they do. That might be a problem for someone who's hiding out."

Ellie picked that location as Pritchard has a history of hiding his victims in abandoned mines, caves, and... fallout shelters.

"Are there any suitable spots up there where he could be hiding?" Beau asks. "Like old miners' cabins or shacks?"

Ellie shakes her head. "No idea. I haven't been up there to take a look. There is an access road here." She taps the map with her finger. A black line meanders through the foothills as the elevation lines tighten together. "It stops, then maybe under a mile on foot to the actual place."

"We'll come back to that later, Ellie. That's good work. What else have you got?" There's another red cross she has marked.

"Cullen's Slaughterhouse," she says, moving her finger to the spot.

"Slaughterhouse?" Beau asks.

"Correct. It was closed down decades ago. However, here's an

61

interesting fact. It was where Dylan Cobb was hiding out when he was caught. He had abducted a woman and had taken her there. Apparently, Cobb turned one of the underground rooms into some type of torture chamber."

Ellie looks at me, and I can tell what she's thinking. Did Joel Renner know this about Cobb, and did he pass that information on to Sam Pritchard? It sounds like common knowledge around the town. But would Pritchard know of this place as well?

"Do you think it's a viable hiding place for Sam Pritchard?" Beth asks, turning to me.

I step closer to the map and study it for a moment. A slaughterhouse. It sounds ominous and intriguing at the same time. Judging from the map's scale, it's only four miles out of Ravenwood. Secluded and isolated, it's likely to be a large structure full of abandoned rooms and basement areas.

"What else do you know about the place?" I ask Ellie. "Alfred Beckett. What did he say?"

Ellie smiles. "He was also an absolute treasure trove of knowledge and local history. The Cullen family owned it—it had been in their family for generations, going back to the eighteenth century. It was closed down in the fifties... something about chemicals leaching into the soil and ending up in the creeks. Beckett seems to think that all the buildings are still standing. He also said that it is part of local history that people around here would rather forget."

I turned back to everyone. "What do you think?"

Beau nods. "Seems logical."

"It's definitely worth checking out," Beth says.

I look at Ellie. "It's on my list," she says.

"Then, it's settled," I say. "Today's plan, as discussed... Ellie, you will go into town and see what else you can find out. And the rest of us are going to this slaughterhouse. We'll check out the Dark Rift after."

"Let's saddle up," Beau adds.

14

MAP

"Are you certain you didn't get a look at their face?" Perez asked. "Anything will do."

"Like I said last night," Shaw replied, "it was too dark, and they may have been wearing a hood or something. But it was definitely a male."

They were sitting at the kitchen counter, drinking coffee.

Perez thought for a moment. "Did it look like they were going to or were already leaving from a place?"

"What do you mean? Like leaving a possible crime scene?"

"I'm just trying to figure out... when you saw them, were they about to do something, like break into a place, or had they already done something?"

Since last night, there had been no reports of prowlers or break-ins around Denise Glover's neighborhood, where Shaw had seen the person and given chase.

"I think they had just come from a place," Shaw replied. "It's how they moved—like they were leaving in a hurry. Not loitering like they were about to commit a crime and just waiting for the right chance. They seemed guilty, like they had already done something."

Perez nodded. She understood, even though Shaw hadn't gotten a look at their face. It was all about how people behaved. Their demeanor, their posture, whether they loiter, meaning they're about to break the law, or if they are quickly and purposefully moving away from a location after they've already committed a crime. But nothing yet had been reported. Maybe Shaw had gotten it wrong. Maybe he caught them in the act, about to perpetrate a crime, and scared them off.

After Perez had finished up with Denise Glover, she was leaving the house when she received a call from a woman who said there was an intruder in her backyard, and his name was Ben Shaw. As Shaw had the keys to her police SUV, she had to run two blocks to the woman's backyard, then convince her he was no threat and was with her.

The woman had a permit for the shotgun. She berated him during the ride back to her place, and he just sat silently in the passenger seat.

"How's the head?" she asked.

"Sore. So, what now?"

Perez didn't have a game plan. Despite having the next two days off, after just completing a ten-day roster, she intended to go back into the station today for a short while and use her computer to see if there was anything new on Sam Pritchard. But she doubted it.

"I don't know," she said. "Like I said yesterday, there have been no new updates on him. And I've also flagged him in the system, so I'll get a notification if there is." Perez wasn't confident that Pritchard was even within a thousand miles of Ravenwood.

"Tell me about this Peeping Prowler case," Shaw said, getting up and refilling their coffee cups.

Perez spent the next ten minutes explaining a spate of complaints about someone prowling the streets at night around a particular part of Ravenwood and peeking through women's bedroom windows.

"It's not him," Perez said. "From what I've researched about Sam

Pritchard and his past cases and victimology, he's not the kind of guy that just watches and observes. He tends to act, abduct, then kill pretty quickly."

"Maybe he's changed his approach," Shaw said. "Maybe he's been here a while and is settling in and doesn't want to be too obvious. So, he's taking his time."

"There have been no abductions reported for over six months now," Perez said. "And those that have been were quickly resolved. No homicides."

"Phantom missing persons?" Shaw said. "No doubt you are aware of the term?"

Perez nodded. She was very familiar with it. It was where the perpetrator would kill, commit a homicide, and then hide it to look as though the victim was alive and just missing for legitimate reasons. A concerned family friend or relative would report them as missing to the police because they hadn't seen or heard from that person for a while, and it was out of character.

The police would follow it up, only to be fooled that the person wasn't missing and that there was a legitimate reason for their absence. In some cases, the killer will take the victim's cell phone and continue to send texts to loved ones, reassuring them that they have just moved away, needed space and that everything was fine. In one extreme case, they would even post pictures, fake ones, on the victim's social media accounts, acting out a chilling charade, pretending to be the victim, and even drawing on their Social Security benefits.

The police would then conclude that someone who doesn't want to be found or has moved to the other side of the country and wants privacy does not constitute a legitimate missing person's case. Whereas, in fact, the person in question was dead and buried. No police force in the land has the resources to dig deeper into such cases.

Perez started cooking eggs while Shaw took a shower. It felt nice making someone breakfast, she thought as she placed the eggs on plates with toast and then poured more coffee.

Shaw came out of the spare bedroom, his hair still wet, carrying his backpack. They sat at the counter, and Perez looked on as he pulled out and unfolded a map. It was creased, torn in places, and bore the ketchup and coffee stains of many meals taken in gas station diners and truck stop roadhouses while he had pored over the map. The map was covered with handwritten notes in various colors of ink, scribbled questions, circles, crossed-out towns, and directional arrows, leaving Perez with no doubt of his disciplined focus in finding Pritchard. He had selected a search field of the entire state, then systematically broken it down into grids and systematically searched grid by grid during the last six months. The result? Nothing. No Pritchard.

As they ate, Shaw scrutinized the map with a fierce look of concentration. Perez preferred to say nothing, to leave him to his thoughts—or maybe his obsession.

Then he spoke. "Can you drop me off in town on the way into work?"

"I have the next two days off," Perez replied. "Where do you want to go?"

He turned to her, his finger pointing to a spot on the map. "What's this place?"

Perez leaned closer. He smelled of soap and that musky male scent that made the hairs on the back of her neck bristle. Then her heart shuddered as she looked at where his finger rested on the map.

"Do you know this place?" he said. "I've been thinking about places where he could be hiding in and around Ravenwood."

Perez knew the place well and had vowed never to go back there again. "It's up in the foothills, just a few miles out of town," she said. "It's called the Dark Rift." She turned to look at him before realizing his face was just inches from hers.

"How do you know of this place?" she asked. She could feel her cheeks flush, and then suddenly, she looked away and began busying herself, clearing away the plates.

"Someone mentioned it in town yesterday before I met you," Shaw said. "I could hardly walk around showing people the sketches, then asking them if they had seen this man. So, I asked a few townsfolk about the area. Local landmarks. Abandoned places. Past history. Likely places where I think someone would be hiding."

Sitting back down, Perez took a sip of her coffee and then spoke. "Just please don't go running after anyone you think is him, okay? Call me. Don't intervene."

"Scout's honor," Shaw said with a smile.

She wasn't convinced. "You never told me you were a Boy Scout."

"Because I wasn't."

Perez let out a sigh and then studied the map. Maybe it was a good idea that she had a few days off so she could keep an eye on him while he was in Ravenwood. "Okay," she said. "If you promise not to go chasing anyone like you did last night, then today I'll take you around and show you some locations. We'll spend the day together."

He seemed pleased. Then, he did something unexpected, something he had never done to her before. He touched her and squeezed her knee. While not intimate, it still sent a current of electricity up her leg.

"Don't worry, Haley," he said. "I won't be performing any citizen's arrests."

Thank God, she thought. She took another sip of her coffee, wondering what the day would bring.

15

SLAUGHTERHOUSE

We skirt around the edge of the forest, keeping a few rows back, hidden within the tree line.

Beau is in front, rifle at the ready, watching for any sign of movement from the hulking shape of the building as we search the perimeter along one side. Beth is next to me, her eyes constantly looking behind us.

"What's up?" I ask.

"I don't know." She takes another glance over her shoulder to where the pickup sits hidden behind a thick row of trees on the other side and out of sight just near the dirt track we had followed from Ellie's map. "I just get the feeling someone is watching us."

"From behind?"

She looks at me. "Maybe."

We trudge on. It has just gone midday, and it's unseasonably warm, I imagine, for these parts.

Beau comes to a halt, and we gather in.

"What now?" Beth asks.

The place looks cold and dead, a shrine to industrial decline and abandonment. The perimeter fence has holes torn out from where I imagine thieves and scavengers have entered and ransacked the place, stripping it of anything valuable: machinery left abandoned, metal wiring, copper pipe, and electrical conduit, all likely pulled, wrenched, stripped, and stolen. What is left is the decaying carcass of an industry long since closed or shipped offshore. There are thousands of places just like this one scattered across the country. Usually at the end of some back road like this or buried deep in the scrub off the main highway or on the edge of a once-populous and thriving town. Once proud factories, serving the community, providing jobs, and sustaining families are now gone, with just a desolate, barren wasteland in its place.

We hold our position in the tree line, and it's like Beau is sniffing the air, his body perfectly still. His eyes are like slits, searching the exterior of the building.

Finally, he speaks. "Let's take a look inside."

"Wait," I reply. "Have you seen anything?"

He turns to Beth and me. "The place looks deserted, but we won't really know until we go inside and look around properly."

I nod, then we move out from the safety of the forest and cross a dirt road that rings the entire building. The ground is hard and crinkles underfoot with a layer of leaves.

The clouds have cleared, and the sky above is bright blue.

Reaching the wire fence, we quickly slip through a large rent, Beau first, then me and Beth bringing up the rear.

We head for a hunk of rusted machinery half-buried among the grass and weeds, crouch down, and then pop up and take another look.

It's about another hundred yards to the side of the building, where there is a raised platform, like a loading dock, with a set of stairs that leads to a large entry door. Everything is smashed windows and vacant openings.

"Let's go," Beau says, taking off and not waiting for us.

Breaking cover, we hustle across the open ground, then up the stairs and enter the building.

Inside, we pause. The interior is cavernous, ribbed with a

network of metal gantries, ladders, and girders, like a massive cathedral made of Meccano. Shards of sunlight cut through the gloom from high above. Entire sections of the ceiling are gone, revealing the blue sky, the tin sheeting worn away from decades of harsh winters and hot summers.

The floor is a confused mass of twisted and scattered debris, leaves and twigs, dead animals, and trash. Some walls are scorched by fire. Others are covered in graffiti. Everything looks covered with layers of grime, filth, and years of abuse.

"This place is a tomb," Beau states, tilting his head back.

The air is thick with the cloying smell of tannin fluid, rust, and freshly tilled soil. The place has a morbid heaviness to it, like it's hiding years of dark, sinister secrets, layer after layer through the ages. A set of wide stairs rises to a framework of overhead gantries and offices, and a pit of stairs leads down to subfloors and drainage tunnels.

"It's the perfect place to hide," Beth says next to me, her eyes looking around in mystic awe. "Someone could be watching us right now, and we wouldn't have a clue."

A chill runs up my spine. "Let's take a look. I don't want to be in here any longer than we have to."

"Me neither," Beth says with a shaky smile. "It's giving me the creeps."

Keeping together and relying purely on the natural light that seeps down from the gaps in the ceiling, we start searching the first floor.

Twenty minutes later, we're done and have found nothing, just a few soda cans, girlie magazines, and a rusted, off-road motocross bike with aggressive dirt tires. It was hidden behind a pile of broken wooden pallets, covered with an old solid canvas tarp. It looks like it has been there for years, and someone cut the ignition cables. The bike isn't going anywhere soon.

"Where to now?" Beth asks, turning to me.

Beau looks at me, too.

"Your show," I say to Beau. "We'll follow you."

He doesn't answer for a moment. And again, he does that thing like he's sniffing the air, trying to pick up on a particular scent apart from all the others. Watching him, I get an uncomfortable feeling in my gut.

"Come on." Beau motions us to a set of steel stairs that leads down into the darkness. "We need to search the lower levels."

The steps and rusted handrail tubing seem to be gradually erased as they angle downward into a black and ominous pool below. Power to the place would have been cut decades ago.

Beau flips on his flashlight at the top of the stairwell and hands it to me.

Beth pulls out her handgun, and I do the same. With me leading the way now, we move slowly down the metal stairs, passing one landing, then down again to the bottom. I hold the flashlight in one hand over the handgun in the other, my aim sweeping the lower metal treads.

In a tight group, we move forward along the passageway. I'm in front, panning the flashlight, my gun raised; next is Beau, with his rifle aimed ahead of me, and Beth is bringing up the rear.

I can feel Beau behind me, calm and methodical, as he swings the barrel of his gun over my right shoulder as we descend. At the bottom of the stairwell, a long passageway stretches away in front of us. The air is thick and damp, like a dungeon. Open doorways run off each side of the passageway, and the floor is pooled with brown, rusty puddles.

Without saying a word, I move forward, the beam of the flashlight sweeping left and right, the aim of my gun following. Graffiti smothers the walls on both sides—no tasteful paintings, just symbols and swirls in neon green and orange. Most of it is just tags —signatures of the various artists. Then, one catches my eye, and I smile. *Trump did win!*

Twenty yards along, I reach an open doorway and pause outside what looks like a room. Looking down, I notice what looks like red paint on the floor and the outline of a boot imprinting the rough concrete in red. Three red footprints lead into the room, into the darkness beyond. Blood or paint? I can't tell. Whatever it is, it isn't fresh.

Beau grips my shoulder from behind, a silent signal that he's there and has my back.

I step into the room, Beau tethered to me, Beth behind him. I pan the flashlight around.

A chair sits toppled in the middle of the room. Silence, nothing. The room is empty.

We turn and get out, back into the passageway. This time, Beau leads. After walking for twenty feet, Beau pauses and cocks his head.

I can hear it, the reason why he stopped. It is a faint sound, like the soft clang of metal echoing through the distance, off walls, along the passageway toward us. Someone is running—away from us, the sound fading fast.

I don't wait. I take off, pushing past Beau.

"Carolyn," he calls out after me, but I ignore him. I keep running, my flashlight bobbing around, holding my gun as steady as I can.

The passageway ends in a set of stairs going up. Clangs echo down to me from above. I begin to climb, my gun pointed up, turning and climbing, my feet on the metal. At the top, I'm back on the cavernous first floor. There's movement to my right—a shape, a person, running from me. I take off again after them.

Through a side door, they disappear, and I follow.

Then, I'm outside. I see them sprint through a swath of long, unruly grass, heading for the tree line. Is it Pritchard? I can't tell. Their head looks strange, rumpled, and deformed—not human.

Then, they reach the trees—and stop. The person turns back,

and I stop and take aim. The face! I lower my gun in disbelief. Confusion swamps me. A ghastly face, dead, evil, soulless, stares back at me.

Then, they are gone.

16

THE DARK RIFT

No matter how many times Perez had been up here, it always gave her the creeps—daytime or in the middle of the night.

"Al Beckett, an old recluse who lives up on Dawson's Ridge, said this place is like a lover's lane. Kids come up here and mess around, build campfires, and make out."

Shaw looked around at the unearthly landscape. "Can't imagine why," he said. "Seems more like one of those huge dinosaur burial grounds from the prehistoric age."

They had driven in Perez's police SUV, left it parked on a dirt area, and made their way through the thickly wooded foothills, using a shortcut trail that shaved at least twenty minutes off the regular trail that most people used and knew about. The main trail led up from the dirt area where most people parked. It wasn't a proper parking lot, just a large clearing where the dirt road that led in off the main road ended. To the untrained eye, the main trail seemed like the only path leading up to the Dark Rift. But a hundred yards along the main trail, another dirt trail, narrower and steeper than the main trail, branched off. Even during the daytime, everyone missed it because the opening was small and camouflaged perfectly by the surrounding foliage.

"If I had someone special," Shaw said, shooting a quick glance at Perez, "I sure as hell wouldn't bring them up here to make out."

They were standing together at the jagged edge of one of the deeper, wider fissures that slashed the earth, leaving a massive, raw wound.

"Oh," she said, raising an eyebrow. "And where exactly would you take them? Considering you have no place of your own."

The undulating ground around them was strewn with rocks of various sizes, some as large as a family sedan, others no bigger than a baseball. Parts of the earth were fractured in a labyrinth of cracks that reminded Perez of the old World War I battlefield trenches, crisscrossing the ground and creating a maze-like effect that stretched in all directions. Some of the cracks were narrow enough to simply step across; others required a leap of faith across the wide and yawning bottomless pit of darkness where light could only penetrate a few feet.

Shaw pressed his hand to his heart and grimaced. "Ouch!" he said. "I'd probably suggest that we go back to her place." He held Perez's gaze, a cocky smile spreading across his face, waiting for a response.

A cool breeze ruffled Perez's hair, and she felt a sudden rush of heat in her cheeks. Then she waved him off, not bothering to respond. He was baiting her. They had been walking around for nearly an hour now, and apart from the odd fire pit with cold ashes and some trash, they hadn't discovered anything remarkable.

"The place is like one huge death trap." Shaw picked up a large rock, held it out over the fissure, and let go. Eight to ten seconds passed before a resounding thud wafted up from the darkness below.

"Deep," he said, turning back to Perez. "Very deep."

"So I was told," Perez said, trying to adjust her focus to see if she could make out any shapes or features in the blackness below. But her focal point couldn't latch onto anything solid. It was like looking into a still pool of oil that swallowed everything and reflected nothing. Dizziness crept into her, and she stepped back for fear of toppling in and landing in some deep, hellish underworld. She took a breath. She hadn't quite conquered her fear of the dark.

"Are you okay?" Shaw asked, taking her arm and pulling her gently away from the edge.

"I'm fine," Perez said, even though she felt slightly unsteady on her feet.

"It's hard to believe no one has gone missing up here," Shaw continued. "Toppled into one of these deep fissures and never seen or heard of again."

"Maybe people have," Perez replied, thinking of the last time she had been up here—for entirely different reasons and in the middle of the night.

Shaw looked at her. His eyes narrowed. "Perfect place to get rid of a body. It would literally slip into a crack in the world and vanish."

Should she tell him? Maybe not yet. It was a dark secret, a pact she had made that she'd vowed never to mention ever again.

"I don't know exactly what we're supposed to be looking for," she said, changing the subject.

"I don't know either," Shaw replied. "I guess I'll know it when I see it."

"But we can't search it all," Perez said. "It would take forever."

Shaw's shoulders dropped a fraction. "It seems unlikely anyone would be hiding out here. There's nowhere to hide unless they like living in one of these cracks in the ground like cave bats." Grabbing another rock, Shaw hurled it into the fissure. "Perhaps this place is just a hang-out for teenagers and nothing more—a place where they can run around, drinking and scaring each other in the night." He turned back to Perez. "You're right, Haley. There's nothing here, and if there were, it would take weeks, if not months, to search the entire area, prodding and poking into every nook and cranny."

The wind suddenly whipped up around them, and a deep, mournful sound floated out of the fissure in front of them.

"Tell me about the guy you mentioned, Alfred Beckett," Shaw said. "The name sounds familiar."

"Maybe you met him in another life," Perez said jokingly.

"Maybe," Shaw replied. "Maybe we should ask him? Does he come up here a lot?"

"Not recently," Perez replied. "He told me it was nearly twenty years ago when he was last up here. He said that he had stood on the edge, looking down, and there was a deep, endless blackness to it that he had never seen in all his days working as a geologist. He said, at times, he could have sworn he heard screams echoing up from the darkness below."

Shaw gave a mock shiver. "Spooky," he said, his voice quivering.

He turned back to Perez. "Probably nothing. Like what we just heard. Just trapped wind, deep underground, moving through the fissures and channels under the crust." He walked back to where Perez was standing. "I'm a bit disappointed," he said. "I thought it would be bigger."

"Bigger?" Perez replied. Then, she gestured toward the edge of the fissure. "That's a small one."

Shaw frowned. "Small?"

"Yep. You haven't seen the Dark Rift yet."

Shaw scratched his head, then threw a thumb over his shoulder. "I thought that was it?"

Perez shook her head. "No. That's not it. Come on." She began stepping down from the plateau of flat rock. "This way."

"How far?" Shaw said, following her.

"About ten minutes to where the earth ends."

17

AAMON

Jessop's Hardware was located on the outskirts of Ravenwood, and Ellie turned into its dirt parking lot just after 10:00 a.m.

The outside of the store was layered with rows of ladders, wheelbarrows, pallets of fertilizer, and an assortment of gardening tools.

As Ellie pushed open the door, the familiar sound of a brass bell rang above her head, and a warm, comforting feeling settled over her. It was like stepping back in time to an era when attention to detail and traditional values meant something and made in America was the norm, not the exception. Immediately, she was hit by the pleasant smell of raw lumber, wood shavings, and beeswax. The floor had seen a million feet over the years, the original stain worn back to a dirty olive smear. There was a long counter along one side of the store, and behind this was a tall wall with built-in pigeonholes crammed full of small tools, parts, cardboard cartons, small boxes, and hardware bric-a-brac, all neatly and carefully stacked. A ladder on a slant ran along a rail halfway up the wall to gain access to the top where larger boxes were stacked, the print on the sides faded, and their cardboard sagging with age.

Every conceivable space was taken, brimming with bits and pieces of hardware.

"Morning." A young man in his mid-twenties with blond hair and blue eyes stepped out from a storeroom in the back. He was tall and well-built, wearing a checked shirt, blue jeans, and sneakers.

"Hi," Ellie said, looking around. The store seemed empty. She peeled off her face mask. "Do you sell prepaid cell phones?"

"Sure do," the man said with a bright, friendly smile. He led Ellie down an aisle toward the rear of the store to a small wall display of cell phones in blister packs hung from pegs. He turned back to her. "Any particular kind?"

He had the most intense blue eyes Ellie had ever seen. "No, not really."

He nodded. "Well, take a look, and if you need any help, just let me know." He paused for a moment and then said, "I'm Aamon, by the way. Aamon Jessop."

"Jessop?" Ellie said. "This is *your* store? You're the owner?"

"Don't look so surprised," Aamon said. "I'm the third generation. My father, Clarence, retired a few months back, and it was his father, Walter, my grandfather, who first opened the store back in the fifties when my father was just a boy."

Ellie was impressed. "A true family business. It's nice to see."

"Yeah, I guess," Aamon said. "I went to community college, did a business course, and now I'm keeping the family tradition going." He looked at her expectantly.

"Oh, sorry. I'm Allie."

Aamon rocked back on his heels. "Nice to meet you, Allie. So, have you moved to Ravenwood?"

"No. Just visiting. I'm writing an article on the local sights, town history, anything interesting in the past."

Aamon's eyes lit up. "Well, maybe we could grab a coffee sometime. Like I said, I'm third generation. Born and bred in Ravenwood. I could help you with anything you need to know."

"Thanks," Ellie said. "I'll keep that in mind."

Aamon nodded. "Shout out if you need anything." He walked away, and Ellie turned and surveyed the cell phones on the wall, surprised at the wide selection. She picked one and checked the details on the back. It would do nicely.

Aamon had disappeared back to the storeroom, so she decided to take a look around the store, walking the aisles, amazed at the size and variety of stock crammed into the place. Then she stopped and looked down at the floorboards, thinking she heard something like a hollow moan coming from under the planks. She listened some more. Nothing. Maybe it's just rats or water pipes groaning in the cold. She made her way back to the front counter.

Aamon Jessop emerged moments later, carrying a carton of wall filler, and placed it on the counter. "How did you do?"

Ellie handed him the phone. "I'll take this one."

He regarded the blister pack. "Good choice. You can easily activate it online and get ten gigabytes of data." He looked up. "Did you break your other cell phone?"

Ellie gave a goofy shrug like she was careless. "Dropped it. This is just temporary until I get a new phone."

"It happens. Cash or charge?"

Ellie pulled out some bills from her wallet. "Cash." She handed him the money, and he rang up the sale. Then, he handed Ellie her change, the cell phone in a bag, and the receipt.

"Thanks." Ellie slipped on her mask and headed for the door.

Aamon called out after her. "Don't forget," he said. "Just drop by whenever, and we can grab that coffee."

Ellie turned back and smiled. Not shy, this one, she thought. "I might just do that." She opened the door and stepped out into the cool fall air.

18

CROSSED PATHS

We left Cullen's Slaughterhouse about an hour ago, after I told Beth and Beau about the person I had seen, then chased outside.

We hung around, searching the woods for a while, but the person had gone. I couldn't tell if it was Pritchard or not, given that the person was wearing a mask. We followed up with another quick search of the sub-basement area but found no evidence that someone was living down there, and given that the place was huge, we simply didn't have the time to search it entirely. There were several outhouses scattered around the exterior grounds and a few tin shacks—rundown smaller structures, nothing more. Someone could easily be living in any one of them.

"Oh, crap!" Beth now exclaims from the passenger seat of Beau's pickup truck.

Beau eases off the gas, and from the back, I lean forward between the front two seats. Through the windshield, I can see a police SUV approaching us along the narrow dirt road leading down from the Dark Rift. Why were the police up there?

"Everyone, take it easy," I say, tapping Beau on the shoulder. "They might just pass us by without stopping."

"The dirt road isn't wide enough for us to pass each other comfortably," Beau says.

The SUV has dark tinted windows, and I can just see a pair of hands gripping the top of the steering wheel and a ghostly partial outline of a person in the driver's seat. There's another ghostly figure in the passenger seat. Both their faces look hazy and featureless thanks to the window tint.

"Just local cops," I say. There's a small shoulder ahead, between the vehicles, where the dirt road widens a fraction, and it looks like we can both squeeze past.

As I watch, the police SUV gets to the shoulder first, swings to the middle of the dirt road, and diagonally blocks us from going any farther.

"Oh, shit!" Beth whispers.

"Everyone, keep calm," I warn again. "Beau, pull up here."

We coast to a gentle stop about ten yards from where the police SUV is blocking the road, their intent now clear. It's like two bulls on one path, and neither wants to budge—a Mexican standoff.

"No one get out and keep your hands visible at all times, Beau. No sudden movements either. That goes for you, too, Beth."

"No need to explain that to me," she says grimly. "I've done thousands of traffic stops in my day. I've just never had one actually done to me."

The driver's side door opens, and a young woman steps out in plain clothes, a detective, I imagine. Her face comes into full view from behind the open door, and a coil of apprehension begins to unravel in my gut.

"Oh, fuck!" Beth says.

Beth seems to be cycling through her entire repertoire of *Oh!* cusses today.

"Well, I'll be damned," Beau croons, his head slowly bobbing up and down thoughtfully, acting as though a deer, a prized trophy stag, has strolled into his backyard at the exact same moment he's just finished cleaning and oiling his favorite hunting rifle, which is fully loaded. And the telescopic sight is dialed in.

Sometimes, life has a strange way of making coincidence seem like fate.

Ellie has shown us all photos of the young woman—lean, five-eight, mid-twenties, with olive complexion, hazel eyes, and pitch-black hair tied into a tight ponytail.

Haley Perez is standing not more than ten yards away from where we are sitting. And we're all armed, too, with Beau's favorite hunting rifle in the back.

"What do we do?" Beau asks.

"I rest a calming hand on his huge shoulder, wondering at the same time if the other cop, her partner in the passenger seat, is running our plates as we speak. "Just go with it," I say. "She's going to ask for your license and registration. Where are they?"

"In the glove box."

"Then tell her that before you reach for the glove box," Beth chimes in with some sage advice of her own. "Ask her permission before you move."

"But wait until she asks," I caution. "Don't volunteer to show her." We might get lucky, and Perez might just be curious as to who is driving up the dirt road to the Dark Rift while she and her partner happen to be driving back down.

"And for heaven's sake, don't accidentally call her Perez," Beth says. "We're not supposed to know who she is."

I lean closer to Beau's ear. "And if she asks why we're here, tell her we're just tourists, which we are. That's close to the truth. We're in town for a couple of days—shit, no. Scrap that idea. Then, she's going to ask where we're staying. Just tell her we're in town for the day, and some locals told us about the Dark Rift. So, we thought we'd come up and take a look."

"No problem," Beau says, "as cool as a cucumber."

Perez is walking toward us, approaching Beau's side.

He powers down his window, and I slip back, keeping my hands in plain sight.

"Now, who could this be?" Up ahead, Perez could see a pickup truck coming up the dirt road.

"Do you usually get people up here during the day?" Shaw asked from the passenger seat of her SUV.

"I wouldn't know. I rarely come here. But I'm going to take a look." She slowed, then angled toward a small section of the dirt road that was wider. Reaching it, she turned back across the center, effectively blocking the pickup's progress.

"Stay here," she said to Shaw. The pickup had dark-tinted windows, and she couldn't make out the occupants.

"No problem," Shaw replied.

She opened the door and slid out, then made her way toward the driver's side window of the pickup truck.

The window powered down. A huge, muscular man sat behind the wheel. His head almost touched the ceiling. He had a thick neck, shoulders like barbells, and hands the size of ham hocks gripping the steering wheel. Next to him was an older woman, late sixties perhaps.

The man smiled. "Hi, Officer. Is there a problem?"

Perez angled herself and then saw another woman in the back seat. She turned back to the driver. "No problem. Just wondering what you're doing up here?"

"We're just tourists," the man replied. "In town for the day. Thought we'd come up here and take a look. Some of the locals back in Ravenwood said that the scenery is spectacular. Is it worth the trip?"

"You're a long way from home," she said. "Iowa plates on your pickup truck."

"Like I said," the man continued, "tourists, just passing through."

Apart from the woman in the back, Perez couldn't see anyone extra in the pickup. "Just the three of you?"

The man nodded.

Perez glanced again at the woman in the back. There was something about her, a certain aura that defied her detached interest in Perez. Perez gave the upfront occupants another look. They hadn't done anything wrong, and this wasn't a traffic violation stop. She was just curious to see who they were.

The man tapped the steering wheel impatiently.

"Just be careful up there," Perez said. "There are a lot of holes in the ground and plenty of loose rocks—places where you can easily twist or break an ankle, or much worse."

"Thanks for the advice," the man said.

"Just take it easy." Perez angled her head and caught the woman in the back seat looking straight back at her like she was keenly studying her now—measuring her up. Law enforcement, perhaps, Perez thought.

"Have a nice day," Perez said, stepping back.

"You too, ma'am," the man replied before powering up his window.

As she walked back to her own SUV, Perez knew the three sets of eyes from within the pickup were watching her, and not just for plain curiosity either.

"All good?" Shaw asked as she climbed back in and closed the door.

"Out-of-towners going up there to take a look. It's their choice. A free world. I told them to be careful, though."

She turned and smiled at Shaw as she started the engine. "What? Did you think it was Sam Pritchard?"

"We're not going to be that lucky," he replied. "But, just for curiosity's sake, what if it was? What would you have done?"

Perez put the SUV in reverse, turned the wheel, and eased off the center of the dirt road and onto the verge behind. Dropping her window, she gave a beckoning wave.

"I don't know," she said. She watched as the SUV approached. It slowly squeezed past with about half a foot to spare.

"That was close," Shaw said, his eyes following the pickup as it slid past.

"Probably arrest him," she said, watching in the rearview mirror as the pickup truck carefully made its way up the dirt road before disappearing around a bend.

She waited a moment before kicking the SUV into drive and pressing the gas pedal. "What would you have done?" she asked.

She imagined he had been thinking about it for six long, hard months. What would he do if he crossed paths with Sam Pritchard again? He probably even dreamed about it.

Shaw's response was instant. "I'd kill him."

Perez gave a thin smile as they moved off again down the dirt road, the SUV bouncing side to side on the undulating ground. "Is that because of what he did to you, that one day you might tell me about, or because of what he's done to others?"

"At first, because of what he did to me," Shaw said, looking out the window. "But now, after what I've learned about him from what you've told me...." He turned back to Perez. Their eyes met, and she saw nothing but pure vengeance there. "I would kill him for all the others."

"What if he was unarmed?"

Again, there was no delay. But it wasn't an answer. It was a question that served as an answer. "Do you think all the innocent women he slaughtered were armed?"

19

SOMETHING BAD

It was late afternoon by the time we left and drove back to the homestead.

The Dark Rift reminded me of Slaughter Falls in Georgia, where I had fought Pritchard on that fateful night and saved Ellie. Even during the day, the place possessed a mournful feeling that no good could take root and exist there. For the two hours we were there, I had felt a malevolent presence. I couldn't see it but knew it was lurking slightly out of frame, making the hairs on my arms erect. The ground, the maze of rifts, small and huge, also made it appear like a place of pilgrimage where evil people went to commit evil acts under the cover of darkness.

Beau thoroughly searched, looking for any traces of a camp or a stash of supplies. Apart from small pockets of discarded trash and the remnants of the odd campfire, which he had judged to be months old, his final conclusion was that it wasn't a practical place to hide for any sustained length of time. Admittedly, the place was too vast to search it all, but I never want to go back.

Now, with all of us assembled in the barn, about to hold our daily debrief, it seemed like we had escaped that place—that we were lucky, and if we were to return, we might not be that fortunate next time.

"What else can you remember about this person you saw running from the slaughterhouse?" Beth asks me.

I rub my forearms, still trying to drive out the stubborn chill that I came away with from that place. "As I said earlier, I didn't get to see their face. They were wearing some kind of horror mask."

"You didn't think it was Pritchard?" Ellie asks. Her arms are folded. A shimmer of impatience is in her eyes. We only have one day left to come up with concrete proof that he is here in Ravenwood. Then, I'll have no choice. I've allowed myself to be backed unwillingly into a corner by one person in particular. I will have to allow Ellie to hatch her kill plot plan.

"I couldn't tell who it was," I reply. "I guess they ran because they saw our guns and not because they were there with malicious intent." Afterward, I wondered if they had put the mask on when they heard us coming to hide their identity. After all, who would walk around all day wearing that rubbery thing?

"How did it go in town?" I ask her. "Any luck?"

With her arms still folded, she gives me a listless shrug. Maybe it's that generation where everything that's not their opinion, idea, or take on the world is otherwise bat-shit boring to them. I love her like a younger sister, but now I feel I've inherited a gnarly, rebellious teenager.

"Pretty much the same as when I was last there," she says. "I asked a few more locals if any strange things had happened in town lately. One person asked me to define 'strange.' A few mentioned a prowler going around some neighborhoods, but it didn't amount to anything."

I hold Ellie's bored gaze for a few seconds. Did she actually ask anyone anything today, or is she just waiting for the countdown clock to expire so she can get her way?

"I guess there are a lot of strange things going on in this town," Beth says, coming to Ellie's rescue. "What about Haley Perez?"

"Since I told her we were only in town for the day, I guess we need to be scarce from now on," Beau says.

"We could always say that we decided to stay longer. For the life of me, I can't imagine why, though," Beth counters.

"Ignore Perez," I say, feeling irritated. "Let's not waste more time thinking about her. She's not part of the bigger picture. We need to find Pritchard. That's our priority. If we run into her again, we'll deal with it then. We haven't broken the law and shouldn't be acting like we have. Let's move on."

Everyone agrees.

"So, what now?" Ellie asks. "Do you think something bad will happen tomorrow night?" She looks around the group.

"I never thought of that," Beth admits, a puzzled look on her face. "Now that you mention it, Ellie." Beth turns to me. "What a frightening prospect."

Ellie's question catches me off guard, too. We've all been so busy focusing on finding Pritchard—looking around the town, driving to various locations—to notice the impending backdrop.

I glance at Beau. "Makes no difference to me," he says. "I never bought into all that garbage as a kid anyway. We grew up dirt poor."

A nail of concern drives into me as I think about what Ellie and Beth have just said. The timing would be horribly perfect, creating the ultimate nightmare.

I look at everyone in the group. "I guess we'll know by tomorrow night."

20

WEIRD FEELING

A raven perched on the town sign bobbed its head in approval as it watched them drive past on the way back from the Dark Rift.

"What's up, Haley?" Shaw asked.

For most of the drive, Perez was thinking about the occupants of the pickup truck she had stopped. They just didn't seem like tourists on a day trip to a place of interest. Like any small town, Ravenwood attracted its fair share of people passing through on their way to bigger and more interesting towns. The trio in the pickup didn't fit that mold. All three seemed focused, more measured, with intent, like they had a specific purpose.

Perez had already described her brief interaction with them to Shaw.

"My instincts tell me there was more to them than just a casual sightseeing trip. The woman in the back seat in particular."

"What about her?" Shaw asked.

"The way she was looking at me. Like she was studying me. Comparing me to a photo or a ready-made expectation."

"I wouldn't read too much into it."

Perez slowed to the speed limit. "They were there for a specific reason, not casual sightseeing. They were looking for something or someone in particular."

"Maybe they were. But they weren't breaking the law. Why didn't you ask for ID? A driver's license, at least?"

Perez let out a long sigh like a smoke signal, a clear message in the sky that Shaw read.

"You regret it now, don't you? So, instead of talking about it, you've been stewing for the last five miles."

"No, I haven't," Perez lied. "It's just... you know that feeling?"

"What feeling?"

"Like when you meet someone for the first time, and they give a look like they have already met you, but you haven't met them. And they give you that, 'Oh, so that's who you are' kind of look." She shot Shaw a glance. "Does that make sense?"

"Did you tell them your name or show them your badge?"

"No. That's what makes it all the weirder."

Shaw seemed to ponder it for a moment, then spoke. "It's like when you see pictures of something, like a place, an attraction, or maybe even a vacation destination. Then, when you actually go there, see it for real, in the flesh, so to speak, in your mind, you are comparing it to the pictures or preconceived expectations you had. Like deciding if you're disappointed or pleasantly surprised."

"Exactly!" He understood. He got it. "You explain things better than me."

"Maybe they recognized you. Maybe they've seen your picture in the local newspapers or on the Internet. In these parts, I imagine you're a celebrity based on what you've done in the past."

Perez threw him a scowl. "I'm not a celebrity." She detested the publicity and her picture being splashed everywhere in the media because of what she had done in the past.

"I'm not saying you're a celebrity, as in people are rushing up to you to get your autograph; it's just that maybe your reputation precedes you. What you did was pretty amazing."

"Now, you're just teasing me," Perez replied.

"I would never tease you about something like that, Haley. It does explain how you were feeling at the time and that lingering feeling you have now."

He was right. She hadn't thought about it like that. It made her uncomfortable when people she didn't know recognized her—not regular townsfolk. They all knew her, and she didn't mind that.

They turned onto the main street. "So, what now?" Shaw asked.

Perez thought for a moment. Nothing had come of the visit to the Dark Rift. And as much as she hated thinking about it, Shaw was right. Maybe Pritchard was communicating with another monster that they both knew. It was something she didn't want to do, and she had vowed never to go back and see him or talk to him. Now, it appeared to be the only viable option left.

"I'm dropping you back in town. I'll give you a set of keys to my place." She pulled to the curb. "Then, I'm going to pay Dylan Cobb a visit."

21

NEW MAN

"To what do I owe the pleasure, Detective Perez?" Dylan Cobb asked, a devious, hot little grin on his face.

Cobb sat across from Haley Perez, his ankles chained and wrists manacled through the thick metal eyelet welded to the top of the metal table. A prison guard stood behind Cobb, his gaze focused on the two of them where they sat.

"Did you miss me? It's been a while." His piercing, hypnotic green eyes seemed to flow across the gap between them and seep into her head, dismantling her thoughts, her fears, and her secrets.

"I missed our intimate conversations," Perez replied, taking in Cobb's new look. It seemed that whenever she visited him, which she avoided like the plague unless she wanted something vital from him, like now, his appearance changed. His previous wavy dark hair was now cut short. Before, he had also added some lean muscle to his frame, especially along his forearms, chest, and shoulders. Now, most of the muscle was gone, replaced with an overall layer of fat, making him look doughy and soft. Cobb was such a disciplined person. His waistline seemed to have expanded a few inches too. She guessed he had finally succumbed to the fact that he was never getting out of here.

But he remained supremely confident, as always. A man full of dark secrets and riddles, who was only willing to drip-feed them to her if it served his purpose. "Like I've always said, sarcasm is not your strongest point, Detective," he said, eyeing her with a broad smile. Then his eyes narrowed to slits, and he nodded slowly, tilting the chair he sat on back onto its rear legs, the chain pulling taught as he moved his hands as far back as he could. He always assumed this pose with her.

Cobb pursed his lips. "So, why are you here, Detective?"

During the drive, Perez had formulated a plan of attack, a strategy to tease what she wanted out of him without being obvious. "I'm concerned about you."

Cobb gave her a sly look, then pointed a finger toward her. "That's why you're here? Because you're concerned about me?"

Perez nodded. "Because you have no one. You're all alone. Didn't you tell me last time that all your friends are dead?"

The chains rattled as Cobb tilted the chair back down and rested his hands on the metal table. "Let's cut to the chase, shall we?"

Haley glanced at the guard over Cobb's shoulder and caught him suddenly looking away from her.

Cobb lowered his voice to his trademark viscous, wet whisper. "Maybe I got me some new friends," he said with a fake southern twang.

Perez felt the first glimmer of hope. Was Cobb just teasing her, or was he giving her another one of his infamous cryptic clues?

"I guess you're surrounded by hundreds of them," she replied disinterestedly. "Day and night. Not exactly friends, are they when you're all locked up together?"

Cobb leaned back in his chair again, pulling the chain with him. "Maybe I got me some new friends on the outside too?" The hot little grin returned to his face. "Maybe some of them know who you are. They tell me all sorts of things about you."

"Bullshit," Perez said.

Cobb gave a smirk. "These walls mean nothing to me. Anything can pass right through them. Words. Whispers. Information. I know and see what's going on outside. I have eyes and ears everywhere in Ravenwood."

"Then, if you know so much about what's going on, if anything, in Ravenwood, tell me," Perez said. "Impress me with your knowledge."

His eyes assumed a transparent quality like a cat's eyes at night, hollow and empty. "You like music, Haley? What did you listen to as a kid?"

Haley could feel her insides squirm, fearful of what he would say next, but she kept the fear from her face. It would definitely be about her past as a child.

Haley shrugged. "I listened to a lot of music when I was growing up."

"And boy!" Cobb exclaimed, eyeing her breasts, his mouth making a wet smacking sound. "Look at you now. All grown up and smelling like sweet cherry pie."

Haley forced herself to blink, to breathe as his eyes crawled all over her. "Tell me, Haley," Cobb said slowly, lowering his voice, then looking her directly in the eye. "Did you have a favorite song? Something that you kept on playing?"

"No."

"Well, I loved the Eagles," Cobb said, a look of immense satisfaction on his face. "Still do. I had a favorite album when I was a kid. *Hotel California.* I used to play the living shit out of it. I had it on vinyl. I'm not into that streaming shit. Vinyl sounds better. Always did, always will."

"You're kidding me?"

"No, I'm not kidding you. My favorite song was on that same album, too. Side One, Track Two." His smile lingered. "You should check it out."

"Maybe I will. But in the meantime, tell me more about your friends on the outside."

The chains rattled as Cobb stifled a yawn. "It's getting late, Haley. Big day tomorrow, and I need my beauty sleep." He glanced over to the guard and nodded.

Urgency hit Haley. Cobb was hinting at something, but what was it? "You can't tell me about your so-called friends on the outside because you don't have any friends on the outside," she said with contempt. "You're full of it."

The guard began walking toward them.

"You'll see soon, Haley," Cobb stated with an amused expression on his face.

"You're full of shit, Cobb! No one is interested in you anymore. You're yesterday's news. You're not famous enough to have any friends left. There are others out there, bigger, cleverer, and more cunning than you ever were—celebrity killers who have thousands of loyal fans. You're not in their league."

"Follow the clues, Haley," Cobb said. "You'll figure it out." With his eyes still locked on Haley, Cobb offered his manacled hands to the guard.

The guard undid the lock and slipped the chain out of the metal eyelet welded to the top of the table before closing the manacles firmly around Cobb's wrists again.

Cobb rose, and Perez did, too. "You know nothing, Cobb. Your world now is just these four walls, and the only thing you look forward to each day is bending down in the shower to pick up the soap."

The guard smiled at the comment.

Cobb turned and began being led away by the guard. Twisting his neck, he then glanced back at Haley. "By the way?" he said over his shoulder. "I hear there's a new man in your life?"

Perez froze, her mouth gaping.

"One of my friends told me." Cobb started to laugh. "Impressed now, are you?"

He disappeared from the room, but Haley could still hear his laughter echoing in the corridor outside, gradually fading before being abruptly cut off altogether by the clunking slam of a heavy metal door.

22

ONE WISH

My cell phone rings, and I check the screen. It's Beatriz Vega. I wasn't expecting her call.

"Beatriz, what's up?"

She cuts straight to the chase. That's what I like about her. "Pritchard has gone active in the last few minutes," she says.

"Gone active? What does that mean?" Dread thickens my arteries, and my blood slows to a crawl. He's killed again—another woman slaughtered. Guilt hits me like a freight train. I glance over at Ellie, and she can see the pain in my eyes.

I turn away, gripping the phone closer to my ear. "Who has he killed this time?" There can be no doubt. Pritchard is not here in Ravenwood, and I've made a tragic mistake thinking he was. Apart from the usual small-town misdemeanors, my police scanner has been silent. He's killed again, and it's my fault. This is all wrong. Another mistake. Another hapless woman that I could've saved if I had just acted sooner. None of this is working, and it's my fault.

"Sorry, Carolyn," she says. "I should have explained. He's become active in the chat room that Joel Renner was using. He's talking to Dylan Cobb as we speak—using a different account login."

There's a glimmer of hope. "So, he hasn't killed anyone yet?"

I feel Ellie behind me now. Beth comes in from the kitchen with Beau. They crowd around me as I clutch the phone even tighter. "Hold on, Beatriz. I need to put you on speaker. The rest of the gang is here."

I flip the phone to speaker mode and hold it up. Everyone huddles even tighter around me—a pack of ravenous dogs salivating over a bone I'm holding in front of them. And we are a pack of dogs. Desperate for a tiny morsel—any scrap of information that can give us a fix on Pritchard right now.

Beatriz's monotone voice comes out of the phone's speaker. "Pritchard is using the same chat room name he used with Renner. I kept the link to the chat room open, just in case. Renner's account was deactivated months ago. Both Cobb and Pritchard know that Renner is now dead, so there was no point in keeping it active. But Pritchard just opened a direct private message chat with Dylan Cobb using a new account."

"But Dylan Cobb is in prison," I hear Ellie whisper.

"It doesn't matter," Beth says. "Prisoners can get access to anything—a knife, drugs, definitely the Internet. Even a cell phone."

I don't meet Ellie's gaze. I haven't looked at anyone. I'm still staring at the ground near my feet at a spot where I thought a big black hole was going to open up a few seconds ago and swallow me whole. He hasn't killed anyone—yet. Thank God. But it's a lead. He's active and talking to Dylan Cobb.

"What did he say?" I ask Beatriz.

"At first, they spoke briefly about Joel Renner. I recorded it all. He was only online for two minutes. Now, he's offline. He thanked Cobb for recommending Ravenwood to Renner—about it being a safe haven."

My heart almost stops, but I rein in my excitement. I need actual confirmation. "Did he actually say he was here? In Ravenwood?"

"Not in so many words," Beatriz replies. "He was just thanking

Cobb for recommending the place. He didn't say specifically that he was actually there. And then...."

Beatriz's voice trails off. I squeeze the phone even tighter, my knuckles white. "What? What else?" I feel like I'm on the precipice, swaying one way that's good, then tilting the other way, which spells disaster.

Everyone crowds around me even more, hungry for anything.

I can hear the keyboard clicks down the line. Beatriz comes back. "As I said, Pritchard wanted to thank Cobb. So, he granted him a wish."

Now, I look up and see confused faces.

"A wish?" Beth speaks.

"What the fuck does that mean?" Ellie demands. "A wish?"

"I'll send you the conversation transcript with Cobb's reply," Beatriz continues. "As a thank-you, Pritchard asks Cobb if there's something he can do for him on the outside. Here it comes, Carolyn."

I pull my phone closer and read the screen. The transcript hasn't landed. Precious seconds tick by. Everyone is restless. Drawn faces. Hunched shoulders. Twisted mouths.

I'm about to explode and tell Beatriz that her message hasn't come through.

Then, my phone pings. I open the attachment and squint at the screen. I read the message—the wish the Death Fairy granted the monster locked up in prison. Cobb's wish of Pritchard. His answer. Three words. A name within.

Kill Haley Perez.

23

TRACK 2

"He will always be an enigma to me," Perez said. "A thorn in my side that I can't get out."

It was well after eight by the time Perez got back from her trip visiting Dylan Cobb in prison. Shaw had organized takeout, and now they sat at a small table on the balcony overlooking the street below. Despite his requests, Perez refrained from sharing the details of her meeting with him until they sat down to eat. She had been plagued by Cobb's last comments for the entire drive back.

Since she had to submit all her possessions, including her handgun and cell phone, before entering the prison itself, it was only when she got her cell phone back that she rushed outside into the parking lot and looked up the particular song on the record album Cobb had mentioned.

Side A. Track 2.

The song's title only drove home further Cobb's claim that he had eyes and ears in Ravenwood.

"So, what did he say?" Shaw asked, sliding a piece of pizza onto her plate.

Haley wasn't hungry, yet she accepted the food nonetheless to please Ben.

"He knows about you," she said.

Shaw paused, the pointy end of the pizza inches from his open mouth. He put the slice down. "How?"

That same question had been bouncing around inside Perez's head for the last hour and a half. "He didn't come out and say it directly," she replied. "He tends to talk in riddles and cryptic clues. He said that he had friends on the outside. His so-called 'eyes and ears' in Ravenwood. That's how he described them."

"Prisoners often have contacts on the outside—a network of people they know who act as informants," Shaw said.

"I know that. I just didn't expect Cobb to be telling the truth on this occasion. He is a compulsive liar, twisting and turning everything to suit his own narrative."

Shaw touched her hand. "What else did he say?"

She slipped out her cell phone, thumbed the screen, and held it up for him to see. "He said his favorite song is on the Eagles album, *Hotel California*. Side A, Track Two."

Shaw read the screen. He looked at Perez. "'New Kid in Town'? That's it?" Shaw stuffed the slice of pizza into his mouth.

"Don't you see?" Perez said, slightly infuriated by Shaw's flippant dismissal. "Coupled with what he said about me having a new man in my life, *you* are the 'new kid in town.' It's you!"

"Did he mention my name specifically?" Shaw said between chews.

"No. That doesn't mean he doesn't know your name."

"If Dylan Cobb knew I was in Ravenwood right now, he would've told you that. He likes to boast about it—show how clever he is. He doesn't know my name."

Perez pointed off the balcony into the distance. "But somehow, word got back to him in prison, over a hundred miles away. Someone saw us together in Ravenwood."

"Did you mention Sam Pritchard? Directly or indirectly?"

Perez shook her head.

"What about that pickup truck and the three occupants? Maybe he was referring to them?"

Perez had thought about it but quickly dismissed it. "They were new faces in town unless they've been hiding here for a while. Whatever friends he is referring to have to be locals—been here a while, not newbies." The thought of it, an underground network of spies in Ravenwood watching her, made her stomach turn. She pushed her plate away while Shaw ate hungrily.

"I wouldn't worry about it," he said.

Perez folded her arms, frustration boiling inside her. "He's locked up in prison, miles from here, and yet I feel like he's now constantly looking over my shoulder and breathing down my damn neck!"

Shaw wiped his mouth on a napkin. "Haley, don't beat yourself up about it. He can't do you any harm."

She glared at Shaw, tears in her eyes. "No. But maybe one of his friends can on his behalf. I've seen it done before in Ravenwood. I know how this movie ends. And it's not good."

"Did he say anything else, Haley? Anything? No matter how obscure."

Haley thought for a moment; then, something dragged up from her memory. "He said something about having to get his beauty sleep and that he has a big day tomorrow."

"Tomorrow?" Shaw repeated.

Their eyes met and then widened at the same time.

Perez felt a thread of dread begin to unravel inside her. And the more she thought about it, the more the thread was unraveling and unraveling and unraveling.

"Christ!" she uttered. It had been there all this time. Yet she had been blind to the obvious because she had been preoccupied with Shaw's search for Sam Pritchard.

She sat up straighter. "I think he's here... Sam Pritchard."

Shaw's own interest had suddenly kicked up a notch. "Go on," he said.

"I think he's been here for a while, marking time. Waiting until now."

"The Peeping Prowler?"

"Maybe, maybe not. I don't know. That seems so... beneath him."

"And what about tomorrow?" Shaw asked. "Honestly, I never even thought about it until you just mentioned it now."

Perez pushed the plate with the slice of pizza farther away from her, almost off the table entirely.

Her stomach churned at the thought of what might happen.

"Tomorrow," she breathed. "It's only one sleep away. Then, we'll know."

24

PIGGYBACK

Kill Haley Perez.

It's good news, great news. Not for Haley Perez, though. It's confirmation. Pritchard is right here in Ravenwood and is going to carry out Cobb's wish.

Kill Haley Perez. It's an act of vengeance for her putting him in prison—a wish granted by Pritchard to Cobb—favors between two despicable monsters.

"What's it say?" Ellie demands. All eyes are on me. "Cobb has asked Pritchard to kill Haley Perez on his behalf."

Like a boomerang, my cell phone makes a quick circuit around the group, eyes reading the screen before it lands back in my hand.

Ellie is the first to speak. "So, Sam Pritchard is going after her."

I can't tell if it's excitement or disappointment in her eyes.

But it's a quandary. Do we tell Perez? By doing so, we're going to blow our cover. But Pritchard is here. That fact is now undeniable. And he's going for Perez.

"So, what do we do?" Beth asks.

I look at their faces. "Perez cannot know who we are. We can't approach her."

Beau looks deep in thought. Then, he smiles like a predator. "The answer is obvious."

I'm trying to read his face. Then, I get it. "Ravenwood is the kill plot, and Haley Perez is the bait."

"We put her under surveillance," Beth suggests. "Like a stakeout."

Ellie nods. "Wait till he turns up, then kill him."

"Hopefully, before he kills her," I add.

"But it's not that simple," Beau says. I need all his hunting wisdom now. "She's not static like a typical stakeout or kill plot. It's a whole town, not a narrow plot of land. And she's mobile, on the move. She's not like a piece of meat on the ground waiting in a snare. Or us sheltering in a hide, guns ready for Pritchard to just waltz in front of our sights."

Now, I see it. It's not as simple as I first foolishly thought—too many moving pieces. "Not to mention the townsfolk moving in the background," I say.

Beau nods. "Who could end up as innocent collateral damage, or worse."

Concern flares in Beth's eyes. "Pritchard might go on a rampage if provoked."

"Especially if we foil his plans and he manages to escape," I add to the unfolding nightmare we're all picturing in our minds.

Beau completes the picture. "And he then decides to enact retribution on the innocent."

Beth looks at me. "We have to tell her. She needs to know. Maybe she can help and be part of the plan. Draw Pritchard away from the town. Isolate him using herself. That would only work if she's in on it too. We need to tell her."

I know it's not what she wants to hear, placing another fellow officer in harm's way. But I know in my heart that it's the right thing to do. "No," I say. "If she gets wind of it, she might take matters into her own hands. She could blow this opportunity we have. And it may be the only opportunity we will ever have to lure him out. It's both perfect and imperfect. Perfect for us. Imperfect for Haley Perez. But what choice do we have?"

"I agree," Ellie says in a rare moment of supporting my opinion. "Carolyn is right. Perez cannot know. This could be our only chance."

Beth is pissed. "Look, I don't know her personally, but she caught the Eden Killer and Dylan Cobb. So, she goes right to the top of my Christmas card list. I don't like it, but it's your show, Carolyn." Her eyes pass across each of us. "We all better make pretty damn sure Pritchard is the only one who gets killed."

"That's where you come in, Beau," I say, turning to him. "It's your show from now on. That's why you're here. You're a hunter. How do you ensure the hunted doesn't realize she is being hunted as well as the hunter, not knowing all of us are also hunting him, too?"

"It's a classic hunter's piggyback," he says with a gleam in his eyes.

Then, it hits me: his look of supreme confidence. He already has a plan. While the rest of us were wrestling with the moral dilemma of telling Perez or not, he's been busy formulating something in his head.

25

GOBLIN HEAD

The next morning, Perez and Shaw split up: Perez in her police SUV, driving through the town of Ravenwood. Shaw, with his backpack slung over one shoulder, walking the streets.

Neither of them had gotten much sleep last night. And so, when Perez got out of bed at 5:00 a.m., she wasn't surprised to see him already in the kitchen, making coffee. They had then sat on the small balcony and watched as dawn broke over the township while drinking their coffee.

Perez turned down the main street for a third time this morning, her head swiveling from side to side, her eyes watching the foot traffic on the sidewalks, wondering which of the people she saw were Dylan Cobb's so-called "friends" who had been spying on her. That was why she suggested they split up this morning and go their separate ways, then rendezvous at 11:00 a.m. at an inconspicuous location on the outskirts and compare notes after they had both completed their individual reconnaissance.

Shaw had given her some suggestions on what to do, while Perez had given him a suggestion of her own: don't tell me what to do.

It was almost eleven, and there was plenty of activity in the stores and along the sidewalks. Perez could now see things clearly, things that she had perhaps seen before, but her brain hadn't registered as relevant or symbolic. Orange bunting was draped in almost every storefront window, with little cardboard cutouts of witches on broomsticks or jack-o'-lanterns dangling beneath. Pumpkins, fat and ribbed, with cut-out faces, sat in planter boxes. Wispy cobwebs hung from store awnings, with impossibly large black spiders hunkered in the corners.

Would Pritchard really mark the occasion and come out with all the other monsters and go on some murderous rampage? Was he also going to be joined by some of Cobb's friends, plunging the picturesque town of Ravenwood into a scene from a post-apocalyptic zombie movie?

She had thought about calling Brandon Kershaw, her sergeant, then decided against it. He and all the other detectives would think she was a loon. In all honesty, she couldn't imagine the town turning into that kind of horror-movie chaos. But just in case, she did stop by the armory and check out some extra magazines for her handgun, as well as an AR-15 assault rifle—the law-enforcement equivalent of the military M4. The armorer on duty didn't quibble once when she asked for the regular optic sight to be swapped out for a night vision one. It was Halloween, after all, when nothing bad happens until after the sun goes down.

Perez did another drive of the town, switching back through the various streets, before heading to Ravenwood Books & Café, where Jenny Langdon, the owner, was standing at the curb, waiting with Perez's order that she had texted through.

Perez powered down the passenger-side window and reached across as Jenny leaned in and handed her two take-out cups nestled in a cardboard tray, separated by a small brown paper bag.

"Thanks, Jenny," Perez said, taking the tray and setting it on the seat. "What's in the bag?"

Jenny smiled. "Goblin head muffins," she said. She lowered her voice. "I'll let you in on a little secret. They're not real goblin heads

—just a chocolate muffin, covered in a mint green frosting with raspberry eyes."

"Nice," Perez said. "Thanks again."

"No problem," Jenny said, stepping back from the window. "I hope you both enjoy them."

Perez pulled away from the curb and drove off.

Ten minutes later, in an abandoned lot on the outskirts of town, she and Shaw were leaning on the hood of her SUV, drinking their coffee and nibbling on the muffins.

"Any luck?" she asked.

"No. Everything looks normal. And you?"

"The same. As normal as anything can be on Halloween." She took a sip of her coffee.

"What's the plan for tonight?" Shaw asked.

Perez sighed. "I thought we might find something or see something in town today, but we haven't. So, all we can do is start driving the streets of Ravenwood as soon as the sun goes down, keeping a lookout together."

"For all things nasty," Shaw said before draining the last of his coffee.

26

TIME TO HUNT

After lunch, we assemble back in the red barn and go through Beau's plan one more time, which we covered last night after Vega's call.

The morning was spent sleeping in, getting in a few extra hours of rest because it would be a long night ahead of us. Beth and I cleaned our handguns while Beau went to the barn with Ellie to clean both his rifles.

Now, Beau has the floor and is standing in front of a map of Ravenwood and the three photos. He taps the photo of Haley Perez, who ironically has been elevated to being our primary focus despite the photos of the two abominations on either side of hers: Cobb and Pritchard. "She's now the bait, but we can't put a tail on her."

"Why not?" Beth asks, even though we went through all this last night.

Beau nods to me.

"We can't put a tail on Perez because she will get suspicious," I say. "We don't have all the resources and experience to do it properly. It takes hundreds of hours of training, utilizing a multitude of different vehicle types, rotating them in and out, and everyone having two-way radios. We simply can't mount such an operation.

Even if we try, we'll either lose her real quick, or she'll see us a mile away."

Beth seems appeased for the time being.

Beau takes over again. "I also want us to work in teams." He gestures toward me. "Carolyn's got the police scanner. She will monitor any radio activity."

"And if I hear anything bad, then either Beth or I will call you on your cell phones. So, for Pete's sake, keep them within reach at all times and turned on and fully charged."

We agree on the teams: Beth and me, Beau and Ellie.

"We all know what Haley Perez looks like, as well as her police SUV and plates," Beau continues. "But she also knows exactly what my pickup truck looks like, and the Iowa plates, too. So, Ellie and I will try to stay well clear if we happen to see her."

"What if she sees you first?" Beth asks. "Like standing at a set of traffic lights?"

He shrugs. "Then I'll go with the story that we decided to stay in Ravenwood for a few more days. She certainly doesn't know the vehicle you and Carolyn will be in. Plus, it's a good thing we're not heading out until after dark."

"What happens if she decides to stay at home all night?" Beth asks, playing her usual role of devil's advocate. "What then? Shouldn't we be staking out her place?"

Beau turns to Beth, and I can see he's growing impatient with her. I can't really blame Beth. She's a veteran cop who's a stickler for detail, whereas I tend to fly a little too close to the sun.

"Absolutely not," Beau says. "What happens if we are parked anywhere near her place, and Pritchard spots us first?"

"But he doesn't know what we look like," she throws back.

"He knows what Ellie and I look like," I interject. "And like Ellie said before, we will only get one chance at this. If we spook Pritchard, he'll disappear again."

Ellie gives me a nod. It seems that in the last twelve hours, our relationship has been patched up somewhat.

"So, we're just going to drive around, hoping to see him?" Beth scoffs. "Like lame delivery drivers who can't find an address?"

"That's all we can do for the moment," Beau adds with a thin smile that's not really a smile. "Keeping our eyes and ears open. We know where Perez lives, so we will keep circling back."

On the map is a red cross marking the street of Perez's apartment, the address of which Beatriz found out for us last night.

"But I don't think she'll be staying home tonight," I say. "Halloween tends to bring out the crazies as well. I think she'll be driving the streets, looking for any problems."

"She's a detective, after all," Ellie says. "I imagine it will be one of the busiest nights of the year for any police department in any town, big or small.

"We just need to make sure we don't directly cross paths with her like we did before," Beau adds.

"And if there is an incident, call out," I say, "I guarantee she will respond to it as well. I think it's just in her nature to jump in and help—to run toward danger rather than away from it."

"We're all like that," Beth says, turning to me. "That's why we became cops."

"Not all of us are like that, Beth. I just need to keep the police channel open, and we all need to be ready to move."

"So, what's left to be done?" Ellie asks.

"Nothing," Beau says. "We just have to wait until the sun goes down and it gets dark. Then, it's time to hunt."

27

WRONG

My cell phone rings, and I check the screen. What can it be this time?

We've been driving the darkened streets for two hours now, and nothing. I take the call. "Beatriz?"

She comes on the line, distress in her voice. "Carolyn. I'm sorry. I'm so, so sorry."

I don't understand. What is she apologizing for? "What's wrong?"

Beth, who is driving, shoots me a glance. "I got it wrong, Carolyn. The message from Dylan Cobb."

My heart lurches.

She continues. "The transcript between Cobb and Pritchard that I told you about yesterday. I thought it was the entire message, but there was a missing part to it."

"What part was missing?" My mind races. It was clear and concise. *Kill Haley Perez.* What else did Pritchard say? Or what else had Dylan Cobb requested Pritchard do? "I thought Cobb just asked Pritchard to kill Haley Perez on his behalf," I say.

Beth throws me another concerned look. "Should I pull over?" she whispers.

I shake my head and speak again to Beatriz. "Dylan Cobb asked Pritchard to kill Hayley Perez. Isn't that what Cobb said? Kill Haley Perez?"

"That was only part of what he said," she replies. "It turns out the message was fragmented. A few words were missing at the beginning of that sentence. I didn't know until I went back and thoroughly went through it all again."

"Who cares about a few words? How could that change the meaning of Cobb's answer? He wants Pritchard to kill the female detective."

"No, Carolyn. It changes everything."

Everything? "Stop the car," I tell Beth.

"What's the problem?" she asks.

I cover the mouthpiece. "Stop the car, now!"

We pull to the curb with a screech of the tires, startling a group of kids on the sidewalk who are comparing their candy haul. Beth turns, then mouths, *What's the problem?*

I shake my head and return to Beatriz. "Beatriz, what was the full message then?"

"The partial message, the fragment I told you was, Kill Haley Perez," she says. The entire message is, 'Free me, so I can kill Haley Perez.'"

Free me, so I can kill Haley Perez.

Free me? My mind starts doing backflips.

Beatriz is in my ear again. "You see how it completely changes the message. Cobb doesn't want Pritchard to kill Haley Perez on his behalf. He wants the pleasure of doing that himself. He wants Pritchard to help him escape from prison so he can kill Haley Perez himself."

Dylan Cobb escape from prison? A maximum-security facility? Is that even possible? I can't believe what my mind is contemplating. "How can Sam Pritchard possibly help someone escape from a maximum-security prison? I don't think Pritchard has the resources to accomplish such a feat."

"I don't know," Beatriz replies. "But I've been monitoring local police chatter around the prison, and there's nothing. It's been quiet. Believe me; if someone had escaped, the airways would be crammed with alerts. But there's been nothing."

I need to wrap my head around what Beatriz just told me. *Free me, so I can kill Haley Perez.* The nightmare has suddenly become infinitely worse. Apart from Sam Pritchard, I can't think of a worse person to let loose on the public than Dylan Cobb.

A new twist to the nightmare hits me, and it feels like a knife has been plunged into my heart. Surely Cobb and Sam Pritchard aren't thinking of teaming up? If Cobb does escape, and I don't believe for one moment that is possible, would he risk coming back to Ravenwood just to kill Haley Perez? Is revenge his sole motive?

Beth looks grim-faced. From fragments of the conversation, she's figured out the gist of it.

"Are you certain, Beatriz, this is now the full and correct message? There's nothing else missing. It's complete?"

"Carolyn, I've checked it more than a dozen times. It is the complete message. Dylan Cobb asked Sam Pritchard to help him escape so he can kill Perez."

I look around the streets and see kids in costumes, hand-in-hand with their parents, dressed up as ghosts, ghouls, goblins, and zombies. I see others, too, adults more likely, dressed up as horror movie characters. I spot Frankenstein's monster across the street, lumbering along in his big boots. He salutes Dracula, who is walking the other way and is wearing a high-collared black cape. Under a tree, not far from where we are parked, is Michael Myers from *Halloween*, complete with mechanic's overalls and that ghastly Captain Kirk rubber mask. I swear he is looking right at me. He's carrying a big knife. He then turns and walks away, high-fiving a little girl he passes on the sidewalk. Another person, carrying a machete and wearing one of those creepy hockey masks from *Friday the 13th*, cuts across the street. Reaching the other side, he meets Freddy Krueger at a red fire hydrant, where they fist bump.

Has the world gone truly mad? It's like someone has let out all the monsters from the asylum, and they're now roaming the streets of Ravenwood as though it's perfectly normal. Well, it is perfectly normal—tonight. It's the only night of the year when monsters can walk around freely without so much as a second glance.

I end the call with Beatriz and update Beth on the bad news.

"Holy crap!" she says, looking around, seeing what I'm seeing. "What if Dylan Cobb has already escaped?" she says. "And the prison authorities haven't figured out that he has?"

We turn to each other, and now I feel sick.

Beth goes on. "What if he escaped hours ago? Ellie said the maximum-security prison is only about a ninety-minute drive north of Ravenwood."

Then, she says what I've been thinking. "What if Dylan Cobb is already in Ravenwood? And what if he's walking the streets with Sam Pritchard right now? Two real monsters disguised as two fake monsters."

28

PATTERSON

"Hey, Patterson! Come in here for a minute. I've got something for you." Dylan Cobb sat on the bunk in his prison cell, a small, gift-wrapped box on the thin mattress next to him.

Escape from Alcatraz, and *The Shawshank Redemption* were two of his favorite prison escape movies. Along with *The Great Escape,* of course. He had watched each at least a dozen times since being inside.

The prison guard, Stan Patterson, appeared on the other side of the cell bars. He was roughly the same size and build as Cobb. Same dark, short hair, too. If anyone had bothered to notice over the last six months, especially Stan Patterson himself, they would have picked up on Cobb getting his hair cut in the prison barber's store like Patterson's. He'd also put on a few pounds, mimicking Patterson's girth around the stomach. And when no one was look-ing, Cobb would practice inside his small cell the same slouchy gait Patterson had. Patterson also had a slight lean to his left when he walked. A college football injury Patterson had told him—which was horse shit. Cobb had overheard the guards saying that Patterson had slipped getting out of the tub five years ago and was too tight to go see a doctor.

Patterson wore thick-framed Elvis Costello spectacles, leaving Cobb to wonder how he would manage to see anything once he had put them on his own face. It's a minor detail, though. Luckily, Patterson was also a hypochondriac. Hence the face mask he still wore—and not a small one either. It was one of those big 3M N95 respirator types that practically covered everything from below the eyes down once strapped on. These were just a handful of the reasons Cobb had singled out Patterson six months ago and then dutifully gone about nurturing a relationship with the father of five and devout Ravens fan.

At first, Patterson was cautious, not wanting to get too close to Cobb, and was reluctant to share any personal information with the inmate. But Cobb was determined, and slowly, over the months, Patterson began opening up to him.

"What do you want this time, Cobb?" Patterson asked, staring at him through the bars.

Cobb patted the box on the mattress. "Like I said. I got something for you. A gift. A thank you for getting me that book." A month back, Patterson had brought Cobb, *The 48 Laws of Power* by Robert Greene. The book on the art of manipulation and psychological seduction was banned in most prisons across America. Patterson had charged Cobb six times the RRP to get the book, which Cobb hadn't bothered to read. He knew everything there was to know—and a shitload more—about its contents.

As he regarded the little package next to Cobb's thigh, Patterson's small, beady eyes almost looked normal-sized behind the thick lenses. "What is it?" he asked.

"Come in, and I'll show you. It's a gift, like I said. A thank you. I want to give it to you in person."

Patterson didn't move. He was always a cautious little bastard. "Bring it over here and slip it through the bars then," Patterson replied.

Cobb had anticipated this response. "It won't fit through the bars, dumbass," Cobb said playfully. He picked up the wrapped box and stood up but didn't step forward. "And I don't want the other guards seeing me pass this to you," he said in a low, syrupy whisper, adding to the intrigue. "They'll know. They'll see it on all of them security cameras, especially that one up on the wall on your left."

Patterson glanced to his left to where a camera sat on the wall at the end of the cell passageway. The entire prison bristled with security cameras, but not inside the individual prison cells.

"They'll know. Especially that prick, Rudy. He'll want his share," Cobb continued like he was trying to explain things to a two-year-old. He shook the box, and it made a rattling sound like he was rattling a dog's dinner bowl. "Come and get it. I know you're going to like it."

Patterson took one more look over his shoulder before slipping off the keys and unlocking the cell door. He took out his baton from his belt and held it ominously in front of him. "Don't fuck with me, Cobb. Any funny business, and I'll crack your skull like a melon."

Cobb smiled. "Now, is that any way to talk to a friend?" He stood his ground and waited for Patterson to come to him, lifting the box.

"I hope you like it," Cobb said.

Patterson's eyes dropped to the box in Cobb's extended hand.

And that was all Cobb needed. With lightning speed, he delivered an upward, brutal punch deep into Patterson's throat while at the same time dropping the box. He grabbed the baton with the other hand and twisted it out of the prison guard's grasp.

Wide-eyed and clutching at his throat, Patterson staggered back, rasping sounds coming from behind his face mask, its sides billowing in and out as he fought to breathe.

With both hands clamped on the baton, Cobb brought it up horizontally and drove it hard up against Patterson's windpipe, steering the man toward the wall near the toilet, where there was a small privacy screen that shielded that section of the cell from the passageway outside.

With a choking cry that was muffled by the face mask, Patterson clawed at the baton, trying desperately to pull it away from under his chin as he was shoved back.

Reaching the wall behind the screen, Cobb pushed harder into Patterson, pinning him to the wall with just the baton rammed up hard against his throat. Patterson's eyes bulged, and he started turning purple. Cobb pushed harder, using his legs and hips.

"Mo-ther-fuck-er!" Cobb hissed, his face just inches from Patterson's bulging head. Then came a sickening crunch, and Patterson's body went limp. But Cobb kept the pressure on, holding the man's dead weight up now with just the pressure of the baton. Another thirty seconds passed with Cobb pinning the man to the wall, pressing as hard as he could. Then, he leaned back and glanced around the privacy screen.

Outside, all was quiet.

It took just minutes to swap clothes, Cobb putting on the guard's uniform, Patterson in prison coveralls. Cobb adjusted the utility belt around his waist that held all the usual guard goodies and the most prized possession of all: the security key card on a retractable cord that opened every door inside the prison. He slipped off Patterson's mask and secured it on his own face, ignoring the stench of sweat and bad breath. Next, he popped the lenses out of the thick frames and slid them on. No one would notice. Last, he pulled the guard's ball cap tight over his head. Between all three, the face mask, glasses, and ball cap, nearly all of his face was concealed.

He rolled the body onto the bed and covered it with the blanket, leaving only a tuft of dark hair at the top of his head showing.

It would be lights out in thirty minutes.

Perfect.

Dylan Cobb, dressed in full prison guard regalia, had become Stan Patterson and walked out of his own prison cell and locked the door behind him.

Using the key card, he unlocked the first door he came to before passing through effortlessly.

Keeping his head low, he immediately dropped into Stan Patterson mode, mimicking his slouchy swagger as he walked, even whistling the stupid little tune he always whistled. *"Heigh-ho, Heigh-ho. It's home from work we go!"* The next security checkpoint would be the real test. It was the main fortified exit out of the cell block, beyond that: freedom.

The passageway emptied into a wide, well-lit circular space. A bulletproof glass-enclosed guard control room for the entire cell block sat on the right next to a double-door gatehouse with an intercom panel on the wall. Both reinforced steel doors could only be opened by the guards on duty inside the control room, and not at the same time. Inside the glass-enclosed control room—which the guards affectionately called the fishbowl, while the inmates called it the toilet bowl—Cobb could see four guards sitting at the desks, monitoring the screens and doing paperwork.

Rudy, a brutish hulk from Texas who was sitting at the gate control desk on the other side of the glass, looked up as Cobb approached, then reached across to the microphone lance.

"Hey, Patterson. What did the dipshit Cobb want?" Rudy asked, his Texan drawl coming out of the speaker box of the intercom panel next to the gatehouse.

Cobb bristled but composed himself, then conjured up Patterson's accent he had been practicing too. "For me to wipe his sorry ass. He's got explosive diarrhea. Been butt-hugging that damn bowl and shitting out his intestines for the last ten minutes. You'd better not go in there."

"Fuck me," Rudy said. "You off shift now?"

Cobb kept his face tilted away from the control room and on the door in front of him. "Yep. Let me out, will ya?" Cobb kept his focus on the first security door, waiting for it to slide open.

"You good for another twenty on the Ravens-Patriots game this weekend?" Rudy asked through the intercom. The door still remained closed.

"Yeah. I'm in. It'll make up for the twenty I lost last week backing the shitty Steelers." Last week, Patterson had whined to Cobb for almost an hour about losing twenty bucks by betting against the Ravens when they had played the Steelers.

Rudy reached for the door release button, then stopped. "You got a cold, Patterson?"

Cobb turned his head but not fully. He pointed to his face mask. "Wearing this thing makes me sound like a robot. But it's better than picking up that shitty virus again."

Rudy smiled. "Your choice." He hit the button, and the first door slid open.

"Deal me in for fifty against the Patriots." Cobb stepped in, and the door closed behind him. "They ain't been the same since Brady left."

"Ain't that the truth," Rudy replied. He opened the second gate.

Without looking back, Cobb threw Rudy a, *see ya later* wave over his shoulder and kept walking.

Cobb passed through three more automatic doors, using the keycard without seeing another prison guard. Ten minutes later, he was outside in the parking lot. Keeping to the shadows and away from the security cameras, he hugged the wall and made his way to an external gate that he opened with the card.

Moments later, he crouched in the darkened tree line two hundred yards away from the outer perimeter fence, staring back at the floodlit prison structure.

He was out—a free man. Cobb always had the first part of the plan on how to escape figured out. It was just the second part of the plan—putting as much mileage as possible between him and the prison walls once he had escaped—that he hadn't figured out because there was no one on the outside to help him. Now, there was. Patterson's body would not be discovered until morning roll call at 8:00 a.m., a good eight hours away, and Cobb would be hundreds of miles from here by then.

It was time to see if his friend was true to his word and had delivered on the second part of the escape plan.

Cobb stood and then sprinted off into the dark woods.

29

MASK

The car was exactly where he said it would be parked. Half a mile east in the woods, just off a dirt road, it is nestled in a small hollow among a thick tangle of brambles so the casual passerby couldn't see it.

Reaching down, Cobb felt along the passenger side front tire, then snatched out the keys.

He'd been told to dump the car once he had arrived at his destination and that there was a surprise for him in the trunk.

Dylan Cobb unlocked the trunk. A small light came on, illuminating the inside. He smiled. Reaching in, he first took out the ice hockey mask, a goalie mask nonetheless, admiring it as he turned it in his hand. Immediately, memories came flooding back from his childhood and those gory, slasher horror movies he'd watched without his mother knowing. The mask reminded him, in particular, of one of his favorite villains. As a child, he wasn't ever scared of the character, nor did he feel squeamish at the ensuing bloodbath. It was the opposite. Cobb dreamed of being the character, wanting to enact the violence himself on others.

He pressed the mask to his face, then looped the two heavy elastic bands over the top of his head, adjusting them until the fit was snug. There were two holes for the eyes and a protrusion for the nose. The mask was dotted with circular holes, adding to the scary effect.

It fit perfectly.

Keeping the mask on, he looked at what else was in the trunk. His eyes caught the glint of something long and sharp in the moonlight. Reaching in, his hands wrapped around the wooden handle, and almost reverently, he withdrew the object out of the trunk. Holding it up, he took a moment to admire the long, wide blade. Using his thumb, he gently tested the sharpened edge. Even with a feather touch, it drew a line of blood along the pad of his thumb. Like the mask, the machete was perfect, too, and in keeping with the horror movie theme. But this wasn't some movie prop. He took a few swings, slashing and hacking at an imaginary torso, soon to be a real, living, breathing person.

After placing the mask and the machete back into the trunk, Cobb closed the lid and climbed into the driver's seat. On the passenger seat sat an envelope. He opened it and read the letter.

Dear Mr. Cobb:

I thought you would appreciate the costume, given what tonight is. I hope you don't mind, but I took the liberty of selecting it for you. In the glove box, you will also find a map of how to get to your destination quickly. There is a full tank of gas, and as I said in my previous communication, please dump the car on the outskirts of town when you arrive, leaving the keys in the ignition. I'm sure by morning, some lucky soul will take it.

I hope you enjoy this evening's festivities. I will

also be joining them. So, who knows? We may even cross paths.

Given that you have been imprisoned for over three years, you must have built up quite a thirst that needs quenching. I have provided you with the necessary tools and the camouflage to do so. Only on such a night like this, which only happens once a year in the fall, will you, like me, be able to walk freely through the town, unnoticed and unchallenged. Take full advantage of this opportunity.

I am glad that I could be of help. We are kindred spirits but on different paths, and I wish you well with your pursuits tonight. And I do hope that you find Haley Perez.

However, allow me to offer you some words of advice on that matter. Please note that I do not mean to be condescending. Being locked up and devoid of what you crave, I simply want to ensure that you savor the delights of the revenge you no doubt intend to reap from her for as long as possible. Take your time with her. And when you do, think of me. But before you find her, slake some of that pent-up urge to kill on others in the town. Kill as many as you like just to take that edge off.

They say that you should not arrive at a banquet table completely ravenous. Otherwise, it'll be over too soon. Vent some of that anger, that lust for revenge on others first. That way, when the time comes for you to confront Haley Perez, you can take your time and drain every drop of blood from her young, tender flesh because you have satisfied some of your appetite first on the festivities tonight. You will thank me for this advice.

Your friend,
Samuel J Pritchard

Cobb sat back and closed his eyes.

Pritchard understood. He *really* understood. Yes, he needed to blow off some steam first. Otherwise, when he confronted Haley Perez, he knew the demon deep inside him would overpower his own self-control, and he would kill her too quickly. Killing her slowly was the only penance she deserved for what she had done to him. She had shot him three times and humiliated him. Then, she had incarcerated him for over three long, hard years. And her visits had been nothing but torture for him as she sat there, barely inches outside his reach while he was chained to a table—seeing her there and smelling her musky, womanly scent as it drifted up from within her delicate panties. To watch her lick her moist lips with that serpent's tongue of hers. To marvel at her smooth, young skin. No. There was no release from all she had made him endure while inside prison.

He had all night to ease his thirst first, as Pritchard had put it. Otherwise, as they say, he would blow his load all in one go if he went after Perez right away.

He thought of the mask and machete in the trunk. There was no better way than to make up for lost time and feed his immediate, insatiable desire on tonight of all nights.

Inside the glove box, he found the handwritten map.

It was simple. In just three turns over the next two miles, he would be out on the highway. In under ninety minutes, he would be in the town of Ravenwood.

Cobb took the keys, started the engine, and shifted into reverse, then carefully backed out of the hollow among the brambles. After turning the wheel, he straightened onto the dirt road and pressed on the gas. He began drumming his hands on the steering wheel as he drove and then started whistling to himself. If he were anatomically capable, he would've had an erection by now. But the joy of killing Perez, dragging it out over weeks, was better than any sexual thought he had experienced. And for the carnage that was about to happen, the body count, the blood and gore, the lives he was going to take under the blade of the machete, the blame was entirely Perez's. She alone would be responsible for every life he would take between now and dawn.

30

GREEDY BILLY

The rubber mask was hot, and the two holes for eyes restricted his view, shrinking the world around him to a single, merged aperture.

He didn't care.

Groups of children clutching their parents' hands passed him by without a care in the world. It was the one night of the year when vampires, goblins, ghosts, and all manner of monsters could walk freely among the living without question, without being stopped, without so much as a second glance.

Darkness, thick and inviting, had descended on the streets of Ravenwood. Most homes were laced with lights, and jack-o'-lanterns sat in windows or on front porches, beckoning the young and young at heart to where candy bowls were placed. There were shrieks of excitement, a few screams, and plenty of laughter.

He paused under a sprawling tree on the sidewalk and watched the house across the street, its windows filled with a warm, soft glow. It was a nice house—two stories, white and blue—a stone path set into a green-trimmed lawn led to the wooden steps of the front porch. A 1978 black Trans Am was parked in the driveway. The safe, secure, and homey feel of the neighborhood was just a prequel to the true horror that was about to unfold.

"Hey, man. Nice costume." A father holding his son's and daughter's hands walked past. The two children were clutching bags full of candy—Little Red Riding Hood with a knife in her head and the boy dressed in a skeleton costume. Even the father had made an effort. Frankenstein's monster, with a bolt on each side of his neck, hair dyed black, and his face painted ghostly gray. The trio moved on.

Across the street, the front door of the house opened.

He would have pulled back farther behind the tree trunk, but not on this night. *Trick or treat?*

A woman stepped out—blonde hair, young, trim, all-American type with a tight T-shirt and cut-off shorts. She was carrying a big plastic bag of wrapped candy, which she tipped into the bowl on the porch that sat next to a glowing jack-o'-lantern. Then, she looked up, saw him standing across the street, and waved. She actually waved! *Definitely* a sweet treat, he thought as he watched her disappear back inside.

Carrying the knife in his hand, he lumbered across the street toward the house, passing two kids who were running along the sidewalk, screeching with delight when they saw him. "Hey, Myers, you ugly fucker! How come you never seem to die?" one kid called out to him before they disappeared around a corner.

Indeed, he thought.

He went up the path and onto the porch. A welcoming glow seeped through the side window near the front door. Then, there was movement from behind him. He whirled around, knife in hand.

"Trick-or-treat?" A group of five kids ran up the footpath, then onto the porch. Ignoring him, they clustered eagerly around the candy bowl like ants around a pile of sugar cubes. "Hey, stop pushing!" one kid yelled, jostling the others. "Wait your turn, Billy. You got enough candy already," he quipped.

"Whoa, peanut butter cups!"

"Leave some for the rest of us!" the kid Billy whined.

A sign was stuck to the post. *One handful only, please!*

Holding his ten-inch chef's knife, he stood patiently and waited, watching as some kids took two and three handfuls of candy, stuffing them into their burgeoning bags.

Then, four of the kids tore away back down the stairs in a chorus of laughs and giggles. Billy, with freckles, thick glasses, and short red hair, stayed behind and kept digging into the bowl.

He looked up as if noticing the man standing behind him dressed in the mechanic's coveralls and rubber mask for the first time. "Hey, mister, that's a cool-looking knife. It looks almost real. Why don't ya come back to my place and stick it in my mom's new boyfriend? He's a real asshole."

He said nothing.

Billy resumed his deep excavation into the candy bowl. "Aw! No fricken' peanut butter cups left!" Cussing, he then took off down the steps to join his friends waiting on the sidewalk, and the gaggle tumbled to the next house.

With the kids finally gone and with a real knife in his hand, he turned back to the front door and pressed the doorbell.

31

TRICK OR TREAT

Nick Castle gave Nancy's right breast another hard squeeze. Her tits were small, but Christ, were they firm. And she had those puffy nipples that seemed to make him hard just thinking about them.

Then, the doorbell rang.

"Who the fuck is ringing the doorbell?" he groaned, turning and looking back over his shoulder where they were reclined on the sofa in the living room.

He turned back to Nancy, her T-shirt bunched up above her naked breasts. "You filled up the candy bowl, didn't you?"

She nodded, pulling him closer. "Ignore it," she whispered, her voice husky. "There's plenty of candy out there and in here."

Nick smiled, leaned down, and sucked hard on her left nipple, teasing it erect with his teeth.

"Ouch!" Nancy gave a playful yelp, slapping Nick on the back of his head. "No biting. I don't like it when you bite."

He smiled and then began kissing down her midriff, moving slowly down to her belly button and then to the top of her lacy panties, where a tuft of soft, dark curls protruded. "Ooohh," he crooned, nuzzling his nose deep into the furrow that lay hidden behind the translucent material. "Dark chocolate is my favorite."

"Then hurry up and get eating before I change my mind."

The doorbell rang again.

"Damn it!" Nick growled. He rolled off the sofa and up onto his feet, ready to punch someone—even a little kid—in the mouth. Shirtless, he zippered up his jeans and stomped out of the room.

Nancy pushed up onto one elbow. "Hey, Nick!" she called out after him. "Go easy on them. They're just kids having some fun."

Out in the hallway, Nick stormed to the front door. "Just fucking kids, my ass!" After unlocking the door, he yanked it open. "Hey, you little fuck—"

He stopped, the door wide open, a person standing there, his frame filling the doorway, blocking out the street behind him.

Nick's heart kicked in his chest. "Holy shit, bro! You scared the shit out of me." Nick looked the kid up and down. The kid was bigger than him! He was too thick and muscled to be a kid, in fact, even if he was on the googie juice. It was a man. It had to be.

"You really went to town on the costume, bro." Nick caught a look at the big knife in the man's hand. "You've nailed it, bro. The knife even looks like the fucking real deal. That movie scared the shit out of me when I was a kid."

The man just stood there, two black hollows for eyes, like two little dark train tunnels.

Nick felt a shiver creep up his spine. "Take all the candy you want, bro," he said uneasily. Then, his eyes dropped to the man's forearms. The sleeves of the mechanic's coveralls he was wearing were neatly rolled up, the skin darkly tanned, old, wrinkled, and covered with black hair.

"Aren't you a little old for this shit?" Nick asked with an uncomfortable laugh. "I thought Halloween was just for kids, not adults."

The man said nothing—just stood there.

Nick shrugged. "We don't really grow up, do we?" He dropped his voice to a low whisper and snickered. "That movie, I gotta tell ya —just between us men. That Jamie Lee Curtis was hot as all hell in it—sweet, firm rack on her too."

Still nothing.

"Hey, bro. What's gotten into you? You, okay?" Nick waved his hand in front of the man's face, trying to get a response.

Nothing.

"Hey, babe!" Nancy's sultry voice floated out from the hallway behind Nick. "What's going on? Leave the kids. My candy store is closing soon."

Nick glanced behind him, then turned back to the man and smiled. "Sorry, bro." He began closing the front door. "Got my own candy to eat." Nick wanted to close the door quickly. The man was giving him the creeps now—like he was some kind of zombie. Maybe he was playing the part too seriously.

Nick swung the door shut faster—then it stopped with a shudder. Looking down, he saw a big military-style boot stuck firmly between the bottom of the door and the jamb.

"Hey! What the fuck—?"

The man shouldered the door inward, pushing Nick back. Then, a huge hand smothered Nick's mouth, cutting off his protests. White-hot pain sliced into Nick's chest, burrowing in deeper and deeper. He went to scream but instead belched up a mouthful of hot blood that sprayed out between the fingers that were clamped over half his face. He felt himself shunted back farther, the pain in his chest spreading like wildfire. Looking down, all he could see was the handle of the knife protruding from his chest. The rest of the blade was buried to the hilt.

The man closed the door behind him with a kick of his heel. Then, he pressed Nick up against the wall and began twisting the knife.

Nick felt like his chest was being eaten by a massive set of sharp, gnashing teeth, churning and tearing through his ribcage.

"Hey, babe. Get your ass in here quick, or you'll go hungry." Nancy's words again.

Tears filled Nick's eyes as his vision began to fade, all life seeping out of his chest, down his stomach, then his legs, and forming a spreading, red puddle around his bare feet. All thoughts went back to Nancy. He wanted to cry out, to tell her to run—that there was a monster in the house, and to get out. Then, he thought about his silky-black Trans Am parked a few feet away in the driveway and the driver's seat where Nancy had first straddled him all those months ago when they had parked up at the Dark Rift one moonless night. His beloved Trans Am. The '78 model he cherished so much. He was never going to ride in her again, or Nancy either.

His heart stuttered, squeezed out a few more beats along with a few more ounces of blood, then stopped.

32

NOT MARK

Was that the sound of a window breaking? Like glass shattering?

Sue Gill grabbed the stereo remote and turned down the volume. *On the Border* by the Eagles was playing on the record player. Maybe she had the sound up too loud, trying to muffle all the shrieking and laughter outside from kids going up and down the street. Perhaps someone had dropped a soda bottle outside?

Moving to the window, she parted the drapes and looked out. There was no one around. The bushes swayed in the wind, playing shadows across the lawn.

Sue was a striking figure at just twenty, with short blonde hair cut into a bob. So many guys had asked her out tonight, but her parents had booked a restaurant for their anniversary, which meant Sue had the whole house to herself. She was too old for trick-or-treating anyway. Maybe it was Mark Birmingham outside, the guy from whom she had borrowed The Eagles record? He was always playing jokes, trying to scare her at times. She closed the drapes. Mark had insisted Sue's mom cook another batch of cupcakes for him in return for lending Sue the record.

At the front door, Sue checked the three locks. All secure.

She turned—and nearly jumped out of her skin.

A man was standing there, right behind her. He wore an old army jacket over a T-shirt and a face mask. In his hand was a huge knife, the biggest Sue had ever seen. She sighed. "Mark, you nearly scared the bejesus out of me!" She slapped his arm.

She cocked her head, then folded her arms. "Thought you weren't into all this dressing up for Halloween?" She looked at the knife. "And where the hell did you get a fake knife like that?"

The man in the mask looked down at the knife in his hand, then back up at Sue.

"Anyway," she said, pushing past him, "Mom made you a fresh batch of angel cupcakes this afternoon." She headed toward the kitchen. "They're on the counter."

The man turned and obediently followed her.

In the kitchen, Sue saw that the back door was wide open. "So, that's how you got in," she said over her shoulder. "I mustn't have locked the back door."

She took one step, and her bare foot crunched on something. Stinging icicles of pain sliced into her foot, and she cried out. Broken glass littered the floor on the inside near the door. Looking closer, she saw that one of the small panes was broken, and jagged edges ringed the inside of the wooden frame. "What the—?"

She whirled around.

The man was standing in the kitchen with her.

"Mark?" Fear boiled in Sue's stomach, and she began backing away toward the back door. More glass sliced into her feet, and she cried out in pain again. "M-Mark?" she whimpered, tears rolling down her cheeks.

On the kitchen counter near her stood a block of knives. Sue grabbed at one, slid it out, and held it up threateningly. "Who... Who are you?" She slashed the knife in the air. "Stay away from me!"

The man stepped toward her, bringing up his own knife. At that moment, Sue realized it wasn't a fake he was holding. It was real and much bigger than the one she had in her own hand. Sue pictured her cell phone on the sofa back in the living room, and the man was blocking her only escape to get to it.

There was a phone on the kitchen wall, but it was behind the man. She would never be able to get past him and reach it in time, let alone dial 9-1-1.

The man stepped forward again, and Sue backed away some more, her feet now slippery with blood, leaving a trail of red footprints but in reverse—as though she were walking backward in time toward a previous version of herself.

Suddenly, the man lurched. The big knife swept horizontally through the air in a wide arc, just inches from her face. The tip of the blade scraped across a cabinet door next to Sue's head, leaving a deep, jagged scratch in the wood.

The man gave an animalistic, guttural grunt of frustration. "You dirty little bitch!" he hissed through the mask.

Sue backed away until the door was at her back. She couldn't go any farther.

He swung the knife again. Searing pain cut across Sue's upper arm, and she cried out. Blood poured from a deep slice in her skin. Survival instinct took over, and she lashed out with her own knife, cutting a deep gash across the back of the hand holding the knife.

He growled like a rabid dog.

Blood began seeping from his wound and onto the kitchen floor.

Sue froze in horror, holding the knife, unable to comprehend what she had just done. But he was going to kill her. So, she had to defend herself, right? Her free hand groped behind her, found the doorknob, twisted it, and pulled the door. This time, she lunged forward, burying the knife into the man's chest before turning and fleeing out through the open doorway.

Sue's feet slipped out from under her on the porch's top step, and she toppled down the steps, landing hard on the grass below. Her heart caught in her mouth when she glanced over her shoulder. The man was there, standing in the doorway, a dark, monstrous apparition. She watched in horror as he slowly reached up, then pulled the knife from his chest and tossed it aside.

He began walking down the steps toward her.

Sue staggered to her feet and looked around wildly. Tall fences —too tall for her to climb—boxed in the backyard. Her only hope was to run down the side of the house and get to the street out front. There would be people there. She could flag down a passing car and get help.

Clutching her bleeding arm, she ambled down the side path of the house.

33

BIG KNIFE

Perez was driving with Shaw in the passenger seat. The windows were wound down.

"Did you ever celebrate Halloween as a kid?" Shaw asked.

"No need to," she replied.

He gave her a strange look, but thankfully, he said nothing more. During her childhood, it was Halloween almost every night when she was shoved under the stairs by her father. It had given her enough nightmares to last a lifetime.

Shaw had his arm bent out the window, drumming his fingers on the sill. "Can't believe all these people."

"What about you? Did you celebrate Halloween?" She doubted it.

"No. I just wasn't into it."

Perez took a left, down a street that seemed more secluded and away from the main commotion of trick-or-treating.

At first, she thought it was a ghost, someone dressed in a white sheet for a costume, running out onto the road, the headlights making them almost translucent.

"Shitttttt!" Perez hit the brakes. The car skidded to a stop so close the person's hands came to rest on the front of the hood as though they were pushing back the vehicle.

It was a young woman, maybe in her late teens, her face deathly white, wearing shorts and a white T-shirt—that had one red sleeve. No. That didn't seem right to Perez. The woman's arm was coated in blood. But before she could respond, Shaw was already out of the car, helping the woman. He glanced back at Perez as she swung her door open. "She's been injured, attacked. For real. Hit the lights."

Perez flicked on the lights, and blue flickered across the surrounding houses. The young woman was babbling, clinging to Shaw, wide-eyed and fearful. "He... he tried to kill me. A man. Big knife. A mask. Tried to kill me."

"She's in shock," Perez said. Together, they carefully eased the woman from the road, across the footpath, and onto the front lawn of the closest house where the lights were on inside. The woman looked toward the house, her body shaking.

"Ma'am, what is your name?" Perez asked.

Horrified eyes switched between Perez and Shaw, her lips trembling.

"Your name, ma'am? What is your name?" Perez repeated. She had to keep the woman talking; otherwise, she would go into full shock.

"S-Sue. Sue G-Gill."

The shirt she wore was soaked in blood, and blood spatter criss-crossed her face.

Perez clamped her hand over the deep gash in her arm where the blood was seeping. "There's a trauma kit, Ben, in the back. Grab it."

Shaw came back moments later carrying a large medical pouch, tore it open, and wrapped a tourniquet on Sue's upper arm, cinching it tight with the Velcro band to stop the hemorrhaging.

Perez watched, suitably impressed. "Done that a few times, have you?"

Shaw looked at her. "That and more."

Perez glanced over at the house. The front door was shut.

Sue followed Perez's gaze. "That's my house. He-he was in there. I couldn't come out the front. The door is locked. I ran around the side, the back door. That's how he got in. He's in the backyard. Big knife. Wearing a horrible mask."

"Ma'am, calm down," Perez said as she took a heavy dressing pad from the kit and pressed it hard against the wound. "I'm going to radio for help." Using her spare hand, she called for paramedics on her two-way as well as for backup, then checked the woman's pulse. She was still trembling, and her heart was racing.

Sue gripped Perez's arm, a manic look in her eye. "You must stop him. Others. He'll hurt others. He's got a big knife."

Perez had to do something if there was a man with a knife. She had to stop him. There were kids around. She looked up. "Ben, you stay—"

It was then she realized she was alone with the young woman.

Ben was gone.

34

MONSTERS

Beth is driving, and I'm in the passenger seat, looking out the window as we drive through leafy neighborhoods, passing groups of children with their parents.

Jack-o'-lanterns, fat and glowing orange, sit on porches, and the warm lights from windows light the streets. The police scanner sits silent, nestled in my hands. There's been nothing—no incidents to report. In yellow pools beneath streetlamps, kids and adults huddle with open bags, comparing their candy hauls.

I never really celebrated Halloween. Little did I know as a child that I'd be chasing real-life monsters when I grew up. I'd had no idea about today's date. Now, I understand what Ellie said about everyone masking up.

"Jesus!" Beth exclaims, hitting the brakes. We come to a screeching halt.

A huge figure in a grotesque mask, wearing pale blue coveralls and carrying a knife, stands in the glare of our headlights. Michael Myers is standing in the middle of the road. Slowly, he turns his head toward us.

Even now, years later, no longer a kid anymore, that hollow-eyed face mask that looks like it has been stitched together from pieces of human skin still gives me the creeps. The big fake knife he is carrying glints under the glare. He gives us his trademark vacant stare for a few seconds before turning and resuming his lumbering walk across the street.

"I thought he died?" Beth says as we take off again.

I manage a smile. "He dies in all of the movies but still keeps coming back for more."

We pass more monsters, vampires, skeletons, and a few Frankenstein's monsters. Freddy Krueger, I see leaning against a streetlamp, his knife fingers opening and closing.

The cool night air flows in through my side window.

Then, a blood-curdling scream shatters the peaceful calm.

Beth hears it, too, and she hastily pulls to the curb. We sit in silence, both windows down, straining to listen. It was a woman's scream, I'm certain.

It comes again, a woman's scream, up ahead. I reach for my gun in its holster.

Then she appears from around the corner, running hard and being chased by Jason from *Friday the 13th*. He is wearing his white goalie hockey mask and swinging that machete he always carries. The woman's screams sound more like hysterical laughter now. He catches her, and they embrace before walking arm-in-arm down the sidewalk.

"How the hell are we going to find Pritchard with all this going on?" Beth says as we pull away from the curb and resume our search.

"It's the perfect night to hide in plain sight," I say as I scan the sidewalks on both sides. I see another Michael Myers, smaller than the one Beth almost ran over but equally as creepy. Then, there was another Jason, again sporting the same type of goalie hockey mask, and two more Frankenstein's monsters. A cluster of vampires huddles—little kids, mini vampires, I guess—under a streetlight, swapping candy.

Beth makes a right turn, and we enter another street. Kids and parents are milling around—more of the same. Ghosts, ghouls, and monsters in costumes—plenty small and a few big. Adults never growing up—doing the whole nine yards.

Then my police scanner crackles to life, startling me. I turn it up so both Beth and I can listen. A stabbing—a woman has been attacked by an intruder. The dispatcher is calling for all units in the vicinity to respond. I punch the address into my cell and bring up the map. It quickly plots the fastest route to the address given.

"How far?" Beth asks, all grim-faced.

"Under two miles." I start giving her directions, and she hits the gas.

"What about Ellie and Beau?" she asks. "Should you call them?"

"Let's see what we've got first," I say. "I don't want all of us to turn up at once."

At an intersection, we hang a left and head down a darkened street, the streetlamps not so frequent here. Not as many people about either. Beth is a good driver. She knows the urgency but is also mindful of children out on the streets tonight. I check the map on my cell. We're eating up the distance. "Take the next right. We're nearly there. And if the place is already crawling with cops, just keep our distance," I tell Beth.

She nods.

Clearing a bend, flashing blue lights hit us, and there's only a single police SUV pulled up in the middle of the road. There's a woman lying down on a nearby front lawn. Another woman is crouching next to her. "Pull over," I say to Beth. Is it real, or is it just another elaborate Halloween hoax? Then I see the SUV more clearly. It has the same license plate we saw on the police SUV up at the Dark Rift yesterday.

We come to a stop, our headlights flooding the two women on the lawn. The woman on the ground is covered in blood. The woman crouching turns, and I see her face in full... pale and drawn in the twin beams.

Something rips deep in my chest as I recognize her.

"Hell!" Beth sees her, too.

We climb out and start running.

35

HELPING HAND

Perez looked up as the car skidded to the curb, then two women climbed out and ran toward her.

To her shock, Perez recognized the younger of the two women. She was in the back seat of the pickup truck she had met on the drive down from the Dark Rift. Then she recognized the second, older woman. She had been in the passenger seat. What were they doing here?

Reaching Perez, the younger woman knelt. "Haley Perez?"

Shock hit Perez. "How do you know my name? I'm not even wearing a name badge."

Ignoring the question, the woman touched Perez's arm. "My name is Carolyn Ryder." She gestured to the older woman. "And this is Beth Rimes."

The two women looked at Perez, and the one named Ryder spoke. "You look like you could use some help. What happened?"

"She's been stabbed by a man wearing a Halloween mask," Perez said. "Paramedics are on the way, but the bleeding has stopped." She regarded the two strangers closely. "As I said, how do you know my name?"

Again, no answer. "Haley, it's important," Ryder said. "We're here in Ravenwood searching for Sam Pritchard."

Sam Pritchard? None of this made sense. Perez was confused. "Who are you?" Perez demanded. "Why did you say Sam Pritchard?"

Ryder spoke again. "Sam Pritchard is here in Ravenwood. We saw him. He could be the one who stabbed her. We think he was hiding out at—"

Perez cut her off. "There's no time to explain. A man attacked this woman. He's in that house. My partner has gone in after him. I need to go and help before my partner kills him."

Ryder and Rimes exchanged looks, and then Ryder asked slowly —like she was trying to get her head around the situation, "Why is your partner going to kill him?"

Now, the woman was starting to irritate Perez with her questions.

Ryder stood and looked at the house. "I'll go after him and help. Pritchard is extremely dangerous."

Perez pulled her back down. "No, you stay with her. Her name is Sue. Keep her talking. Paramedics are on the way. This is a police matter. You're just a civilian. Stay out of it."

To Perez, Ryder looked like she had just been punched in the face by her. Then Rimes sat down next to Sue and took her hand in her own to comfort her. "Hi, Sue. I'm Beth. It's going to be okay. You're with me now. You're safe." She threw Ryder a pleading look.

"But I know Pritchard," Ryder stated, turning back to Perez. "I can—"

Perez saw red. She was losing control of the situation and didn't take kindly to being pushed around by some bystander wannabe cop. "I don't care if you know the fucking Pope!" Perez hissed, pulling Ryder up and away from listening ears. "Stay here, or I'll arrest the pair of you for police obstruction."

Perez could see anger flare in the woman's eyes. But then it faded, and she just nodded in acceptance.

Perez drew her gun and took off toward the side of the house.

36

CHASE

"Jesus, I nearly shot you!" Perez whispered, aiming her gun up and at the person standing at the top of the porch stairs at the rear of the house.

"If I were Jesus, then it wouldn't matter," Shaw replied, not looking at her.

Perez lowered her gun and moved to the bottom step. Shaw's eyes looked almost transparent in the milky darkness—like a cat's. He swiveled his head back and forth, searching the backyard.

Holstering her gun, Perez scanned the backyard as well. It was fenced in on three sides—tall fences, six feet at least by her estimate. The roofs of neighboring houses were just visible.

Shaw came down the steps and stood beside her. "I've cleared the house. He's not in there."

Perez couldn't believe he had gone inside without a weapon—nothing, just his bare hands, grit, and determination. Sue kept repeating that her attacker had a big knife. "It could be Sam Pritchard," Perez whispered.

"What do you mean, Pritchard?" Shaw commanded a raw edge in his voice. "He's here? How do you know? Did the woman say it was him? How would she know? Did she recognize him somehow?

I thought he was wearing a mask?" The questions came thick and fast.

Perez held up her hand to shut him up. "Wait a sec. There's a woman—two women—looking after Sue at the front. They pulled up just after you took off without telling me. One of them told me they were hunting Pritchard."

"Hunting Pritchard?" Shaw gave her a skeptical look. "They're cops too. FBI, maybe?"

It was a good question. Perez had just assumed they weren't. "Look, we don't have time now. I'll explain later." Perez didn't know how she was going to explain something she was having trouble understanding herself. The two women just appeared out of nowhere. They knew her name. And tonight, where was the man who had been driving the pickup truck the other day? Was he also looking for Pritchard? Were they a posse of bounty hunters? A ragtag vigilante group of Boba Fetts minus the jet packs and laser guns. After all, there was a one-million-dollar reward for any information leading directly to Pritchard's arrest.

Shaw stepped into the yard and walked a few paces. Perez followed.

"What?" she asked.

He held up his hand, shushing her. A dog barked—close, to the left—maybe a few backyards over. Shaw took off like a hunting dog catching a scent. He scaled the fence before Perez could blink and disappeared over the other side.

"Damn it!" It took her two attempts to clamber over the fence, her utility belt catching on the top of the pickets, before landing unceremoniously on the other side with a thud on her ass.

In the next backyard, she could make out Shaw in the darkness, standing next to a kids' swing set. He was doing the hunting dog thing again, sniffing the air.

A flashlight beam suddenly cut across the backyard, hitting Perez squarely in the face. "Who the fuck are you?" a gravelly voice came from the shadows under the patio at the rear of the house.

Perez held her hand up against the glare. "Police business, sir," she said. "Go back inside."

"Someone was in my backyard before," the man said. "Jumped over the fence. That's why I'm here."

"Did you see which way he went?" Shaw snapped. The flashlight swept across the yard and then ended on the fence on the left. "That side. Just a few moments ago."

Shaw took off again without waiting for Perez and vanished over the fence and into the adjacent yard.

Perez followed. On the other side, she found herself not in another backyard but in a narrow alleyway that seemed to run behind several properties.

Shaw was running away from her, sprinting fast, with no gun, no flashlight, chasing a person who was limping down the alley. It was like watching a cheetah running down an injured gazelle with the same animalistic, single-minded ruthlessness.

Perez took off after Shaw.

Then, up ahead, something came out of the darkness and jumped at the person Shaw was chasing. There was a growl, then several wild barks.

The person who was limping suddenly stopped, lifted their arm, and brought it down. The dog whimpered, then came back twice as fierce.

Perez ran harder. She needed to catch Shaw before he got to Pritchard. She wanted him alive and knew Shaw was going to kill him on the spot.

The dog's barks intensified and then suddenly cut off.

Perez watched as Shaw barreled into the person, and they crashed to the ground and began struggling.

Pulling up and gasping, Perez drew her gun and aimed it at the tangle of arms and legs thrashing about on the ground in front of her. A few feet away lay a German Shepherd, its body almost hacked to pieces. The front sight of Perez's handgun wavered as she struggled to keep her aim steady on the person who wasn't Shaw, but it was no good. They twisted and slithered—two people meshed as one.

Then Shaw was on top, straddling Pritchard's chest, pinning down his arms with his knees, hooking punches down on either side of Pritchard's head, behind the sides of the ugly thick white mask he was wearing.

One of Pritchard's hands held a huge, long knife, the biggest Perez had ever seen. He was struggling to get it free from under Shaw's crushing knee. But it was pinned firmly to the ground.

Thrusting his hips up, Pritchard tried to buck Shaw off. Then he rotated under Shaw's body, trying to slither out from under him. Shaw obliged, smoothly transitioning Pritchard to his stomach, while at the same time, he came up to a low squat and stomped viciously down on the hand holding the knife. Pritchard screamed and released the knife, and Shaw kicked it away. Pritchard was now flat on his stomach with Shaw's knee pressing hard against his back, holding him in place.

Perez stood over Pritchard, aiming her gun down at the back of his head, which was wrapped with the thick elasticized straps of the mask. "Don't fucking move, or I'll shoot you," she snarled.

Shaw slipped one arm under Pritchard's neck, lifted his head off the ground and into a chokehold from behind, and began squeezing.

Pritchard gasped and began struggling, his hands clawing at Shaw's arm, which was clamped under his chin and crushing his throat. "Time to die!" Shaw hissed into Pritchard's ear, pulling him back more. "For what you did to me."

Pritchard's spine inched farther back, bending at an unnatural angle, his own body weight being used against him to crush his own neck.

Panic rose in Perez. "Ben! No! I need him alive."

Shaw didn't seem to hear. He kept pulling like he was going to wrench Pritchard's head clean from his neck.

Gurgling sounds came through the round holes in the face mask.

"No! Don't kill him," Perez pleaded. But she felt powerless. It was like Shaw was possessed by some dark, heinous demon that was determined to kill Pritchard.

Even Shaw's voice seemed inhuman. "You motherfucker," he rasped. "What you did to me. I've searched high and low for you for six long, hard months. Now, I have you, and you're going to die."

Perez gripped her gun harder. "He'll go to jail, Ben—for the rest of his life. I promise. He'll get justice. But not if you kill him now. It will be too easy for him."

Still grappling with Pritchard's head, Shaw looked up and glared at her. "There is no justice for people like him. This is the only justice he deserves."

"Ben, I've got him covered. I'll shoot him if he resists. Let him go. I'll cuff him and take him in."

Shaw twisted Pritchard's head sideways—a few more inches and his neck would snap.

"Please, Ben. Don't do this."

Shaw relaxed his arms a fraction, his chest heaving, his breaths short and ragged. Then, he let go.

Pritchard flopped down, his face smacking the ground hard.

Pushing himself off, Shaw got to his feet. His hands were bunched into fists, his face contorted, his neck muscles bulging. He started pacing back and forth like a ravenous dog Perez had just stolen a meat bone from.

Perez held her aim on Pritchard's head. He was face down, making gurgling sounds into the dirt. Next to him lay the knife. Perez looked at it closer. It wasn't a big knife, as Sue Gill had said repeatedly. To the untrained eye, it could easily be mistaken for a big knife, which, in a way, a machete was. But it was more suited to chopping and hacking, not thrusting and slicing like a more conventional knife. Her heart crumpled in her chest when she glanced to where the poor dog lay, butchered by Pritchard.

Shifting to a one-handed grip, she reached down with her other hand and ripped the mask off Pritchard's head. He was still face down but breathing, not moving.

She held the mask up, examining it, turning it left and right in her hand. It wasn't a rubber mask that fully enclosed the head as she first thought. Instead, it was a white goalie hockey mask. The creepy kind with two large holes for the eyes and dime-sized holes drilled across the face for ventilation.

Tossing the mask aside, she went back to her double grip on the handgun.

Pritchard began to stir, small movements at first. Then he coughed and sucked in a lungful of air, then coughed again.

"Stand up," Perez commanded. "If you try anything, I will shoot you."

Shaw stopped his pacing and came over.

Pritchard stopped coughing, then began laughing—a twisted, manic laugh.

"Shoot him," Shaw said scornfully. "Do society and taxpayers a favor. The man is clearly insane."

The machete lay within reach, but Perez ignored it.

"Get up," she demanded, her finger tightening on the trigger.

Slowly, Pritchard pushed himself off the ground and staggered to his feet. He stood, swaying slightly.

"Turn around and face me," Perez said. If he tried anything, shooting him in the back would be more complicated to explain.

"Well, well, well," Pritchard said. "If it isn't Haley."

Perez's aim wavered. *My name? How does he know my name?* His voice sounded croaky, hoarse from almost being choked to death by Shaw. But she had heard it. Her name. *Haley.* And the way he had said it, too... dragging out the *E.*

Haleeeeey.

It was just the way someone else she knew did.

Raising his hands, Pritchard began to slowly pivot around with his feet. When he completed his turn and was facing them, he smiled at Perez. "Hello, Haley. It's good to see you so soon again."

So soon again? All the air in Perez's lungs shot out of her mouth in one crushing gasp, leaving her breathless as she looked straight into the eyes of Dylan Cobb.

Cobb turned as if noticing the man standing beside Perez for the first time. His expression instantly changed from one of joy to one of seething hatred. "You?" he hissed at Shaw.

37

BAD NEWS

I'm so tempted to draw my gun and take off after Haley Perez. It's me, not her, who should be chasing after Sam Pritchard.

Sue Gill is still shaking, but at least the bleeding has stopped, and her breathing appears back to normal. I can't leave her. Beth is more than capable, but other variables are in play now, namely Perez and her partner. If I draw my gun and join in the pursuit, they could mistake me for Pritchard and shoot me instead. Plus, more cops will be arriving soon to complicate matters.

"Where are the damn paramedics!" Beth grumbles.

"They should be here soon, I hope." I glance over my shoulder toward the side of the house where Perez had disappeared just moments before. If she doesn't catch Pritchard, and he escapes again, he will flee Ravenwood for certain, and that thought kills me inside. All of this would have been for nothing.

The wail of a siren cuts into my anxiety. The sound is rapidly growing louder. People across the street have now come outside to see what is happening. An ambulance appears around the corner, lights flashing. It pulls up to the curb. Paramedics jump out, carrying their equipment, and hustle to where we are on the front lawn. I give them a brief rundown on the victim. They take over, and Beth and I retreat into the shadows.

More neighbors are out now, milling around, trying to get a look at the commotion on the front lawn. Then, there are more wailing sirens in the distance, getting closer. A police car appears from the opposite end of the street and screeches to a halt. Then, another one pulls in from the other direction. Officers pile out from both, guns drawn. They swarm the property, stopping for a moment to talk to the victim before approaching the house. Some go down the side of the house to the back, while others leap up the front stairs. Moments later, they breach the front door with a hard kick and disappear inside.

Thankfully, I left my police scanner back in the car; otherwise, they would've been suspicious if they had seen me with it—the paramedics, too.

My cell phone rings. It's Beatriz. Beth and I slink farther back. I don't even manage to get a word out before Beatriz yells in my ear. "Cobb has escaped! Cobb has escaped! He has broken out of prison."

My head spins, and blood pulses inside my skull. I watch as the paramedics load the victim onto a gurney and then wheel her toward the open doors of the ambulance.

I glance at Beth. Her face is pale and drawn. She would have overhead Beatriz's bellowing voice. Beth huddles closer, and I tilt the phone between us. "When did he escape?" I ask.

"They don't know," Beatriz replies. "The alarm call just came through now on the radio. I've been tuned into the local police channel up at the prison. They just found a dead prison guard inside Cobb's cell and no sign of Cobb. They've also raised the alarm and notified the local sheriff and State Troopers. They've started a search of the grounds, and the entire place is going into lockdown. Someone did a random check of Cobb's cell after lights out—which was more than two hours ago—and found the dead prison guard in his bed instead of Cobb himself."

"Lights out more than two hours ago?" Beth growls, "And they've just discovered him missing now?" She's seething, and I don't blame her. "Pritchard damn well didn't waste any time in helping him," she sneers.

I check my watch. The prison is about a ninety-minute drive from Ravenwood. I look around at the darkened streets. A few of the neighbors milling around are looking in our direction. Is it possible? Is Dylan Cobb here right now?

Beatriz is back in my ear. "I'll keep monitoring the radio broadcasts from the prison and let you know any updates."

I end the call, and Beth and I exchange looks. She nods. "He's here. Cobb is. Right now. He would have found the quickest way he could to get back here to Ravenwood, especially if he's on the run from the authorities. He's going to make good on his promise to kill Haley Perez."

She's right. I've got to tell Haley Perez about Dylan Cobb. That is, if she survives her pursuit of Sam Pritchard.

More police arrive. With our heads down, Beth and I walk quickly back to the car, climb in, and slowly drive away.

Now, we have two monsters on the loose in Ravenwood.

38

UNARMED

Dylan Cobb looked from Shaw to Perez. "The two of you?" he said in disbelief. "Together?"

Cobb's nose was flattened into his face, and blood dripped down his upper lip and onto his teeth, making him look like a vampire who had just been feasting off his last victim's neck.

Perez held her aim, pointing a gun at the center mass of Cobb's body. "Don't move an inch, or I will shoot you."

Cobb glanced down to where the machete lay a few feet from him.

"Don't," Perez warned. "I will shoot you."

Cobb raised his hands more. "As you can see, Haley, I am unarmed, and I surrender." His voice sounded nasal, blood dripping down his chin now.

Perez stepped closer. "I don't know how you escaped. But now you're caught."

Cobb nodded at Shaw. "And this guy is your new friend? Your boyfriend? Do you know what he did to me in Erin's Bay?" Cobb turned to Shaw, pure hatred in his eyes. "He disfigured me."

"I should've killed you," Shaw replied, his voice cold and calm. "One of the biggest regrets of my life."

Cobb tossed his head back and gave a manic little laugh. "Well, well, well." He looked back at Perez. "Seems like *déjà vu,* doesn't it, Haley? Like it was before. You have cornered me. You're holding the gun."

"Don't call me Haley."

Cobb's eyes narrowed. "I could always call you by your real name if you like?"

Perez tightened her grip. It would be so easy just to shoot him here and now.

"Yes," Cobb said, his voice soft and taunting. "I could tell your boyfriend here all about your sorry little past."

"Shut up," she snarled, applying more pressure to the trigger.

Shaw looked at Perez. "Don't fall for that old trap, Haley. Don't let him get to you. Scum like him doesn't deserve anything—especially a third chance."

Cobb twirled one of his raised hands. "Fourth chance, fifth chance, who cares?" he scoffed. He lowered his voice, and those hypnotic eyes Perez had come to know so well settled on her. "You caught me before. Both of you have. And yet...." He gave a little bow. "Here I am, a free man."

"Not for much longer," Perez retorted. She still couldn't comprehend how Cobb had escaped. That here he was, back in Ravenwood, dressed in a Halloween costume and almost murdering another woman.

She was glad Shaw was by her side. Cobb was capable of anything. Him standing here right now in front of her was proof. Cuffing him on her own meant holding her gun one-handed. He would undoubtedly escape.

Then, Cobb did the unexpected. Dropping his hands, he held them in front of him. "Handcuff me," he said. "Go on." He pivoted his hands toward Shaw and offered them to him. "Handcuff me. Arrest me. Take me in. But no prison can hold me. I'll escape again. That's my life's mission."

Perez glanced at the machete on the ground. This had to end.

Cobb stood there with his hands outstretched. "Come on. What are you waiting for? I'll be tucked up in bed soon. Back to three square meals a day. I'm looking forward to it."

Perez made up her mind. "Put down the weapon, or I will shoot you," she said in a stern voice.

Confusion flickered in Cobb's eyes. "What?"

"You heard me. Put down the weapon, or I will use lethal force."

Cobb gave an uncomfortable laugh. "What do you mean, put down the weapon? I have no weapon." He glanced down at the machete. "I'm not holding any weapon."

"This is your last warning," Perez said. "Put down the weapon, or I will shoot you."

Cobb's face went still like a switch had been flipped inside his brain—the kind of expression you get when something sinister suddenly dawns upon you. He pleaded with Shaw. "What the fuck is going on? She can't do this. It's against the law." Now, he was very animated. Panic eased into his voice. He turned back to Perez. "You fucking bitch! Don't you dare. I'm unarmed." Cobb stepped and then kicked the machete farther away. "See! You can't shoot me."

"Unarmed just the way all your victims were?" Then, in a calm, almost detached voice, Perez continued. "There'll be no escape for you again, Cobb. Because there are some things in this world that you cannot escape from."

Alarm flared in Cobb's eyes.

Perez raised her aim twelve inches, away from Cobb's chest to up between his eyes, aiming for the bridge of the nose.

"No, no, no!" Cobb spluttered. "You can't do this. I want justice. I deserve justice. It's the law."

Perez tilted her head and gave Cobb her own twisted, little smile. "There's no justice for people like you," she said, repeating Shaw's words. "This is the only justice you deserve—that all your victims deserve."

Cobb dropped his hands and stepped toward Perez. "But Prit—"

Perez pulled the trigger.

A single shot rang out. One shot. Not three as she had taken before when she had captured him. One shot could be explained. Three would be more difficult in this instance.

One shot was all that was required.

Cobb's head kicked back violently, tugging his body back with it. His arms flew up as the bullet entered the nasal bone between his eyes, shattering it into a dozen tiny shards. Then it sliced through the bottom inch of the frontal lobe, that part of the brain that suppresses socially inappropriate behavior—the part Dylan Cobb had never used since birth. The bullet continued its destructive trajectory, tearing through the temporal lobe next before finally exiting the back of his head as though a steel fist had been punched through. The top half of his skull sheared off in one piece. Everything from his eyebrows up came away from the rest of the cranium in one bloody chunk of bone, cartilage, and scalp hair.

It was only after the echo of the shot began to fade that Perez heard the thumping sound of blood in her ears.

She lowered her gun and began shaking.

Shaw placed a gentle hand on her shoulder. "It's okay. Holster your weapon."

Perez did as she was asked. Then she walked a few feet and looked down at the almost decapitated body of Dylan Cobb. There would be no sequel. No reincarnation. No come back.

Perez felt like she was in a daze. She was still shaking, blood pounding in her ears.

"Haley."

She turned to see Shaw standing behind her. "It was a bad shot," he said softly. "That's all." Gently, he placed both hands on her shoulders and looked deep into her eyes. "That's all."

Tears filled her eyes. Tears of sadness and tears of joy. Sadness for all the victims Dylan Cobb had killed. Joy that she had killed him herself.

She nodded.

He squeezed her shoulders. "As I said, it was just a bad shot.

Cobb had the machete in his hand. You had no choice but to use lethal force to protect yourself and other innocent people."

"Bad shot?" she repeated. But it was a good shot—right on the money. Right between the eyes as she intended.

Shaw nodded. "When they ask you. There'll be an investigation —an inquiry. You stumbled back when he rushed at you, the machete in his hand, ready to kill you. You tripped and lost your footing. Your aim was then thrown high as you pulled the trigger. You had already warned him three times to drop the weapon. That is what I saw and heard. Agreed?"

Perez said nothing.

He shook her gently, then said more firmly. "Agreed?"

She nodded.

Then he kissed her on the forehead, his lips warm and soft.

"What was that for?" she asked, the kiss breaking her from her daze.

Shaw smiled. "For saving my life, too."

39

THE OTHERS

"I just want to say thank you for not saying anything back there," Ryder said. "When I called you, it sounded like you were in the thick of it."

Haley Perez stood, leaning against the hood of her police SUV, arms folded, feeling distinctly outnumbered. They were parked three blocks away from Sue Gill's home, out on the main drag in a dimly lit parking lot of what had once been a large store selling imported tractors and spare parts. Now, it was just a dilapidated shell of a building boarded up with ply.

In the time that had transpired since the shooting death of Dylan Cobb, local police had descended on the neighborhood, led by her boss, Kershaw. Sue Gill had been packed off to the nearest hospital, and Cobb's body had been bagged and sent to the morgue. Perez had given her initial statement, and as was standard procedure with an officer-involved shooting, she had surrendered her weapon. The Independent Investigation Division, in the coming days, would give her a more thorough interview and debrief.

"How did you get my cell phone number?" Perez asked. Ryder had called Perez after the shooting and begged her not to mention what she had said to her about Sam Pritchard being in Ravenwood.

She said that they needed to talk in private right away. And that was how Perez found herself now, in an empty parking lot with Carolyn Ryder, Beth Rimes, and Beau Hodges. All three of them were in the pickup truck she had stopped on the dirt road going up to the Dark Rift. There was a fourth person Perez hadn't seen before—a young woman who had introduced herself as Ellie Sutton.

"It's not important how I got your cell number," Ryder said. "What's important right now is finding Sam Pritchard."

"You'd better make it quick," Perez said. "Tell me what you know about Sam Pritchard and why you think he's here in Ravenwood."

"Where is your partner?" Rimes then asked. "The guy that you said first chased after Dylan Cobb?"

Perez had already told them it was Cobb who had attacked Sue Gill, not Pritchard, and that she had shot him dead. "He is busy back at the crime scene." Truth be known, Perez had no idea where Ben Shaw was. He told her he didn't want to get involved with the police right now unless he was called upon as a witness later. But Sue Gill wasn't blind. It would only be a matter of time before she was interviewed and told the police that a second individual was on the lawn, helping her initially—a young man with Haley Perez. After Cobb's death, Shaw had taken off into the darkness from the alleyway after telling her he would call her in a few hours once the dust settled down.

"You lied to me," Perez said. "You told me you were just tourists."

"We're all on the same side," Ryder said.

Perez looked around the group. They were all watching her intently, especially Beth Rimes, the retired police officer from Utah.

"Get on with it," Perez said impatiently. "Why do you think Sam Pritchard is here and that it was him who had stabbed that woman?"

"That's what we originally thought," Ryder replied. "That it was Pritchard who had attacked Sue Gill, and that's who you and your partner were then chasing. We made a mistake. But we know Pritchard is here in Ravenwood."

"And how do you know he's here?" Perez asked. "You seem to be clueless as to what is actually going on." Her cell phone rang. It was Kershaw. She pressed the side button twice quickly and declined the call. She would give Ryder five more minutes, and then she would leave. She really needed to get back to the crime scene in the alleyway.

Ryder glanced at Ellie Sutton, who gave a slight nod.

For the next ten minutes, Ryder explained to Perez what had happened in Erin's Bay a few months back—about Sam Pritchard being there, her encounter with Joel Renner, and the communication between Renner and Dylan Cobb while Cobb was in prison.

"How do you know Renner and Cobb were talking to each other?" Perez asked. She had read about Renner—The Thriller Killer.

Up until now, Sutton had remained quiet. But now she spoke. "Because I hacked his laptop and then got into a dark web chat room that Renner and Cobb were using to send messages to each other."

"And you believe Sam Pritchard was hiding out in Erin's Bay and was responsible for two murders there, despite no official evidence that he was or actual sightings of him?" Perez countered.

"I saw him," Ryder insisted, her voice hard and determined. "He *was* there. Renner told me he was working with Pritchard."

Perez rubbed her forehead. This was all getting to be too much. First, Cobb escapes prison after killing a guard. Then, he shows up in Ravenwood. Now, a group of vigilantes, admittedly one ex-FBI and another an ex-police officer, turn up saying they'd followed Pritchard to Ravenwood. No wonder she didn't say anything to Kershaw. He would have blown a gasket.

"Otherwise, we wouldn't be here in Ravenwood," Ryder continued; she was the apparent leader of the little group. "We first thought Sam Pritchard had come here just to hide. To lay low, given Renner told him via Cobb that the town was a safe haven."

Safe haven? Perez's ears pricked up.

"Then, we discovered that Cobb wanted help in escaping from prison so he could return here and kill you. He and Pritchard were talking to each other. Pritchard said he would help."

"How did you know that?" Perez asked.

"We've been monitoring Cobb's online communication," Ryder replied.

"And you didn't think to fucking warn me!" Perez yelled. She couldn't believe it. She felt like arresting them all—throwing all their lying asses in jail.

"We didn't know for certain when or how or if such a thing was even possible," Ryder said. "Please, you must believe me."

Sutton stepped forward, an angry look in her eyes. "And what would you have said?" she snapped, "if we had walked into your office waving our arms about. 'Hey, Haley, guess what? We think Sam Pritchard, the most wanted person in the country, is here in Ravenwood, and we think he's about to spring Dylan fucking Cobb out of prison.' You would've thought we were insane."

Perez held the young woman's gaze and saw the seething twist of her lips, the smoldering fire in her eyes. She had an attitude, this one.

Some of the previous anger Perez had felt began to ease. She took a deep breath. "Don't call me Haley," she said.

Sutton gave a dismissive wave. "Whatever."

"I'm sorry," Perez said. "You're right. I would not have believed you."

"Thank you," Ryder said. "You probably would have driven us to the funny farm yourself."

Perez nodded. Yet she couldn't understand why Cobb just didn't seek her out. Why did he dress up in a Halloween costume and walk the streets looking indiscriminately for victims? Maybe he wanted to enjoy his freedom first—make up for the time he had spent in prison by indulging himself in a sick, demented killing spree. God knows what would have happened if Sue Gill hadn't managed to escape, and she and Ben hadn't been driving down her street at the exact same moment she fled her home.

"So, where is Pritchard now, and does he know Cobb is dead?" Perez asked.

"We don't know, and I doubt it," Ryder replied.

"He could also be wandering the streets dressed up like a horror movie killing machine, and no one would bat an eye," Rimes added.

"Great," Perez said, thinking about the menagerie of horror movie villains she had seen so far tonight. It was a perfect disguise, though.

"Believe me, we are just as shocked as I'm sure you are about Cobb escaping," Ryder added.

"And how did you find out he had escaped?" Perez asked. Within a few minutes after killing Cobb, an urgent APB came over on Perez's two-way radio, saying that Dylan Cobb had escaped.

"I have a police scanner," Ryder admitted. "It's all perfectly legal."

Perez could tell the woman wasn't being totally truthful with her. She looked over at Hodges. The huge man just stood there, watching her. Then, he finally spoke up, his voice deep with a rich, smooth timbre to it. "Maybe Pritchard has teamed up with Dylan Cobb, and they went out hunting in a pack—like wolves do. And it was just Cobb who got caught and shot by you in self-defense, as you said before."

Perez's eyes narrowed. "And what exactly do you do, Mr. Hodges?" When introduced, Hodges didn't say why he was there; he just hung in the background.

The cold look in his eyes deceived his smile. "I'm a hunter, Detective."

Perez almost rolled her eyes.

"I disagree about them teaming up," Rimes interjected. "Pritchard is a loner. While he did team up with Dolores Gruber, I don't think he would have liked the arrangement. I think he helped Cobb escape, then left him to his own devices."

Perez turned away for a moment. All of this was making her head spin, and she had a crushing headache. She checked her cell and saw nothing from Ben. Where was he? She could surely use him right now. He needed to be here to listen to all this and give her his honest take on it.

"I just need time to process all of this," Perez stated, turning back and rubbing her eyes. She hadn't yet fully processed the shock of seeing Dylan Cobb, let alone killing him, and now being told that Sam Pritchard was also in Ravenwood and had helped Cobb escape.

Ryder took a step forward. "Look, we may not have time. Pritchard is here, and he will wreak havoc upon this town. That's what he does everywhere he goes."

Suddenly, Perez felt bone tired. Her ears still rang from the gunshot, and every part of her ached. "But you haven't visually sighted Sam Pritchard, have you? In Ravenwood?" Solid proof was what was required right now. She waved to the others in the group. "It's all just speculation, what you've told me." She could tell Ryder was thinking.

Finally, Ryder spoke. "No, we haven't actually sighted him. But...."

"But what?" Perez cut her off, her patience almost gone. She should be back at the crime scene, helping out, not stuck here with the adult version of *The Goonies*.

"We saw someone." Ryder looked sheepish.

"Up at the Dark Rift? Is that why you were up there?" Perez said. "You were searching for Pritchard, thinking that's where he's hiding out?"

"No," Ryder said. "It was at an abandoned slaughterhouse a few miles north of here where we saw someone."

Perez felt her stomach twist. Bad memories of the place Ryder was referring to came flooding back to her. "And?"

"There was someone there. We went to have a look, thinking that it was also a possible location where Pritchard could be hiding."

"And what did you see?" Perez demanded. This was getting absurd now.

"Someone was there, but they ran."

"What did they look like?"

"They had a mask on."

"A mask?"

Ryder nodded. "I know it's going to sound crazy, but the way you described how Cobb was dressed, like a horror movie character—this person was dressed similarly."

"Could have been anyone," Perez snapped. "Getting ready for —" Her words died in her throat, and she realized what she was about to say.

"Tonight," Ryder said. "Halloween. Exactly the way I'm sure Cobb got ready for tonight, too."

Perez thought for a moment. "And you think Pritchard has done the same?"

Ryder's eyes frosted over, and her voice became low. "I have no doubt Sam Pritchard is here. And I also have no doubt that he is walking among us right now, among the good people of Ravenwood in disguise—in a similar costume to how Cobb was dressed. And let me tell you, Detective"—she pointed a finger at Perez—"You may know a lot about Dylan Cobb since it was you who caught him once. But I know a lot more about Sam Pritchard." Ryder's jaw tightened. "And Sam Pritchard makes Dylan Cobb look like a bed-wetting Boy Scout."

40

AX

He had found the ax in the garage.

It wasn't that he didn't find the knife useful. It was just that he thought it was more appropriate, leaving it where he had—buried in the man's chest—like making a statement. And where the man had slid to the floor, that was where he had left him—in the hallway by the front door.

He placed the ax on the nightstand, stepped back, and looked down at the mess on the bed. He didn't mean to be so aggressive with her. At first, after he had bound and gagged her, he sat in the chair in the corner of the bedroom and just watched her and listened to her muffled moans and whimpering cries. He watched tears cascade down her pretty face and marveled as sweat broke out across her naked skin and she shook in fear. Then she wet the bed. He didn't care. It just added to the glorious thrill he had felt.

Was it too self-indulgent to sit there for at least an hour just watching? Perhaps it was. Time. He had plenty of it tonight. And he wasn't going to rush. He wanted to savor the next few hours—perhaps the last hours of his life.

His eyes returned to the mess on the bed—a tangle of separated limbs and a torso riddled with deep cuts. He had never experienced such a frenzy before. He hadn't planned it. Halfway through, he had another episode like a white-hot rod was being driven into one ear, then out the other.

She was alive before the episode started. And by the time the blinding light and the skull-tearing pain had subsided and his vision had returned, it was too late. He couldn't remember what he had done, but he had done it. The blood-covered ax, both his hands gloved in her blood and the mess on the bed were proof.

He went into the bathroom, and without turning on the light, he washed his hands, then dried them on a towel before dropping it at his feet when he was done. Back in the bedroom, he picked up the ax, then his cell phone chimed.

He frowned. Light from the streetlamp outside cut lines across the darkened bedroom through the window blinds. He stared at the phone and checked the screen. It didn't make sense. He brought the cell phone closer to his face and read the message again. It was quite detailed, a few paragraphs. He looked away for a moment and thought. It was a diversion from what he had planned, but what he had planned wasn't as wonderful as the message that had just landed on his cell phone. It contained certain corroborating details that only he knew about.

It still didn't make any sense. Then again, his ability to make sense of anything was deteriorating by the minute. Placing the ax down again, he walked out of the bedroom and into the hallway where the man's body lay. He thought about the message again. Maybe he was hallucinating? His grip on reality slowly surrendering to the blinding episodes of pain and irrational thought. He pulled out the cell phone again and called up the message. No, it was real, a gift.

His car was parked several blocks away, which meant precious time would be wasted walking back to retrieve it. He looked down at the man's body and then came up with a better idea.

Crouching down, he began rummaging through the man's pockets, then pulled out a set of car keys. Yes. This was a much better idea.

41

MANNEQUIN

Three blocks to the west, Shaw stood under the shadows of a sprawling large oak tree on the sidewalk of a leafy neighborhood street.

Kids dressed in various Halloween costumes and clutching their parents' hands were going door-to-door, skipping and running, laughing and cajoling, seemingly oblivious to the violence Shaw had left behind.

He told Perez that he would call her in a few hours, check in, and see how things were going in the aftermath of Cobb's demise and how Sue Gill, the woman he had attacked, was.

He just needed to get out of there, not get involved with the police, unless he needed to jump to Perez's defense later and corroborate her story.

He took a moment to get his mind in order as he watched a woman wait patiently on the opposite curb while her two young kids ran excitedly up the path of a house across the street, where a shiny black '78 Trans Am with gold trim was parked in the driveway, a big firebird emblazoned across its hood. Shaw had always liked the '78 Trans Am or the '79. Maybe someday, he would get one.

The kids scaled the stairs to the porch, where a large plastic bowl filled with candy sat. "Hey! Take only one piece of candy," the woman called out after them.

Dylan Cobb? Shaw thought to himself as he watched the kids decide which one piece they would take. He still couldn't process seeing Cobb again, let alone him escaping and then coming here to Ravenwood. He thought he was chasing Sam Pritchard down that alleyway, not Cobb dressed up like a horror movie character.

Then again, from what Perez had told him, Cobb was probably returning to Ravenwood, seeking revenge against her for what she had done to him. It didn't explain, though, what he was doing at that woman's house, trying to kill her. Maybe he thought he would indulge himself for a few hours before tracking down Perez and killing her.

After making their choice, the two kids ran back down the porch steps, giggling and pushing each other.

Shaw glanced up again at the house, noticing a flicker of movement from behind the drapes of one of the windows.

With their mother in tow, the kids moved off down the street before disappearing around the corner.

Shaw pushed off the oak tree trunk—then stopped.

The house's front door across the street opened, and a person stepped onto the porch.

Something made Shaw slink back into the shadows and watch.

It was a man, Shaw figured, despite the person wearing a pale rubber mask, which looked like flaps of loose pallid skin crudely sewn together—and the faded blue coveralls of an iconic horror movie character that Shaw had already seen several versions of tonight.

And yet, as he watched the person look up and down the street, there was something genuinely malevolent and disturbing about how they stood, their exaggerated, ghoulish head pivoting slowly from side to side. The person went back inside, leaving the door open. Moments later, they returned carrying a body.

No. It must be a mannequin, a prop to scare kids. It looked real

JK ELLEM

enough. There was a large blood stain on the shirt with a large knife buried in the middle of the chest.

The person gently sat the mannequin upright on the porch, resting it against a post next to the brimming candy bowl.

Shaw should have turned away—nothing unusual here. But there was something about the person... How they moved... Their mannerisms.

He continued watching as the person disappeared inside again, only to come out again carrying a blood-covered ax this time—another prop, Shaw imagined. Except this time, the person ignored the mannequin, came right down the porch steps with the ax, and walked along the paved path toward the driveway, all the time having a slight limp, favoring their right side—a distinct gait Shaw had seen before—The Peeping Prowler.

Shaw eased out of the shadows, his eyes trained on the man. Unlike when he had last seen him crossing the street that night near Denise Glover's house when Shaw was sitting patiently in Perez's car, Shaw now had a clear view. Their head had been overly large then because the man, like now, had been wearing the large rubber mask that covered their entire head, not just their face, giving the appearance of having a disfigured, bloated head—just like the fictional horror movie character. Except, as Shaw watched, the man looked anything but fictional now. This was wrong, all wrong.

Shaw glanced at the body propped up on the porch. He saw the blood-soaked shirt and the huge knife buried not in plastic but in flesh and bone.

Shaw moved out from the shadows and began walking toward the house.

The man opened the driver's side door of the Trans Am and then looked across the street to see Shaw walking quickly toward him.

The hideous rubber mask, two hollow black holes for eyes, an orange tuft of rag doll hair—something black and foul churned in Shaw's stomach. He sped up.

The man climbed in, and the Trans Am roared to life.

Shaw ran, then swerved as the car's rear end hurled toward him in a screech of tire rubber.

The man was trying to run him over.

42

OFF AIR

It's getting late, and by the time we get back to driving the streets of Ravenwood, looking for Pritchard, there's only a handful of tired-looking parents being dragged along the sidewalks by their energetic kids.

It's the parents, not the kids, who concern me the most. Pritchard has never touched kids. Maybe that's why he wanted Ellie to kill Dolores Gruber high up on the cliffs that night. He tolerated Gruber as she served a purpose in providing the perception of false trust in having an older, motherly woman with him when he approached his intended victims.

"Let's grab some coffee," I say to Beth as a Sheetz gas station, lit up like a Christmas tree in the darkness, comes into view up ahead.

"Works for me," she says.

In brooding silence, we stand together, leaning against the hood, drinking from take-out cups with a billion stars smudged across the pitch-black night sky above, and the cool air clears my mind. I think back to the meeting we just had with Perez. Is she as convinced as I am that Pritchard is here? Maybe. Then there was how Ellie and Beau were standing next to each other, slightly closer than I would have expected—friendship, not intimacy, which seems to have developed in such a short space of time.

Beau is a natural hunter who can adapt to any situation. Snow. Wilderness. Urban. It's in his blood, calcified deep into his bones. Ellie was never a hunter until Pritchard abducted her. Now, she's hardened, has a raw edge, and a hunter's gleam in her eye. As she did with Beatriz, Ellie seems to have sought out another mentor when it comes to hunting people, and she's covering all her bases: the virtual hunt with Beatriz and now the physical blood hunt with Beau.

And what's with that unnerving smile I've seen from her? The "I know something that you don't" smirk. It's a trait of hers that I find the most unsettling of all. She's dialed down her wild impatience, though—or maybe it's just for my benefit... a veneer that is hiding something more determined beneath.

"What are you thinking?" Beth asks.

"Sorry," I apologize. I untangle from my preoccupation with Ellie. "Just wondering if he's really here." Beth and I stand shoulder to shoulder, connected, arms touching. It's like a sisterhood, the three of us. Ellie, me, and now Beth—bound together by shared pain and suffering thanks to one man.

"I'm still reeling from Dylan Cobb escaping," Beth says. "And I'm glad you didn't tell Perez back there about Beatriz calling you while we were outside Sue Gill's house and telling us that Cobb had just escaped."

"I could have warned her if Beatriz had called sooner. But by then, it was too late," I say. "Perez had already taken off, going after whom we had mistakenly told her was Pritchard."

"How were we to know?" Beth says, shaking her head. "None of us in our wildest nightmares thought it was Cobb who had attacked that poor woman."

We are silent for a few moments, trying to comprehend the recent turn of events. Then I say, "I need your advice, Beth."

She stares off into the distance, and it's as though she knows what I'm about to ask. She's as wise as she is clever.

"I've got a bad feeling about Ellie and Beau," I say.

Beth takes small sips of her coffee and gently nods. She knows it, too. She's seen how they act around each other.

"We all want to kill Pritchard so badly," I say. "But perhaps some of us want it more than others."

She takes another small sip and then turns to me. "She's young, Carolyn—brash, impulsive. She told me all about what happened in Georgia with Pritchard and Gruber. She's the girl that got away. But she can't keep running, and I guess she knows it too. You're younger than me, and she's much younger than you."

"Geez, thanks."

"I didn't mean it that way. What I mean is that she can see her whole life spread out in front of her as one horrible nightmare running on a loop while he's still alive. Survivors need closure just as much as victim's families do."

"It's the same for all of us," I reply. "As it has been for you ever since you retired. As it has been for me since he nearly killed me in that hell hole mine in Utah. I've thought of nothing else, and neither have you."

"But Ellie's different," Beth continues. "Out of all of us, she's experienced Sam Pritchard more in person, as his prisoner. He has messed up all our heads, but I'm sure he's messed up hers the most."

Wise words. True. It makes sense. We all fell down the same dark well of fear and anguish, but Ellie fell deeper and has further to climb out.

Beth continues, "For Ellie, it's personal."

I think of Frances Pridmore... slaughtered before my eyes. "It's personal for all of us, Beth."

"But not how it is for Ellie. She experienced him far deeper than any of us. She was a victim, don't forget. You and I are...."

"Are just a distraction to him," I finish.

"Correct. We're good at getting in his way. But Ellie is the real prize that slipped through his fingers. He won't stop until he finds her again. And it will cloud his judgment. She's become his obsession."

And that's what worries me the most. For Pritchard, she is the prize, shiny and new and untainted, brighter than anything he has ever wanted or desired, simply because the Emma Block I know, and the Ellie Sutton she has become, escaped from him, and he's bitter about that fact.

Beth drains the last of the coffee, then pivots around and faces me. "And that is why she is the bait Pritchard cannot resist. You must understand that, Carolyn. I've never hunted in my life." She smiles and looks up to the heavens. "Christ, it breaks my heart to even see a sick or injured animal on the side of the road." She looks back at me. "But from what I know about Pritchard and how he thinks, the cold and meticulous logic on the left side of his brain can just as easily be overrun by the impulses, emotions, and urges on his right side."

Darkness, thick and unsettling, fills me when I hear her words. I slip out my cell phone and hold it up to her so she can see the recent calls I've made while she was driving. All of them were to one cell phone number—eight calls in total. All unanswered. No voicemail. Nothing. For the last three calls, there was no service at all. Ellie has turned off her phone.

Beth's eyes look up from my cell phone screen and meet mine. She knows. She understands.

"The stupid girl," I whisper.

Beth touches my hand. "She's not stupid—a little reckless, maybe. She just wants it to end. She's got Beau with her, don't forget. He won't let any harm come to her. Have you tried calling his cell?"

"He doesn't have one."

"Well, I don't see how they are going to find Pritchard on their own," Beth says.

I pull my cell phone back. "I think I've got an idea of how she's going to try."

I speed-dial Beatriz Vega. She answers almost immediately.

"I hear Dylan Cobb is dead," Beatriz says. "Shot by a police officer a few hours back."

"Haley Perez," I say. "Thanks for the heads up too."

"No problem. Remind me to buy Perez a drink if we ever meet."

"Have you heard from Ellie?"

"Not in the last forty-eight hours. We've had no reason to talk."

"Joel Renner's account in that secret chat room—is that still open?"

"I deactivated it weeks ago. Remember?"

So much has happened in the last few days that I'm lucky if I can remember my own name. "And it can't be reactivated?"

"No. You would have to set up a new account. But he's dead, and dead people don't message you. Pritchard would get suspicious if Renner suddenly messaged him again. He must know Renner is dead. That's why we shut down the account."

Then it hits me like a sledgehammer—Beatriz's words. *We shut down the account.* I grip the cell phone tighter. "Does Ellie know how to set up a new account in the same chat room?"

"Of course. I taught her."

I feel sick. I walk a few yards away from Beth and drop my voice. "Beatriz, remember you were digging into Ellie's past as Emma Block, and you told me about those two high school students who disappeared from Ellie's class?"

"Yes. She was a suspect in their disappearance. She had broken the nose of the female student, her supposed best friend, all because they had been arguing over the same guy. I remember, but I found nothing more. If I had, I would have told you about it." Beatriz pauses. "Why? What has happened?"

"Nothing; I was just wondering if there was more to the case."

"Still unsolved as of today. Any sign of Pritchard?" she asks.

"Still looking."

I end the call and walk back to Beth.

"So, where are Ellie and Beau?" Beth asks with concern in her voice. "How can we find them?"

I thumb the screen on my cell phone and activate an app. "We are about to find out."

43

HORROR MOVIE

Shaw glanced through the rear windshield to the rear-view mirror up front and saw those dark, empty eyes staring back at him as the rear end of the Trans Am sped toward him. Turning side-on just before impact, he tilted at the waist and bent over the flared rear spoiler, swung his legs up, and rolled onto the trunk of the car, which scooped him up like a shovel. Otherwise, he would have gone under the rear wheels. The car braked hard, and Shaw barreled into the rear windshield, shattering it. Then, the driver threw the car into drive, and Shaw rolled off, landing on the road. The car sped off, tires squealing in a haze of blue burning rubber, but not before he noted the license plate.

Uninjured, Shaw got to his feet and ran across the lawn and up onto the porch. The man was dead, his pale, open eyes staring at nothing. The knife was real, buried deep into his chest. Shaw tried the front door. It was locked.

Headlights cut down the street, and he ran back onto the road, waving his arms. A Buick Enclave SUV came to a stop, and Shaw wrenched the driver's side door open and pulled out the male driver, the only occupant.

"Hey, man! What the fuck do you think you're doing?" the man shouted.

"Commandeering your vehicle. Police business." Shaw jumped in, gunned the engine, then performed a one-eighty skidding turn and took off in the direction of the Trans Am. A cell phone sat in a cradle suction-cupped to the windshield. He thought about calling Perez but wasn't certain who the person he was chasing was.

Two blocks later, he caught up to the Trans Am and eased off the gas, keeping his distance—no point in scaring them.

With one eye on the road and the Trans Am in front, he quickly dialed Perez's number on speaker.

"Who the hell is this?" She didn't sound happy.

"Haley, it's me. Where are you?"

"Heading back to the crime scene. Where the hell are you? I didn't recognize the number. It sounds like you're in a car. What's going on?"

"I'll explain later. There's a dead body at an address three blocks west of Sue Gill's house. It's the same guy I saw—your Peeping Prowler. He's killed someone. The body is on the front porch. You can't miss it."

No sound came out of the speaker. "Haley, are you still there?

"It's Sam Pritchard."

The Trans Am up ahead made a left, and Shaw followed, still keeping his distance. "Sam Pritchard?" He wasn't sure if he'd heard Haley correctly. "You said Sam Pritchard. Do you know for certain?" Shaw's insides suddenly went cold. The man he was pursuing was dressed up like a horror movie character from the seventies—just the way Dylan Cobb was—not identical, but similar. Were people going crazy or...?

"Talk to me, Haley," Shaw said. He could sense hesitation in her voice.

"It's just that... new information has just come to hand," she said.

"Just come to hand. What the hell does that mean? Do Cobb and Pritchard know—"

She cut him off. "Dylan Cobb and Sam Pritchard have been communicating with each other. Cobb recommended that Pritchard come here to Ravenwood. I know that for a fact now."

"They know each other for sure?"

"Ben, I can't explain everything at the moment. But Cobb escaped, and it looks like Pritchard helped him."

This was insane, Shaw thought—two monsters dressed as monsters roaming the streets of Ravenwood on Halloween night. One had a machete; the other swapped his cook's knife for a damn ax. Two horror movie nightmares had become a murderous reality. Shaw gripped the steering wheel harder, his eyes focused on the Trans Am thirty yards in front. He pressed the gas pedal, and the SUV lurched. Then he caught sight of a group of smiling children in costume skipping along the sidewalk, a woman pushing a baby stroller following close behind. He cursed, then eased off the gas.

"So, they've teamed up. Cobb is dead, but Pritchard is in Ravenwood? Right now?" he asked.

"I think so. I can't be certain." Again, there is more hesitancy in Perez's voice. She wasn't telling him everything.

"Describe the person you've just seen," she went on.

"Dressed in a Halloween costume—similar but not exactly the way Dylan Cobb was dressed. He's wearing faded blue mechanic coveralls and a Captain Kirk rubber mask, except he was carrying an ax. He buried the knife in some poor guy's chest."

Perez gave a sharp intake of breath. "Oh, my God. The person is walking around like Michael Myers?"

"Seems like that. But I've seen about six Michael Myers so far this evening. So have you."

"And you've got eyes on him? You're following him?"

"He stole a car, and I... borrowed one—an SUV."

"Ben, the kids—"

"Haley, I know. I'm just tailing him at the moment. If he pulls up and starts anything, I'll stop him. I'll take his head off with his ax."

"I need to know where you are," Perez insisted. "It's too dangerous. Whoever it is, he must be stopped."

The Trans Am pulled up at a set of lights, and Shaw eased in behind. He couldn't clearly see the driver with the rear windshield shattered into a spider's web of cracks. A group of kids crossed in front, and Shaw tensed. One kid strayed behind the group, paused, smiled, then pointed at the driver before running to catch up with the others.

"Tell me exactly where you are and which direction he's heading. Also, the make, model, and license plate of the car he's driving," Perez asked.

The light turned green, and Shaw let the distance between them stretch to about thirty yards before easing on the gas again. There was virtually no other traffic, so losing him wasn't a concern.

"Ben? Are you there?"

Up ahead, the car performed a right turn, and Shaw followed, keeping his distance. "It seems like he's heading out of town," Shaw finally replied.

"Tell me where you are. What street? An intersection? Any stores?"

Leafy streetscapes and nice houses with green lawns gave way to big blocks, industrial sheds, and vacant lots. Shaw passed a Sheetz gas station. "Can't see anything. I think we're heading out of town."

"Tell me the license plate." Perez sounded angry now.

Shaw thought for a moment before replying, "No."

Suddenly, Perez's angry voice filled the interior of the SUV. "What the hell do you mean, no?"

"No police involvement. I want this person, Haley, especially if it's Pritchard. I've waited six long months for this."

"But he's extremely dangerous. He's a danger to the public."

"The only person who's in danger is *him*, from *me*," Shaw

growled. "Just trust me, Haley. I trust you. But it's my way or the highway."

"I can't let you do this," she replied. "I need to call it in."

"And tell them what? You don't know where I am."

"God dammit, Ben! You can be so pig-headed at times!"

Shaw pulled a face. *Pig-headed?*

Perez gave a sigh. "Okay. You win. Just me. No one else. I'll come alone."

Shaw smiled. "You'll tell no one else? Not the rest of your colleagues?"

"No. I promise. You have my word. I'll come alone. Just tell me where you are or where you're heading."

The Trans Am in front accelerated—smoothly, not in panic or alarm. Shaw let the distance open up. They were heading out of town now on a stretch of road that looked familiar. In the rear-view mirror, the lights of Ravenwood were slowly shrinking into the darkness.

"You know that place you took me to, up in the foothills? I'm not certain, but it looks like we're heading that way."

"Why the hell would he be heading up to the Dark Rift?" Perez questioned.

"No idea."

Shaw reached an intersection and turned right as the Trans Am had, and the speed limit ticked up to sixty. The route seemed familiar. The driver was definitely heading up there.

"That's where he's heading, Haley. I'll call you back if anything changes. No lights or sirens, please. I'll call you again."

"Ben, wait a sec—" Shaw hit the end call button on the steering wheel. Everything around him was a curtain of velvety black, including the cutout outline of hills in the distance. He tightened his hands on the steering wheel as his whole world narrowed to just the taillights in the distance—the glowing red eyes of a demon lying in wait within the dark recesses of Shaw's mind.

44

DARK CLIMB

Beth and I had to deliberately slow our pace to avoid a sudden tree root, partially submerged rock, or the multitude of rain-plowed furrows that snake through the dirt trail of grit, rock, and gravel.

Obstacles that were welcome footholds or additional traction up the slope now only served to sneakily catch an ankle or jolt a kneecap. The dark sky is clear, and there's enough moonlight to navigate our way. My worst fears were confirmed when we arrived, and Beau's pickup truck loomed out of the darkness, parked in the exact spot we had pulled into before on our last visit. I imagined they had gotten an hour's head start on us to plan and set up whatever they were planning to do. We then drove back and found a secluded hollow in the thick brush that couldn't be seen from the dirt road, even with headlights, and Beth nosed the car into it.

Now, as we make our way up on foot, I see it's a lot different at night than it was during the day. A ghostly blueness seeps through the interlaced branches of the trees farther up the incline. The landscape has transformed into the surface of some unearthly forest shrouded in perpetual shadow and filled with black angular silhouettes and vertical pools of ghostly light that shimmer and ripple.

We each carry a small pocket flashlight but keep them off.

I stop now and take a moment to establish our bearings again, following the same rough trail we had when there were three of us.

"How much farther?" Beth asks, her breath labored.

"Just take a moment, Beth," I reply, looking around. Beau and Ellie would have given themselves plenty of time. Then, it would become a waiting game. Beau once told me back in Willow Falls that he sat alone in a hide he had built, waiting almost two days for the deer he was hunting to wander innocently into his trap. Somehow, I don't think it will take that long tonight.

Beth sits on a large rock and waits. God bless her. She's done her best without so much as a word of complaint. I know the climb is taking its toll on her, but it's much cooler than before. Yet the fear and apprehension burn scalding hot inside me. Is it going to work? Maybe he's already here, and we're already too late?

"Not much farther, Beth." I offer her my hand; she gladly takes it, and I haul her to her feet. "We've already navigated around some of the smaller rifts in the earth, and I know we're close."

Twenty yards up the incline, I look up and almost draw my weapon. Brittle, icy fear flutters in my heart, and then I relax. Yes, I am fearful—fearful that it might not work. Fearful for Ellie, Beth, and Beau. Fearful that one or more of us are going to die this night. Fearful that he will get away again, and the nightmare will reset itself, and I'll begin this never-ending torment all over again.

A familiar copse of trees, one tree in particular where the branches look like someone holding up their arms in surrender, is what spooked me.

Beth is a few feet behind me, and it's comforting to know she drew her gun fully based on sensing my sudden movement. She's got my back.

"What is it?" she whispers, aiming past me.

"Just that stupid tree we saw before that looks like a person. It's up there... maybe another thirty yards or so. We're nearly there."

She lowers her gun but doesn't holster it.

Moments later, the ground flattens, the trees thin, and the canopy of branches pulls back to reveal a wide clearing awash with moonlight. We pause again. There's a sudden shift in the atmosphere like we're passing a thermocline—an invisible wall of coldness. Something unnatural is here—an oily, dripping malevolence that I didn't feel during the day. Then the hairs on the nape of my neck prickle like a ghost has just floated up behind me and licked the back of my neck with its cold, sandpapery tongue.

Something feels wrong.

"We need to go around," I whisper to Beth. "Otherwise, we'll end up being the prey in the trap."

Beth nods. Her face is gaunt and furrowed in the moonlight. "I can't see anything," she admits.

"Just stay close behind me," I say. "Just don't shoot me in the ass." The humor does little to settle my nerves, which feel like stretched violin strings about to snap.

I step off the trail at a right angle and move to my left, where the ground is hard, compacted dirt and stone layered with slabs of flat, sheared rock. No one is going to hear us. Together, we traverse the stony ground, the brush around us shielding us. I can't see the Dark Rift, but it's there on my right. I can feel its gigantic emptiness. That massive tear in the earth is like part of the planet is missing.

A dark chasm yaws before me, a fathomless expanse of nothingness. But a flat, long slither of rock bridges it, and we cross over to the other side after a few perilous wobbles of the rock.

"Creepy place," Beth murmurs behind me. "Much worse at night."

"Be careful," I say as I step across the ragged edge of a smaller rift. The ground is dotted with these open wounds oozing black blood.

Then comes the sound of someone running, crashing through the undergrowth behind us. I whirl around, gun drawn. So does Beth.

My eyes track the sound as it curves away from us, fading with each heartbeat. It came from where we just were, near the trail. It's too big for an animal.

"What was that?" Beth gasps.

My mind folds in on itself. No. It's too soon. It can't be. I've misjudged.

We're too late.

Pritchard is here! He's running up to the Dark Rift.

"Ellie!" I almost scream before covering my mouth, muffling a desperate cry.

A solitary gunshot thunders through the darkness.

45

THE KILL PLOT

She stood there, on the edge of the abyss, a swallowing chasm of darkness below.

The exact spot reminded her of that fateful night on the clifftops, the moon beaming down, painting everything in a ghostly light. There, next to the shimmering top of the waterfall, she had waited for Pritchard and had lured him with Dolores Gruber to come to her.

This time would be different. There was no Gruber, and Ellie was more prepared. Nothing would go wrong this time. Pritchard would die.

She checked her cell phone, logging back into the new account she had set up in the chat room she had used to reach out to Pritchard. It was her new prepaid cell phone, the one she had bought at Jessop's Hardware in Ravenwood, when she had decided to fully commit to her plan, regardless of Carolyn's objections. She had hidden it in the barn and retreated there to retrieve it when the others were in the main house. And in the dusty solitude, she plotted her revenge. Carolyn knew nothing. More importantly, Beatriz couldn't trace the phone. No one, other than her and, of course, Beau, knew her secret cell phone existed.

The cell phone served only one purpose: to act as the long string attached to the piece of meat she was now dangling in front of a very ravenous monster.

The details of how to find her were very clear in the message she had sent. Inspired by what Beau had shared with her about his own kill plots to lure Whitetail, this was *her* kill plot. Her own simple design in cyberspace. A lush virtual valley of temptation that would lead Pritchard right to her. Sending several recent photos she had taken of herself, together with some key facts about her previous abduction that only he would know, acted as the tender saplings to draw out the monster. And it had. Pritchard had made contact.

Did she feel she had betrayed Carolyn's trust? No. Simply because the ultimate price she was destined to pay as the only alternative was too much. The darkness that had plagued her, clung to her, invaded every pore of her skin, every fiber of her flesh and bone was only days, not weeks, not months, away from consuming her entirely. And once that tipping point was reached, Ellie knew she would die by her own hand. Only one of them was going to leave Ravenwood alive.

Turning her back to the huge rift of darkness behind her, Ellie made sure her feet were placed equally between the two small rocks that had been placed at her feet. Then, looking up, she focused on the dark tree line twenty yards away. That's where he would be coming from.

Standing just a few feet from the edge, with the Dark Rift behind her, she felt like she was at the very edge of the known universe.

Then, she saw movement—a slight bulging of the shadows among the trees.

Hold steady.

Ellie tensed and watched as a large shape detached itself from the darkness and floated toward her, its dull edges growing sharper by the second.

Hold steady.

No matter how hard she had prepared for this exact moment, for being reunited with Pritchard, her courage began to wane. Long fingers of fear scuttled up her throat as if she had swallowed a large, bony spider.

Hold steady.

The bony fingers then curled their sharp tips around the edges of her mouth. She stifled a moan as someone—a thing—stepped toward her.

Hold steady.

He was wearing coveralls and a hideous rubber mask that hid his true face. In one hand, he held an ax coated in blood.

It was him: Pritchard... dressed similarly to how Perez had described Dylan Cobb. It had to be. Only he knew where she was. She had drawn him to her. She was the bait.

Hold steady.

He regarded her with those dark hollows in the mask. Then he peeled off the rubber mask and dropped it at his feet.

This time, Ellie could not stifle her gasp.

His face caught the moonlight; the true horror, his facial disfigurement, revealed itself, and for a moment, she wished he had kept the rubber mask on. She only knew his previous face before Carolyn had taken to it with a rock. Now, it looks like cruel fingers had sunk into a hunk of molten wax, then twisted, pummeled, gouged, and tore before the wax had finally hardened.

"Hello, Emma." That voice from her nightmares. He lifted the ax and then took a step forward.

Ellie shuffled her feet slightly but kept within the rock markers.

Then, there was more movement to the left, in the tree line from where Pritchard had emerged just moments ago.

Pritchard turned at the sound—a person running hard and fast, crashing through the trees.

A man emerged.

Ellie had never seen him before.

He stumbled toward Pritchard.

Yes, she had seen him before. Now, she remembered. The bookstore in town. She had taken a mental snapshot of him seated at the window. Lean, late twenties, dark hair and eyes, sharp features, faded blue jeans, white T-shirt under a weathered brown leather jacket, and sensible boots.

Turning back to Ellie, Pritchard growled at her, saliva drooling from an opening she gathered was his mouth. "You fucking bitch!"

Ellie shook her head. She had no idea who the guy was behind Pritchard or why he was there.

Pritchard leaped toward Ellie.

There was a spurt of light from within the tree line and a thunderous crack a millisecond later—light traveling faster than sound. The hypersonic bullet was traveling faster than everyone could move or think.

Pritchard buckled sideways as though a Thai fighter had just kicked his entire knee joint into outer space, leaving behind only the femur and tibia.

He screamed, a high-pitched, unearthly scream, tilted sideways, and then toppled to the ground.

46

THE BLOODLETTING

Guns drawn, Beth and I break through the tree line and arrive in the clearing near the edge.

Precious moments are lost as my brain takes in everything I see. The moon, huge and yellow, coats everything in a surreal, iridescent light—a thin rind of glowing orange on the horizon, the darkness fading, the sudden edge of the world beneath—the gaping Dark Rift beyond, looking empty, soulless.

Three people stand just back from the edge.

My heart leaps. One of them is Ellie, and the other is Beau, a hunting rifle topped with a large scope cradled in his hands, the barrel pointed down at a bulky shape on the ground. The third person? I can't see their face clearly. The shape on the ground at Beau's feet is squirming, moaning, and writhing in obvious pain.

With our guns holstered, we approach. It's Pritchard on the ground, a bloodied ax next to him.

The person, the stranger, turns to face me, and the earth stops rotating as I look at him, all wide-eyed in disbelief. "No," I breathe. It... How? What? No.

With all the stress, anxiety, and fear, I must be hallucinating.

The man steps toward me, and it's like I'm seeing a ghost from

199

my past solidifying into flesh and blood before my very eyes. "Ben?" I say, my voice barely a whisper.

"Carolyn," he replies with that fucking roguish smile that used to crush my heart. It still does.

"You know this guy?" Beau asks.

With my eyes still fixed on what surely is an apparition, I just nod. Questions begin to numb my brain, and I can't think straight. Ben Shaw. After all these years. Then, I remembered my vow to myself if I ever saw him again. I step up until we're face to face, then slap his face. "You walked out on me. I woke up the next day, and you were gone."

Beau turns to Ellie and smiles. "Don't you just love reunions?"

I back away from him and look him up and down. He is real? Flesh and blood? "What the hell are you doing here?" I say, feeling angry and euphoric at the same time.

Shaw rubs his chin, and my slap did little to remove that heart-crushing smile from his face. In fact, it looks more intense now.

"I was about to ask you the same thing." He looks down, and I follow his gaze. Sam Pritchard. The common denominator.

Pritchard stirs, and Beau puts a firm boot on his chest, keeping him in place.

I turn back to Ben, ignoring the man on the ground who has poisoned my mind for the last twelve months, and replace him with the man who filled my heart for years, even long after he was gone. Just the mere thought of Ben, what we had, wonderful memories, staved off the wretched blackness of Pritchard for a while.

"But how? How do you know him?"

Ben steps up to me and is now standing in front of me. My God. It's really him. Tears fill my eyes. I want to touch him. Hug him. Kiss him. Even slap him again or kick him this time.

But I don't, for fear that if I reach out and touch him, he'll disintegrate into a billion atoms and be carried away on the wind. So, I rest my fingertips ever so gently on the dusty leather jacket he is wearing.

He looks deeply into my eyes, then says, "We've got a lot of catching up to do, Carolyn. But that can wait."

I understand. We have time. Plenty of time. But I can't get distracted. There's still the matter of Sam Pritchard.

I nod, then move to Ellie. Her expression is cold, her posture rigid. "What happened?" I demand.

Beau steps up. "Blame me if you must, Carolyn. It was my idea to set a trap for Pritchard."

"I find that hard to believe. More like Ellie coerced you to, using her as bait."

"And it worked," Beau adds.

Ellie just looks at me. There's no joy or warmth there. The void between us is wider now than it's ever been.

"I just didn't want you to get hurt," I say, trying to melt some of the frostiness she is radiating.

"Well, it worked," she says with a slightly upturned chin. "My plan worked."

"Thanks to Beau," I say. I squeeze Beau's massive arm. Ellie was never in any danger. Beau would have ripped apart the planet if it meant protecting her from Pritchard. That and more, I'm certain.

There'll be plenty of time later to discuss, argue, and understand how we ended up here. But now, it's time to get serious again.

Beth comes up to Ellie, gives her a hug, and then walks to Ben and looks up at him like he's a mirage. "Ben Shaw," she says. "Didn't think I'd ever see you again."

Ben nods. "Good to see you again, Beth."

"Strange how the universe works." She gives him a hug, too.

I crouch down near Pritchard and study him properly for the first time. The others gather around me.

Pritchard is semiconscious. One leg is shattered at the knee, leaving a bloody pulp of splintered bone and blown-out cartilage. The rest of the leg—from the top of the shin bone down—is barely attached, hanging by a thin twine of muscle and loose skin. The pain must be unimaginable.

Good.

"The ax?" I ask without looking up.

"His," Beau replies.

"What happened to his face?" Ben asks from behind me.

"I did." I stand again. "I happened to his face."

To the east, the sky is brightening by the minute. Dawn is creeping toward us—the promise of a new day. But before it arrives in full, we need to put an end to this day, once and for all.

"Why didn't you kill him?" I gesture toward the rifle that Beau is holding.

He looks at Ellie. "When it comes to women, I just do as I'm told."

Elle meets my eyes, and finally, Lot's wife speaks. "The plan was never to kill him," she says. "Not at first. Beau was just to bring him down—immobilize him."

"Why?"

"Because it's her kill, not mine," Beau replies.

Her kill? Of course, it is. *Her* plan. *Her* kill plot. *Her* as bait.

"So, what now?" Beth asks.

What now, indeed?

Ellie withdraws something from her pocket. It's a Swiss Army knife. The same knife Pritchard deliberately dropped for Ellie so she could cut the ropes that bound her hands and then escape from that fallout shelter. The same knife Ellie then used to attack Dolores Gruber, turning the woman's face into Swiss cheese.

Ellie opens the main blade and then stands over Pritchard. Beau has him covered with the rifle, the barrel aimed squarely at his deformed forehead. His good leg convulses, but he can't move. Then, leaning down, Ellie plunges the blade into the side of his neck. "This is for that father and daughter you killed at the camp-ground," she whispers. "And for everyone else you have killed, you sick fuck!" She twists the knife. "You picked the wrong woman to kidnap that day." She withdraws the knife, and blood immediately seeps, not pumps, from the wound. Her aim was deliberate, avoiding the carotid artery. He will bleed out if not attended to, just not in the usual two to three minutes I would expect if she did hit the right spot.

Now, I realize why. It's not just *her* kill. It's *our* kill. To us all, the spoils of the hunt will go.

Ellie turns to me. "That's just for starters."

Reaching down, she picks up Pritchard's ax, then hands it to me. No words. No instructions. Just the presumption of revenge by my own hand.

Without hesitation. Without any second thoughts. Without any internal debate on ethics, morality, or what separates us humans from wild animals, I take the ax—my personal invitation to the purge that is about to happen.

Let the bloodletting begin.

47

BEYOND CRUEL

In my hand, I hold an ax, warm, slippery, and wrapped in blood.

I think of all the faces stuck to my basement wall—all the women he has killed. And plenty more, I imagine, if we had not found him. Never did I think I would see this day. Pritchard is helpless at my feet. All the power is in my hands to kill him. I tried before. I won't fail now.

His eyes open and swivel up to look at me. Gurgling sounds come from his mouth, and blood continues seeping from the hole in the side of his neck—liquid so diseased and toxic, being squeezed out by a heart so black.

Stepping over him, I pin his arms down on either side with my feet, swing the ax, and then crash it down. The blade cleaves into his chest, and he hollers in pain. "Frances Pridmore sends her regards," I say, then step away, tossing the ax.

I nod to Beth, passing the mantle of vengeance to her—to avenge all those who can't anymore because of him.

Beth doesn't hesitate. In one smooth, fluid motion, she draws her handgun, aims, and puts a bullet into Pritchard's groin.

He convulses.

Then another bullet, and finally... a third. She holsters her gun.

In turn, she looks at Ben. I don't know why he is here, but it must be a damn good reason.

He steps up and shakes his head. "If I start," he says, "I won't be able to stop."

What did Pritchard do to him?

He looks down at Pritchard with pitiless eyes, squirming on the ground. "He'll be dead soon," Ben says. "I'm just happy to sit and watch until he is."

Next is Beau. He shrugs. "Don't look at me. I've done what I was asked to do."

The circle is complete, and all eyes return to me.

Despite his injuries, Pritchard begins to move. The ground, soaked with his blood, squelches as he starts dragging himself up onto his good knee. He is growling like a dog. He truly is inhuman.

"Shit!" Beth says, drawing her gun. "He's trying to get away." She shuffles closer, the barrel aimed down, just inches from the top of Pritchard's lumpy skull.

"He's not going anywhere but Hell," Beau replies, passing his rifle to Ellie, who shoulders it.

Beau crouches down and cranes his neck to look at Pritchard one last time. Then, he stands and takes a step back.

"Are you certain?" Beth says. She touches the end of the barrel to the top of Pritchard's head like she's about to put a lame dog out of its misery.

Pritchard stops moving. Now, he's almost cowering.

"Let's just end him now... once and for all." Beth looks up to Ellie for confirmation.

Ellie nods. "You've been hunting him the longest, Beth."

Beth looks at me. It's only fitting that she delivers the final—

Then, it happens so fast that before my brain can comprehend, it's too late.

With cunning speed, Pritchard weaves his head away from under the gun barrel and reaches up and grabs Beth's gun. He twists, and before she can react, the gun is now in his hand.

Ellie slips the rifle off her shoulder.

I reach for my gun.

Ben lurches forward.

With the gun in one hand, Pritchard claws up Beth's body with his other hand, using her like a human ladder. Then he's upright, hopping around on his good leg, waving the gun wildly.

I bring my gun up—but Beth is blocking my shot. I can't get a clear shot.

Ben is fast, but Beau is faster. He scoops up the ax.

Pritchard swings the gun toward me and begins squeezing the trigger.

With almost no backswing, Beau brings down the ax. The heel of the blade cleaves into the top of Pritchard's shoulder and sticks there.

The bullet zings past my head before shooting off into the trees behind me.

Beau's got Pritchard from behind in a bear hug, his massive arms around Pritchard's torso, crushing his arms, then lifting him off the ground, the ax still stuck in his shoulder.

The gun falls from Pritchard's hand.

"I have a better idea," Beau says into Pritchard's ear. "Let's send you back to where you belong. Hell!"

With the ax still protruding from the top of Pritchard's shoulder, Beau swings him around and then starts carrying him toward the edge—toward the Dark Rift.

Reaching the edge, Beau pauses, both facing the wide plain of blackness. Arching his back, he lifts Pritchard even higher in his python-like embrace so he can throw him clear.

Pritchard's leg kicks out over nothingness.

Then, Beau wobbles like there's a tremor.

"No!" I scream. "The ground!"

It's too late, and I watch in horror as the edge crumbles and collapses beneath Beau's feet.

And they are gone.

Not worried about my own safety, I reach the edge and look down. A slice of earth three feet wide, where Beau was standing just seconds before, has sheared away, revealing a plateau of rock—a black vertical drop below.

A torrent of misery and anguish crashes down on me, and I sink to my knees, burying my face in my hands, and I weep.

Beau is gone, and Pritchard, in his last dying act of defiance, has claimed another victim.

The world is beyond cruel.

48

PERSEUS

Riddled with sadness and disbelief, we huddle together at a safe distance from the edge, hoping and praying when it seems like all hope is lost and that God is an uncaring tormentor.

Ten minutes pass. Nothing.

Then, twenty minutes. Still nothing.

The sun breaches the horizon, bathing my face in a warm, rejuvenating glow. Yet inside, I am cold and dead.

After thirty minutes, Beth, the voice of reason, speaks. Her voice, like my heart, is broken. "He's gone. He's not coming back. No one could survive that."

Ben nods but says nothing.

"No!" Ellie cries, her face brittle with dried tears and her eyes ringed red. "He might."

I'm numb, hollow inside, like my guts have been ripped out. Like part of me has been torn away and tossed over the edge. But deep inside, I know he is not coming back. It is a sheer drop into nothingness—a rift in the earth that seems to go all the way to its very core.

"We need to head back," I say. There is nothing we can do. Beau is gone, swallowed up into the bowels of Hell with the Devil as an eternal companion.

I turn away, my heart in shreds.

"No! Wait!" Ellie screams, stepping forward. "I hear something."

"Be careful!" Beth warns her. "More ground may give way."

I turn back to see a hand with fingers the size of an excavator's log grapple claw into the crumbling edge, pulling soil and rocks with it.

The hand releases and reaches farther forward this time as it gouges at the earth some more like it's pulling itself up and out. A huge black forearm, muscled and corded as though with steel cable, slaps up and over the crumbling edge. Next comes a cannon-ball-rounded shoulder. Then another shoulder followed, finally, by a head crusted thick with dirt.

A black phantom slithers up from the burning pits of Hell. A winged Gabriel, my Gabriel, rising from the Dark Rift, collapses chest-first onto solid earth.

My heart now swells as I watch in awe his convulsing body, coated in a bloody, sweaty, gritty afterbirth. The Dark Rift didn't claim him—didn't want him. So, it vomited him back up and spat him out to where he now lies.

He clutches something in his other hand.

Beau stirs—death coming back to life. New hope within me also stirs from the depths of my previous anguish.

Using his spare hand, he pushes it into the ground like a huge piston. Slow, tentative, still fragile, he levers himself up—rebirth, not new birth. First to one knee and then into a low, hunched crouch, all the while still clutching the thing in his other hand as though it's the most prized possession in the world.

Slowly, Beau rises, unfurling to his full height—tall, proud, monumental.

Dark eyes survey us—a god looking down upon a ragtag flock of mortals—nonbelievers who didn't believe the unbelievable.

Blood is splattered across his heaving chest, face, neck, and arms.

Then, the other hand comes up. The hand that refused to let go of what it held... Something precious—more precious than anything. Something many have died for unnecessarily. Now I see it. The nightmare has ended. It's not a dream I'm witnessing. It is reality in all its beautiful horror.

Just as Perseus had lifted high the severed head of Medusa, Beau Hodges now holds aloft for all of us to bear witness to—the decapitated head of Samuel Pritchard.

Minutes pass as we drink in what we have just done and the gift Beau has brought back from near-death to share with all of us. Despite the horridness of the sight, it will ensure sweet dreams from now on.

Beau lowers the head. Then, with a flick of his wrist, it tumbles through the air toward us and lands with a meaty thud at our feet. Strangely, the head comes to rest at an angle so that the eyes, now stretched wide in shock, are looking straight at me.

Still, we remain rooted to the ground, a garden of statues cemented firmly in place, savoring the moment—the victory.

Ellie breaks free first from the speechless trance, rushes to Beau, and embraces him. "I thought you were dead," she sobs.

He shields her with a massive arm, and she nuzzles into his flank. He grimaces and clutches at his side.

"What?" Dismay flares in her eyes, and she looks up at him.

"It's nothing," he says. "I think I may have just broken a few ribs when I tumbled down to that hellhole."

Ellie smiles and nuzzles deeper.

Beau turns to me and nods a look that says, *We did it. We killed another monster.*

His words come back to me from when we first gathered in the barn. *Pritchard is no different. He's not some mythical beast out of Greek mythology that can't be killed or can rise from the dead. He's human. He will bleed. He will be killed.*

"Damn straight," I murmur.

49

REUNITED

It is a somber mood. No fanfare. No high fives. Everyone is alone with their own thoughts as we make our way back down.

Beau leading, then Ellie next, Ben next to me. Beth bringing up the rear.

The sun is up, and the woods are cool and quiet. It's much easier traversing the rocks, twisty tree roots, and deep furrows in the earth in the daylight than at night.

I keep stealing little glances at Ben as we move.

"You're staring," he says.

"Sorry. Just thinking."

"About?"

"You need to tell me why you're here. How did you know Pritchard was up here at the Dark Rift?" It's strange. He hasn't asked me a single question yet. But I can't hold off any longer.

"I've been in Ravenwood for a few days. I've been searching for him for the past six months."

"Six months? What happened? What did he do to you?" The floodgates open, and I'm acting like a curious child. Sam Pritchard has touched all of us, and I need to know where Ben fits into all of this.

"Like you and your friends, I was searching for Pritchard last night," he says. "I was just walking the streets. I had no clue where he was. Then I saw a man dressed in coveralls and a rubber mask come out of a house. He was carrying what I thought was a mannequin, a Halloween prop. Turns out, it was a body—a man he had killed. He had an ax with him, too. He dumped the guy on the porch, jumped in a car, and took off. I flagged down a passing vehicle, jumped in, and followed him up here."

So, like Cobb, Pritchard was running wild in Ravenwood on some kind of killing rampage. I shudder to think how many others he killed.

"And you thought it was Pritchard?"

"Just had a feeling," he says. "Had no idea, really, until I got to the clearing and saw your two friends standing over him. Still didn't know until Beau told me it was him." Ben shakes his head. "Pritchard's face...."

"Was different. I know," I say.

"And you did that to him?"

"A long story," I say. "I'll explain it all later. I just want to get out of this place." Even during the day, the place still gives me the creeps. There's an eerie silence in the woods around us as we descend. The place is unnatural.

"Can I borrow your cell phone for a second?" Ben asks.

Who's he going to call? I slip it out and turn it back on. Beth and I both turned our cells off just as a precaution.

He taps in a number, stops, then frowns.

"What's wrong?" I ask.

He holds the phone up. The name Haley Perez is on the screen. As he tapped in the number, the phone pulled up her name from my contacts list.

"You know Haley Perez? The cop in Ravenwood?"

"Sort of. Why?" Now, I feel guilty.

As we continue down, I explain how Beth and I were driving around, looking for Pritchard, too, last night. And how we happened on Haley Perez's police SUV, lights flashing, and found her tending to a woman called Sue Gill who had been stabbed.

"Haley wanted to go after her partner, who had gone after the attacker. So, we looked after the victim until the paramedics arrived."

Ben doesn't say anything.

Now, it makes sense. "Was she referring to you?" I ask. "The partner?"

"She was helping me find Pritchard. That's why I came back to Ravenwood."

I pause. "Wait, hold on. You came *back* to Ravenwood? You've been here before?"

"It's a story for another day," he says. "She probably referred to me as her 'partner' but not in the sense of 'police partner.' She just wanted to keep me anonymous. It was good thinking on her behalf."

"We certainly have some catching up to do," I say. I don't want to press him anymore, so I keep quiet while he calls Perez.

"No answer," he says, hanging up. "Went straight to voicemail."

He hands back the phone. "So, Perez knows about your group here?" he asks. "That you were also searching for Sam Pritchard?"

"I told her after the incident with Sue Gill. I wanted to be honest and upfront with her. Someone like Pritchard in your town could be devastating."

He suddenly stands still and looks around.

"What's wrong?" Beth asks from behind.

He looks unsettled.

"It's nothing," he says.

But I can tell something is troubling him.

"You think we're being followed?" Now, I'm looking around but see nothing but trees.

"No. It's not that. Let's keep moving."

We set off again.

"Maybe she's just tied up with paperwork and everything else that happened last night," I say, trying to appease what obviously now is Ben's concern as to why Perez didn't pick up his call. "Or maybe she saw my name on the screen and chose to ignore it."

"Because you're FBI?" He smiles. "Can't blame her."

"Ex-FBI," I correct him. He gives me that look. "I'll explain later," I say.

His eyes are still darting about at the woods around us as we keep walking down.

"Did you call her last night?" I ask. "After you found the dead man?"

"Yes."

"Did you also tell her you were following someone you thought was Sam Pritchard?"

He nods, looking around some more.

"Where's the cell phone you called her from?"

"Back in the SUV I borrowed to follow Pritchard." Then, he turns to me. "You know there's a shortcut up to the Dark Rift. I've never been this way. I came up here with Haley. She showed me around. There's another path we took. It's steeper but shorter."

"I only know this one. Been on it only twice. It's all new to me," I say.

Haley? First name basis, is it? "Perhaps you should've told us that before we set off from the top—that there was a quicker way down."

He shrugs. "This is your rodeo. Your group. You're the leader. I'm just happy to follow."

We say nothing for a few minutes as we navigate down through the uneven terrain. We must be nearly back at the bottom, where the vehicles are parked.

"Maybe she called you?" he says. "Last night?"

"I didn't get a call from her last night."

"Can you check your phone again? Maybe she left a voice message for you."

"I doubt that. When I turned my phone back on, it would've pinged with any new messages."

"Please, Carolyn. Can you check again?"

We pull up again, and Beth joins us.

Ellie stops and looks back. "Everything okay?"

I waved her off. "Keep going. We're fine. We'll catch up."

Ellie continues on down.

I check my cell phone. "There are no new messages from anyone." I thumb the screen. "Let me check the call log. Maybe there's a missed incoming call, and they didn't leave a message." I scroll down. Then Haley's name pops up. A missed call about an hour after we parted ways after our impromptu gathering in the vacant parking lot.

"There's a call from her in the missed call log, but she didn't leave a message."

"Try her again."

I do. Nothing. "It's the same as you just before, Ben. It went straight to voicemail. She must have her phone turned off."

"Why would she do that?" Beth says. "She's a serving police officer. A detective. She needs to keep it on twenty-four-seven just in case. I always did."

Now, I start getting an unsettled feeling in my gut. "Well, probably for the same reason that Beth and I turned off our phones—because...." Then, it hits me.

"Did you tell her you were coming up here?" I ask Ben.

"Oh, Jesus," Beth whispers. "Did she come up here last night looking for you and...." Her voice trails off.

My stomach lurches. "And ran into Sam Pritchard with his ax on the way up?"

Farther down the slope, Beau's deep voice floats up to us. "Got a body down here!"

50

DYING

Shaw sprinted off, stumbled, then fell and went down in a tangle of arms and legs. He got up and kept going, a wild human snowball, careening down the dirt track, getting faster and faster as he went.

Beau was already there, bent over the body, and Shaw fell in next to him. His heart tore in two. It was Haley. She was lying on her back, clutching at her lower abdomen, the front of her shirt soaked in blood, which was seeping between her fingers, a cloak of red beneath her.

"Gunshot," Beau said, tearing a piece of his shirt, then balling it. "Need to find the entry point and stop the bleeding."

Everything slowed. Haley turned toward Ben, her eyes filled with tears, an apologetic smile on her lips.

I'm so sorry. I'm sorry I got you into this mess. I'm sorry I didn't wait for you.

"No! No! No!" Ryder cried when she arrived, followed by Beth.

"Oh, Christ!" Beth cried, looking down at Haley.

Ellie went to her knees next to Haley and held her hand. "Haley, it's okay. We're here. It's going to be okay. Stay with me."

"How the fuck did she get shot?" Ryder asked, tearing out her cell phone and then dialing 9-1-1. "Hang on, Haley; help is on the way," she said, then shot off a stream of details to the dispatcher.

Haley's eyelids fluttered. She stared at Ellie vacantly, her mouth open, dribbling red, a wheezing, gurgling sound coming from between her lips.

"Come on, Haley; I need you to stay awake," Ellie pleaded.

Haley smiled, then her eyes began to glaze over as life began to hemorrhage out of her.

"No!" Shaw screamed. Blood smudged his hands, slippery and wet, as he ripped open her shirt. Two inches below her belly button, a black hole of punctured skin oozed red.

Beau pressed the balled material into the puddle of blood that was now forming. Almost immediately, it turned soaking red. "She's lost a lot of blood. It's not good. This is bad. Really bad."

It was no use.

Shaw tore off his jacket, then his shirt, then Beau discarded the blood-soaked ball, and Shaw pressed his shirt hard into the bullet hole.

Ryder ended the call. "ETA twenty minutes. They're sending a chopper."

Twenty minutes? Shaw's brain began caving in on itself. He did a quick calculation based on the bloody rags, her pale face, the amount of blood beneath her, and how much a body her size could lose before she dies.

"Come on, Clare!" Shaw yelled.

Dull eyes looked at him. She was fading, but he didn't give up. "Hold it," Shaw said, and Beau took over, pressing the shirt into the wound.

Shaw felt for a pulse on her neck. A tiny, winged creature trembled beneath the skin. She was dying in front of them.

Standing, he looked around and saw a line of cars a hundred yards away parked on the flat ground at the bottom of the slope. One extra vehicle had been added since he had arrived there last night—Haley's police SUV. The trauma kit he had used before was inside. It had HALO Chest Seals for treating gunshot wounds and blood-clotting gauze. He had seen it all when he grabbed the kit to treat Sue Gill.

He tore down the slope—no time to search Haley for her keys.

Reaching the police SUV, Shaw skidded to a halt in a cloud of dust and dirt in front of the side window. His eyes focused on the very center of the glass.

He balled his right hand into a tight fist and drew his arm back. Twisting his shoulders and hips, he tensed, bringing every muscle he had into play, gathering all his strength before channeling it all back down his shoulder, along his forearm, down to his wrist, then deep into his hand and out through his knuckles as he swung his fist forward in one concentrated ball of power, hope, and desperation.

51

BEDSIDE

The others came and went, always alone, never together. They always managed to time their individual visits when the police, the sheriff's department, and the FBI weren't in attendance.

Almost as if they had congregated as a collective in the parking lot in a pickup truck, then took turns going into the hospital separately, spending ten, perhaps fifteen minutes, before leaving again, like a coordinated relay of stealthy compassion.

Coincidence? Too unlikely.

There were four of them: the man as big as a bear, the older woman in her mid-sixties, the younger, willowy woman with flowing dark hair, and the young woman with shoulder-length brown hair, wearing a Baltimore Ravens ball cap.

Then, there was the young man with the plaster cast on his right hand, his arm in a sling. He never came and went. He just came—and stayed. He would sleep on the chair in her room or on the sofa in the visitors' lounge. One nurse caught him dozing in the cafeteria—head down, resting on his free arm at a table.

The medical staff didn't mind. A nice young, good-looking man was always welcome. He was like a loyal dog whose owner was on their deathbed and refusing to leave their side. As she was—on her deathbed. During the first three days, death came for her three times. All dark and poisonous, it crept into her room and flat-lined all the machines. Alarms went off, and people rushed in. Injections were given, paddles were charged, and electric shock was applied. And thanks to their swift actions, the medical staff kicked death out of her body and then out of the room. Three times in three days, all the while as the young man looked fearfully on, as though his whole world, his entire existence rested in her heart restarting again.

On the fourth day, a young nurse finally plucked up enough courage. She went over to him and asked him if he was a relative—perhaps her husband. He smiled politely and said that he was her partner.

On the fifth day, the patient woke, and death never returned to try to claim her again. Her recovery was hailed a miracle. All the medical books said that with the amount of initial blood loss, she should have died on the slopes of the foothills before the rescue chopper had winched her out.

Maybe it was her resilience. Maybe it was a testament to the team of surgeons who had operated on her for fourteen hours nonstop. Maybe it was the post-operative care of the hospital's nursing staff. However, the nurses believed that her miraculous recovery was due to the young man's quick actions when she had been discovered shot. The same young man who had also unselfishly sat beside her hospital bed for five days, holding her hand and talking to her, sometimes in hushed tones, as though sharing a deep secret. Other times, he was animated and smiling as though sharing a joke.

And when she did wake, the first person she saw was him, by her side, holding her hand. And when she spoke, with her lips dry and parched and her voice raspy, her first words were, oddly enough, "Who the fuck is Clare?"

Haley was sitting upright, a swath of puffed-up pillows propped behind her. She had tubes in both arms, and a bank of computer monitors sat to one side, colorful lines, numbers, and symbols scrolling across the flat screens.

"After your call," she said, "I drove up there. I saw the Trans Am you described, a pickup truck, and the SUV, which I assumed you had stolen."

"Borrowed."

"Whatever. Then I went up the shortcut like we had done before. It took a bit longer. It was dark. I had a flashlight but didn't use it."

Shaw sat patiently on the chair he had pulled next to her bed and listened.

"Then...." Haley frowned like she was trying to remember, her memory foggy. "I heard a gunshot. It sounded far off, farther up the slope. So, I started climbing faster. I thought it was you, that you'd been shot."

"That was Beau Hodges shooting Pritchard in the knee," Shaw said.

She nodded. "Then maybe ten, fifteen minutes later, I finally reached the top and began making my way through the trees and...." Her voice trailed off. She squeezed her eyes shut. "I can't remember. I can't remember anything after that."

"It's okay," Shaw said, touching her arm.

Her eyes opened, and she had an intense look on her face. "You need to tell me," she said. "Tell me what happened."

"I already did." For the last hour, Shaw had laid out everything that had happened up at the Dark Rift, leaving out nothing.

In the days he had spent by Haley's side, ensconced in his own dark thoughts, despair and anguish his only companions, he had replayed inside his head in minute detail everything he could remember. There was only one conclusion he could come up with. And then yesterday, he discovered that ballistics had proved it.

"What do you think happened?" Haley asked.

He thought for a moment. He had to tell her. "It was a one in a million," he said. "An unimaginable convergence of poor timing and just plain bad luck."

"What do you mean?"

"The stray shot from Pritchard—from the gun he had wrestled from Beth Rimes." Even thinking about it now, it seemed so unbelievable. "It missed us all, then hit you, Haley. You had just arrived at that exact moment and stood in the exact spot of the bullet's path."

"I don't remember being shot."

"The brain, the body... don't ask me to explain the science when people more qualified than me can't," he said.

Haley's brow furrowed. "But how did I manage to get back down to where you found me? I must have...."

"You must have stumbled back down. Disoriented and with your brain in survival mode, it switched to autopilot—like limp-home mode on most luxury cars. Your brain switched on its internal GPS and navigated you back down the shortcut path. Maybe it was telling your subconscious about the trauma kit you had in the back of your police SUV."

"Like sleepwalking," she whispered to herself.

"More like near-death walking," Shaw replied. "That's why we didn't discover you. We went back down the path we came up, not the shortcut."

"And that's why Beau Hodges didn't find any of my blood," she added, a faraway look in her eyes.

"Exactly," Shaw replied. "I estimated it was about an hour and a half from the moment Pritchard took the shot to when we made our way back down and found you where the shortcut trail and the longer trail converge into one that then leads down to the parking area."

"I almost made it," Haley said.

"You almost did, but you almost died as well. You should've died. The doctors told me you lost more blood than what a human body needs to sustain life."

She gave a weak smile. "What about your hand? How is it?"

He held it up. "It was worth it."

"My car keys were in my pocket. You didn't think to check?"

"I panicked... didn't have time. I just had enough time to get down and back and whack a HALO Seal on the bullet hole." Thanks to his Secret Service training, Shaw prided himself on being cool and calm under pressure and during moments of extreme stress. But this was the first time he had allowed his emotions to get the better of him.

He looked at Haley, and now he knew why.

She smiled and gave him a suspicious but playful look. "Ben Shaw panicked? Who would've thought?"

"Yeah. Just don't go around saying that to too many people."

Seeing her smile made him feel good.

"And I think you called me Clare?" Haley said.

"So, you do remember what happened? Me being there?"

"Just fragments," Haley replied. Her eyes narrowed into a mischievous look. "So, who is Clare? Is she someone else whose life you also saved?"

"Maybe."

"Maybe someday you'll tell me?"

"Maybe I will."

Haley rubbed one eye. "There's something in it. Can you take a look?"

Shaw stood, came closer, then leaned over her, his nose just inches from hers. He looked into her eye. "Can't see—"

A hand covered with tubes reached up and wrapped around the back of his neck, then gently pulled him closer.

And he relented.

But he was uncertain—cautious. He didn't want to presume

anything. So, he let her dictate what was about to happen and where it might end up. And he pursed his lips together, not wanting to overstep some unspoken line of friendship between them.

Haley kissed him, and he kept his lips pressed together, giving her the kind of kiss soap stars give each other on set in front of the cameras when their contracts strictly stipulated nothing more than closed-mouth kissing.

But Haley was having none of it. She hadn't signed any contract and decided she wanted to kiss him however the hell she wanted to. The hospital food was typically not good. And, at the moment, Haley was hungry for something else.

Her lips parted then—tentatively at first—her tongue began probing forward, pushing up against his sealed lips.

And he relented.

Then her tongue came up against the wall of teeth and forced them apart. And he relented.

Then, quite presumptuously, he thought, she used her tongue to leverage apart his teeth farther, and then she flowed inside his mouth—her tongue, her lips, all suddenly warm and wet and welcoming.

For a brief moment, the lines on the monitoring machines climbed upward, the beats-per-minute spiking before settling back into a normal rhythm.

After thirty seconds of succumbing happily to Haley's oratory exploration of his mouth, Shaw pulled back, fearing that he might need to use an oxygen mask to recover. He looked into her eyes and saw her beaming smile.

"What was that for?" he asked, taking a breath.

She tilted her head. "For saving my life."

"I did nothing."

"You did everything. I was just thanking you with a proper kiss."

Now, Shaw tilted his head questioningly. "A proper kiss?"

She nodded. "Not that bullshit, father to daughter one you planted on my forehead before."

"There was nothing wrong with it," he protested, thinking back to the kiss he had given her in the alleyway after she had just shot Dylan Cobb.

Haley made a stern face. "You pull that kind of kiss on me ever again, and I'll kick your ass."

Shaw smiled. "Yes, ma'am."

THREE MONTHS LATER...

52

UNPLANNED

Haley Perez sat on the toilet seat, holding a thin plastic stick.

Two pink lines.

For the last five minutes, that was all she had stared at: two pink lines. Her mind was a mix of emotions: Happiness, Sadness, Excitement, Fear, and Fear of the unknown.

She didn't think it was possible, given the path the bullet had taken. That was what the doctors had said. She was devastated when they told her she may not be able to conceive. So, birth control had taken a back seat.

Two pink lines. It was a miracle. A gift from God. A miracle baby. It wasn't planned, and she did want kids—albeit a little later, perhaps—in a few years' time. If she found the right man, that is.

She glanced up at the locked door and heard someone whistling on the other side, *Roxanne* by the Police, coming from the kitchen.

How would he react?

It had been just over three months since Haley had been released from the hospital, and he had stayed by her side all the time she was there. Then, when she came home, he stayed with her, looked after her, and did everything for her, including wiping her ass when she couldn't herself. That was surely true devotion, wasn't it? When you can't wipe your own ass, and someone does it for you —without complaint—not a single word.

And all during that time when she was at home, recovering, her mobility restricted, he was so patient. He didn't patronize her or make her feel inadequate or like an invalid.

She had found the right man when she wasn't even looking.

Until a few months ago, she hadn't given it much thought. Him. Her future and where he fit into it. The more likely question was where she fit into his future. And where was his future? With her or someone else?

The police investigation into her shooting of Dylan Cobb had concluded that she had acted in self-defense. Perez testified that she had given Cobb ample warning to drop the machete. When he chose to ignore those warnings and run at her, she had no choice but to discharge her firearm. In that exact same moment, she had inadvertently stepped back onto the body of the dead dog and lost her footing, thus causing her aim to be thrown upward slightly, resulting in Cobb dying of a fatal shot to the head. The case was closed, and a commendation for bravery was awarded to her. Shaw had also been called as a witness, corroborating Perez's recollection of events that night.

She glanced down at the stick again. Two pink lines. She would be turning twenty-six next week. She wasn't getting any younger, either, and this might be the only opportunity she would ever get. Would she even make a good mother? Especially given her own childhood. A childhood she hadn't told him about yet. How would he react when she told him she wasn't who he thought she was? Those were deep, dark secrets she hadn't shared with anyone.

Over the last few months, he had shared everything about his own past with her, including his relationship with Carolyn Ryder. She didn't have to pressure him about it. He was an open book, far from what she had been when it came to her past.

The last time Carolyn had visited her in the hospital, she

seemed so sad and heartbroken that she had been shot. She said that what Ben and she once had, their past relationship, was precisely that—in the past—water under the bridge.

"He's one of the good ones, Haley," she had said, kissing her cheek before leaving. "And take it from me, there aren't that many around. And when you see one, a guy like Ben, you grab them and don't let go."

Haley sighed. There was no point in delaying the inevitable. Standing, she pulled up her panties and jeans, slipped the plastic stick into her pocket, flushed the toilet, opened the door, and walked outside and into the kitchen.

Ben was making coffee. His hand was out of the cast and sling and was almost fully healed. Now and then, it would become a little tender.

"Very domesticated," she said playfully, watching him operate her new espresso machine that he had insisted she get and that he paid for.

He turned and smiled. That smile. That incredible smile melted her every time—making what she had to say just that much harder. She had seen him smile at other people on the street, in a café, and in the line at a supermarket, but not like this one. This smile came with a specific look... an understanding that their relationship was at another level. Intimate. Knowing. Trusting. Skin-touching naked-ness. That he had seen everything there was to see. That he was reserved especially for her and no one else. It all made her feel incredibly special.

"Coffee?"

"Sure. But first, we need to talk."

His smile faded. "Sounds ominous," he said. "Is it about the wet towel I left on the floor this morning?"

"No."

"The dirty ice cream dish in the sink last night?"

She gave him a weary smile. At times, he could be the funniest, sweetest person. And at times, she had to remind herself that he had also ruthlessly killed people, sometimes with just his bare hands. So, taking one of them in hers, she led him to the sofa, and they sat side-by-side. She looked deep into his eyes. It was now or never.

She took a deep breath, deciding that reverse psychology was the best strategy to adopt. "You know you don't have to stay. I've told you that."

He gave her that lopsided grin as only he could. "So, you're trying to get rid of me?"

"No. Of course not. But you shouldn't think you have to stay— feel obligated."

Now, he looked slightly offended. Not pissed off. Just offended. Slightly.

Did it come out wrong? She didn't mean to say it like that—like she was some charity case and the only reason he was sticking around was out of pity—and the sex. *Boy, the sex*! He'd already had to reinforce the bed with heavy gauge steel brackets—twice.

"I'm sorry," she said, "I didn't mean it like that."

He squeezed her hand. "Haley, nothing I do when it comes to you feels like an obligation. I want to be here. I want to be with you. I've told you that."

Hearing those words made some of the doubt and anxiety Haley was feeling dial down a tad. She could also feel the plastic stick in her pocket prodding into her thigh like it was nagging at her to get to the point. *Tell him! Tell him!*

"What about the town? Ravenwood?" she asked. "And everything that's happened here?"

He lifted one shoulder. "I like the place. Believe me, it's a lot better than some places I've been. It's different in a quirky sort of way."

Quirky? Okay. She could go with that. "And us? What about us?"

"Us." He seemed to loll the word around in his mouth like he was wine-tasting. "Hmm... us?" Now, he pitched it like an open-ended question. "I like the idea of us," he finally said.

Maybe it's too soon—that level of commitment. "You told me you've traveled a lot and don't like being in one place for too long." Ben had shared some of his travels over the last few years with her. A little place called Martha's End in Kansas, then Lacy, a mountain town in Colorado. Salt Lake City in Utah. A place with a weird name, Ghost Crossing, in Nebraska. The infamous Erin's Bay on Long Island. And more recently, the town of Bright Water, New Hampshire.

"Maybe it was fate," he said. "Three years ago, when I got off the bus here in Ravenwood."

"Yeah, but then you were gone! You vanished like a ghost. Then, for three whole years, I didn't hear boo from you. That's what I'm trying to say. You obviously get restless and are a drifter." It was true. Their lives were in different orbits. Yet, they had crossed paths three years ago in Ravenwood when a stranger walked into town... walked into her life—a guy she didn't like at first. He was too arrogant, too brash, and extremely impatient. Oddly, these were the same traits Haley knew she had herself.

"But I came back," he said.

"Only because you needed my help in finding Pritchard. Now, he's dead. Your search is over. What's stopping you from just upping and leaving one day, and then I won't see you again for another three years or longer." Annoyance grew inside her. "I don't want to get that kind of note on my pillow."

He leaned in, his voice low, and she suddenly got lost in his eyes. "I would never do that to you, Haley," he said.

"Really? Truthfully?"

"Absolutely." He leaned back, stretched, and then yawned. "I'd leave it on your car windshield. Unfolded. Facing outward for all your neighbors to see."

She punched him in the arm. "Prick."

"Sorry." He smiled.

"I'm being serious," she said.

He apologized again and slid closer. "Things change. I've changed."

"In what way?" she asked. It was starting to sound like an interrogation, and she began to feel embarrassed. She should just leave the poor guy alone. This was a bad idea.

"I've had enough of being on the road," he said. "Of drifting around. I've done a lot of thinking over the last few months, being here with you. It's why I want to be here... with you. That is only if you want me to be. If you don't, then I'll go. Just say the words and—"

Haley grabbed him and kissed him hard. Not passionately, just hard like her life depended on it. Like to live another day, a month, a year, for the rest of her life, she needed his breath to fill her lungs each and every day. To sustain her, to help her grow, so she could become everything she knew she could become. To give meaning to her existence on this wonderful but often cruel and unfair planet.

He was smiling when their lips finally parted.

Then dread crept into her voice. "There are things about me that I haven't told you... things I've done. In my past. Bad things."

Shaw shrugged. Water off a duck's back and all that. "We've all done bad things, Haley." Then, his eyes narrowed, and she wasn't sure if he was being humorous or serious. "You haven't murdered anyone, have you?" Then, he quickly added, "Who didn't have it coming to them, that is."

She laughed. It was an odd way to put it. "No, I guess when you put it like that."

She went to speak again. "But I need to tell you. When I was—"

He touched her lips gently with his fingers as though pushing her words back into her mouth. Dark secrets to remain under lock and key deep inside her for a little longer.

Then, he leaned in and whispered, his lips millimeters from hers, "I don't care what you did as long as you love me."

It took Haley a few seconds for her brain to process what he had just said. Love? What? Love? No? Yes? Her heart melted. Tears filled her eyes.

A serious look came across Ben's face. "Have I said something wrong?"

Haley shook her head vigorously. "No! No! It's all good—perfect, in fact. Everything you said is just perfect."

But fear still occupied her. She stood up in front of him, slipped the pregnancy test kit stick from her pocket, and held it out.

Ben's eyes looked at the two pink lines, his face expressionless. Then, he looked up at her, then back to the plastic stick.

He smiled. And that smile said everything about him—the type of man he was.

Without words, because words were not needed, he gently lifted the front of her shirt, exposing her abdomen. His first kiss was on the scar of the bullet wound two inches below her belly button. Butterflies took flight inside her stomach, fluttering and bouncing around as though trapped inside a corked jar. She didn't want the feeling to escape—ever.

His second kiss was slightly lower than the first—a different kind of kiss. To Haley, it felt like it wasn't a kiss meant for her. It was a kiss for the one that was growing inside of her. Part of him. Part of her. Bonded together.

He was kissing their baby.

53

FULL CIRCLE

Leaves of mottled yellow, rust brown, and burnt orange swirl around my ankles as I stand at the graveside. It's not exactly a grave... Just a brass engraved plaque on a small cement base surrounded by a neat plot of grass.

They never found the body of Tyler Finch, and I've often wondered what Ritter did with it. Maybe that was his gift to me, his sick legacy. Punishment that keeps on punishing. A piece of my past forever unresolved.

For some things, there is no closure.

I know one thing for certain. Ritter is dead. Same with Pritchard. And that's closure enough for me and for the families and loved ones. That's all I ever wanted to do when I first started this journey.

Crouching down, I brush away some leaves from around the plaque.

There is no glimmer of hope for Finch. I've read the forensic crime scene report. Finch died there in that abandoned warehouse on the outskirts of town. Ritter had set up a kill plot, clearing a path through the warehouse debris to an upturned chair in a small clearing on the floor. Finch's blood was on the ground and on the chair. The police later recovered the silver necklace belonging to Clarissa Mulligan, the girl who had been first crucified by Ritter here in Willow Falls last winter. On the necklace, they found traces of Finch's blood. The anonymous call to the police was Ritter himself, luring Finch unsuspectingly to his death.

He walked into a trap, and he didn't even know it. And Ritter would have made sure that he suffered.

A cool breeze ruffles my hair, and I stand, tightening the jacket around me. There's nothing left to keep me in Willow Falls. Jodie, my sister, is still here. Last night, I dropped by the house she bought. She has a new man in her life, and she told me they're trying to start a family.

I wish her well.

In the distance, my mother's grave is about twenty yards away, where I spent the last hour having a two-way conversation with her. My words, present, now. Her responses, just memories of how she would have responded, will never leave my head.

Fat, white clouds roll overhead, and there's a sudden frostiness riding the wind. I've come full circle, back to where it all began.

Ellie has moved to New York City into Beatriz's fortress apartment. It seems like that's her calling: to learn as much as she can on how to hunt down those who don't want to be found. Maybe Beatriz can rein in Ellie's temperament a little.

Dinner at Beau's place last night was nice. Walking in, I almost expected to see Pritchard's head stuffed and mounted on the wall alongside his other trophies, even though the police recovered it from up at the Dark Rift where we had left it.

Parking close to his pickup meant I could quickly squat down and retrieve the black box tracker I had attached under one of the rear fenders without him or Ellie ever knowing.

During dinner, he told me he was sorry for going behind my back with Ellie. I told him I understood. All is forgiven. He then told me more about what had happened when the ground gave way, and he and Pritchard plunged into the Dark Rift. Apparently, they landed on a narrow ledge about forty feet below, the slice of earth they were standing on cushioning their fall. They wrestled for a few seconds before Beau realized there was only one way to ensure Pritchard would die. So, off came his head. The internal wall of the rift was hard cubic-like rock with enough hand and foot holds for Beau to eventually climb back out. He apologized that the climb took a while, saying that he was carrying a head, after all, and could only use one hand. A good excuse, I suppose.

"Why no more dogs?" I asked. "The cages are empty."

"Too painful. And they were irreplaceable, those dogs," he said. "And I prefer seeing the empty cages each day. It reminds me of the good times I had with them. Sometimes, I catch a glimpse of movement, a flash of fur out of the corner of my eye like their spirits are still roaming inside those cages."

But then he went all quiet and brooding across the dinner table. "Carolyn, there was something else down there... on that ledge."

"Like what? I guess all sorts of things fall into that hole."

"No," he said. "Something... wrapped up... in a tarp, tied with rope." Then, he said nothing for a while. And when he spoke again, his voice seemed cold, unearthly. "An object. Big."

"An object? You're sure?"

"Pretty certain."

"Did you touch it? Did you... unwrap it?"

"No, but I went up real close to it, though. It was dark, but I've got good eyes in the dark. Hunter's eyes. And... the smell."

"Smell?"

"Just slight. It's not as strong anymore as it once would have been. It had been down there for a while on that ledge."

"An animal?"

"It wasn't no deer. No animal."

Then, he looked at me with dead eyes. "It was a body. Human. I know what a dead person smells like even after they've been left for a while to rot down to just skin and bones."

Then, he shook his head like he was trying to shake off a bad dream. "Like one of those bodies I've seen in photos scattered up the summit of Mt. Everest. People just walk by like it's a normal thing to see. I just wanted to get the hell out of there. I figured they would recover it when the authorities returned for Pritchard. I left his headless body there so they could. As proof he was dead. Could have just as easily rolled him over the side."

A recovery team did rappel partway down into the Dark Rift, but they never found Pritchard's body. The ledge he and Beau landed on had apparently collapsed and broken away. Pritchard's decapitated body had fallen with it—along with whatever it was that Beau had seen down there—into the depths of the earth... gone forever. I imagine that place, the Dark Rift, holds many secrets. Secrets that are best left uncovered.

And Beth Rimes is a million dollars richer, thanks to the reward. It took some coaxing from me for her to get off her ass and apply for it—and more than a few phone calls to Dan Miller at the FBI to convince him that she deserved it—that she'd done the most out of all of us to find Pritchard. The rest of the ragtag posse agreed.

It seems like Pritchard's severed head was enough to get Uncle Sam to cut Beth a check, which she promptly used to snap up a lovely waterfront home in the Florida Keys at a bank foreclosure sale for a fraction of its worth. These interest rates are killing everyone.

Stepping back, I thrust my hands into my pockets.

Ben seems happy, too. He called me last week. Haley is pregnant, and they are expecting their first child in the summer. They asked if I could be godmother. I'd like that, I told him. "It will be my honor."

I'm happy for them. Really, I am. I know we couldn't have gotten back together. It wasn't wishful thinking; it was just a spur-of-the-moment thing when we finally sat down and spoke for the first time in so many years. It's like when your life has been empty for so long that you suddenly crave the emotional security of past relationships, old, familiar surroundings, and dust-covered hopes and dreams you once had. Then, seeing him again after all these years and talking properly to him made me realize that I had moved on from him. That I didn't want what I thought I had wanted. Now, I understand the phrase, *Careful what you wish for.* All those feelings and emotions I once felt for him are gone. Sure, we will remain good friends. But that's it.

However, I can't help but still feel a little resentful that everyone else's lives seem to be dropping neatly into place—all except mine.

One thing I do know for certain is that my body cannot take much more of this. Maybe it's time to settle down. I've been given a second chance, and my last scan showed that I'm still all-clear, which is the best.

The winters in Willow Falls are too cold. It also has too many bad memories for me. I want someplace warm, in the sun, close to the ocean with long walks on the beach, soft sand between my toes, and salty fresh air. It's no fun on your own, though.

Wherever the next stage of my life takes me, I want to share it with someone. Someone who I can see a future with. Family? Kids? Maybe.

After Ravenwood, Aaron Wood called me to see if I wanted to come back into the fold of the FBI. Dan Miller then called me within the hour and tried to convince me as well. He got the same answer that I gave Aaron. I'm no longer the career animal I once was because I'm not the same person I once was.

I crouch down again, kiss my fingertips, and press them to the cold brass plaque. "Goodbye, Tyler." A single tear runs down my cheek.

Trudging back to my car, I think about warm, sunny days and soft sand, sunsets of fire and brimstone, lazy days spent in bed, and a man's recent warmth that I can still feel on my skin as he lay next to me.

Opening the car door, I pause and look up at the fluffy whiteness above. Something icy, soft, and floaty lands on my cheek... then another. I tilt my head back farther, close my eyes, then open my mouth. And like a big kid, I start catching the first snowflakes of the season on my tongue.

It's the first day of winter. A day I never thought I would see again.

54

SISTERS FOREVER

The nightmares are gone, and I hope Carolyn's are too.

Before, when he was still alive, each night, I would wake to see him standing in my bedroom behind the thick window drapes. Those ugly work boots he wore poking out from beneath. Scuffed and scarred, the leather skin of one toe split open like a wound, part of the steel cap showing—the sound of his labored, rasping breath. A sound I vowed to end. And I did. I'm not ashamed to admit that I enjoyed killing him... playing my part in his demise.

Now, I don't see him anymore. All visions of him died the moment he died, as I knew they would. I don't wet my bed anymore. The suicidal thoughts are gone, too. Now, I want to live, to breathe, to live life to the fullest on my terms.

Memento Mori. Remember, you must die. Some day. Just not today.

I still sleep with a gun. It makes me feel safe because there are other monsters out there. I'm always armed, even here, in this state. I know it's a risk, but I don't care. I drive everywhere. I don't fly. It is so much easier.

Central Park is covered in a fresh dusting of snow—a picture from a fairy tale. It's wonderful. The cold morning air is bracing, fresh, and clean. I feel born again, transformed into someone new.

But my old self, Emma, still lives inside me, and she always will. I love her for how she has helped me grow into the person I am today and who I will become in the future.

Emma has her own dark secrets, tucked up and well hidden inside me, too. No one will ever know where I buried them, the two from high school. They both deserved what I did to them. My revenge for what they both did to me, leaving me bloodied and so violated on that cold, tiled floor.

Occasionally, I will walk down that dark passageway in my mind where there are other doors. Doors I have created that open into rooms I have built to house memories I would rather forget. Then, I realized that such memories, no matter how terrible, serve as reminders of what we have endured during our lives. What has made us more resilient, thick-skinned, determined, harder, and at times... colder.

I only have a few such memories. Instead of fearing them as I did before, I now want to harness them collectively and fashion them into my own destructive monster. A monster for the good, to help the innocent and the wronged. A monster that I can call upon at any time, unleashing it from the cage within me, as I have done in the past.

Is my monster stronger, more powerful, more destructive than the ones I will face in the future? Only time will tell.

I see her walking toward me, all wrapped up in a woolen hat and scarf and wearing a stylish jacket. *Carolyn.*

We hug, then sit down on the park bench. Thick, fluffy clouds drag overhead.

"How have you been?" she asks.

"I'm good. What about you?" There's a sparkle in her eyes, and it's not because of the cold air. She looks more vibrant, like me, reborn.

"I feel great," she says. "How's Beatriz?"

"She's good. She's dying to see you again. She's making lunch for us. We can't be too long. But I wanted us to meet, to talk beforehand."

There is forgiveness in her eyes, even before I tell her why we are meeting here like this. I take her hand, then blurt out, "I'm sorry. I'm so, so sorry. I didn't mean to go behind your back. And please, don't blame Beau, either. Afterward, I felt bad, guilty. But I had to do it, Carolyn. I needed it to end, and I was willing to sacrifice myself to achieve it."

Tears build in her eyes.

"There were only two choices for me, Carolyn. Either he was going to die, or I was going to die trying. It couldn't go on anymore."

She squeezes my hand but says nothing. She understands. I'm reminded of that day when I turned up on her porch at her beach house on the cliffs in Erin's Bay, pleading my case. "There was simply no other way. I had to do something in Ravenwood. We were never going to find him, and it had to end there, or I would have ended myself."

Carolyn lets out a deep sigh. "I know. But in the end, I have you to thank. Even though, at the time, I was angry."

I couldn't chase him anymore. Ravenwood was the final stand simply because the demons that were chasing me had finally caught up to me while I was at that homestead—the red barn. No one knew, especially not Carolyn, what I was contemplating before they had all arrived. Inside the barn, there was a thick chain hanging from one of the exposed beams. It was too long, but I had shortened it.

"If he had escaped again from Ravenwood," I continue, "then there would've been no escape for me from that town. I was going to die there."

More tears fill her eyes. "I know," she says. "You had to do it. He imprisoned you. He imprisoned all of us in our own minds. You had to rid yourself of him. You had suffered the most out of all of us under his hand." Carolyn hugs me, then whispers in my ear. "You didn't betray me, Ellie." She pulls back, and her gloved hand touches my cheek. "You could never betray me."

It takes supreme control for me not to start crying, too. "You are my sister, Carolyn; you should know that. And at times, sisters argue. They don't see eye to eye. But that doesn't excuse me for acting like a spoiled brat at times. And for that, I'm sorry. I'm better than that."

She shakes her head. "Don't apologize."

"So, what now for you?" I ask.

She looks around. "It's too cold for me here," she says. "I want someplace warmer." She looks at me. "Someplace close where I can visit you."

"I would like that." I know where she means, and I'm happy for her.

"And Beatriz?" she asks, "what has she got you working on?"

"Victoria Christie. She's like a female Dylan Cobb, only more refined in her methods."

"I know," Carolyn says. "She was involved in that Murder School game right here in New York City a while back. A group of privileged college students terrorized the city by committing the most audacious murders in public at some of the most iconic tourist sites."

"They had an online points tally board and everything," I add.

"The monsters these days seem to be getting younger and younger," Carolyn says, a mix of disgust and disbelief on her face. Then she brightens. "Anyway, enough of this depressing talk. I'm sure Beatriz will be wondering where we've gotten to." We rise together, and she threads her arm through mine.

"You've never been to her place before?" I ask as we begin walking, snow crunching under our feet.

"Never," Carolyn replies. "All I know is that it's like some hidden fortress. I don't even know where it is in the city."

"Well, you are in for a treat. It's like this crazy amazing warehouse, full of security measures and the coolest gadgets."

Carolyn pulls me closer, and we continue walking into the white, arm in arm, sisters forever.

55

SUNFLOWER

He was halfway across the parking lot of the Erin's Bay Police Department when he noticed the woman leaning against his police SUV. What the hell? Clayton Morelli thought.

It was mid-morning, a clear day, the sky that color of deep blue where you knew winter was here. But winters in Erin's Bay were never cold. They were mild, warm even some days, with clear blue skies and gentle ocean breezes just like today.

A silver trolley bag stood at the woman's feet. She stood five feet nine inches tall, with a lean, athletic build and shoulder-length chestnut hair. She had Audrey Hepburn sunglasses on, her face tilted skyward—a beautiful sunflower basking in the sunshine.

His pulse quickened as he approached. She knew he was there, walking toward her. Yet, her face remained tilted toward the sun.

Then, she smiled.

"You shouldn't be leaving your possessions lying around like that, ma'am," he said, trying to muster as much grouchy authority in his voice as he could.

The woman dipped her head to him, her eyes hidden.

"Why the hell not?" she said matter-of-factly.

"It's a quiet town, but there's no telling what strangers come drifting in and out. One minute they're here, the next they're gone, most likely with your bag too." He stood in front of her, his hands on his hips. She had filled out nicely since he had last seen her—in all the right places, too. And her hair was thicker, the sun catching the chestnut highlights just right, like she had tiny jewels among the strands.

"Strangers, you say?" she asked with a tilt of her head, giving him that coy look she seemed to have reserved just to annoy him.

He nodded. "Yes, ma'am. All kinds of undesirables blowing in from time to time, bringing all kinds of troubles with them."

The woman seemed curious. She slid her sunglasses to the tip of her nose, then angled her chin down and gazed at him over the top of the frames.

Then the man felt his loins stir when he saw her eyes—those bright blue-gray eyes that missed nothing.

"Is that so?" she said. She pushed herself off the fender of his SUV and slowly sauntered toward him. "What kind of trouble might you be referring to?" She glanced at his name tag. "Chief of Police Clayton Morelli?"

Morelli rubbed his chin theatrically. "Some people have an unsavory past—a bad history that seems to follow them wherever they go. We don't need that kind of trouble here."

The woman placed her hands on her hips, and what slender, grab-them-from-behind hips they were. "Well, that's good because my past is the past, and I've come here looking for a new life... a fresh start."

"We don't need no celebrities either in this town."

The woman raised an eyebrow. "Celebrities?" she scoffed.

"That's right. Some folk think just because they caught the number one most-wanted criminal in the land, they can just waltz in here, and everyone will just fall at their feet."

"Does that include the chief of police," she asked. "Falling at their feet, that is?"

"Yes, ma'am."

"Then it's a good thing I don't have a big ego."

"Not what I heard," Morelli shot back.

"Is that so?"

"Yep. They come here and do all sorts of damage, then up and leave."

"Damage? What kind of damage? Like break things?" the woman inquired.

Morelli nodded. "Break things—including breaking hearts."

The woman paused. Her coy expression faltered, then she quickly recovered her aloof composure and added a southern lilt to her accent. "Any other damage that you happened upon?"

Morelli smiled. "Yeah, now that I think about it. There was a cypress tree that sat right out on the cliffs a few miles out of town. A while back, someone set fire to it. You wouldn't know anything about that, would you?"

"I cannot tell a lie, Chief. I know nothing about that. Maybe the person did not like the tree. Maybe it reminded them of something that they would rather forget."

"Maybe."

"Well, I hope you catch the person who did it," the woman replied.

"Maybe I just have." Morelli suppressed the urge to laugh. "You just passing through?"

"Maybe."

"Maybe?"

The woman twirled her hand in the air. "Maybe I'll settle down here. It depends on how welcoming everyone is. I'm a stranger in these parts, but I don't want to be treated like one."

"Well, if you stay long enough, you won't be a stranger no more," Morelli replied. "And I can be friendly to the right kind of people."

The woman stepped closer... really close... the toe-to-toe kind of close.

He could smell her, her scent—sun-kissed skin and ocean-fresh.

Reaching out, she touched his name badge, then spoke in a low, husky voice. "How friendly might that be, Chief?" Her fingers began stroking his name badge.

Morelli swallowed hard.

Then, her fingers slid to the top button of his shirt and began teasing it out of its loop. She looked up at him. "I'd like to find out how friendly you can be."

Morelli shifted uncomfortably, his arousal growing slightly obvious. He crossed his hands in front of him.

Her finger slipped into the gap between buttons and touched his chest. "Maybe we should go back to your place, and you can show me some of your small-town hospitality?" she whispered.

Morelli met her gaze. "There's no sheets on the bed," he declared, repeating what she had said to him before their last good-bye. "Being laundry day and all," he added.

The woman's accent shifted into a full southern belle Scarlett O'Hara, and she batted her eyelids at him. "Sir, you are not a true gentleman, then, if you invite a young lady back to your place and your house is not in order."

Morelli slipped out his key fob and unlocked his SUV. "Frankly, my dear, I don't give a damn."

Carolyn Ryder rolled her eyes. "Oh, for Christ's sake!" she said, back in her own voice. His Rhett Butler attempt was genuinely cringe-worthy. "Shut up and get in the damn car."

Turn the page for
A WINTRY KILL, Book #5 and a continuation in
The Killing Seasons

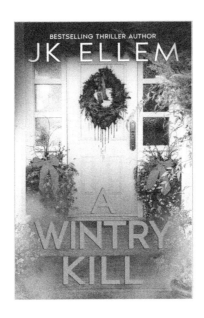

It's Christmas and Santa's Little Killers are coming for you!

Christmas has come to Erin's Bay, and with it, Santa's Little Killers, a sinister trio who sneak into homes at night and leave grisly gifts under the tree.

For Carolyn Ryder, it's her first Christmas in the bay, and she's looking forward to the wintry holidays with her new man, Chief of Police, Clayton Morelli. She's had enough of killers and carnage, and just wants the festive season to be filled with chilly nights, cozy log fires, and spicy eggnog.

But her plans soon take a nasty turn when the killers take a mother and daughter hostage. Can Ryder save them or will Santa's Little Killers Deck the Halls with their body parts?

If your Christmas gift under the tree this year is seeping blood... don't open it!

A Wintry Kill. Definitely not a cozy Christmas read...
Available through Amazon in Kindle and Kindle Unlimited
A Fast-Paced Read

Want more of Carolyn Ryder then
turn the page for a sneak peek of
A DARK KILL
Book #1 in the Erin's Bay Thrillers

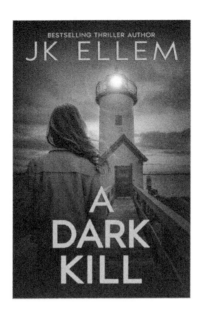

Ex-FBI discovers her hometown is full of hidden killers.

**"Monsters are everywhere.
You just can't see them."**

Spring has returned to Erin's Bay, bringing with it something dark and sinister. Someone has followed Carolyn Ryder back from Ravenwood to the peace and tranquility of the town she now calls home. An unfamiliar killer hides in the township, fixated solely on her.

Chief of Police, Clayton Morelli, doesn't believe Carolyn, thinks that she is overreacting when she tells him about the town's past. Undeterred, Carolyn finds an unlikely ally in the head-strong Abigail Brenner, a young, brash woman who knows all too well about Erin's Bay's buried secrets and evil history.

It's going to take all their courage, strength and cunning to defeat what's coming for them.

"This town's got history, a dark history, every town has. Erin's Bay isn't immune." The seasons come and go, but true evil never leaves.

A Dark Kill is available through Amazon in Kindle and Kindle Unlimited.

Ben Shaw from A Fall Kill is certainly an Intriguing character, with a mysterious past. He has his own series starting with **NO JUSTICE.** Each book in my NO JUSTICE SERIES is a self-contained murder mystery that you can read in any order. However, I do suggest you start with Book #1, NO JUSTICE.

Turn the page for a sneak peek of
NO JUSTICE.

Young man helps desperate woman from being bullied off her ranch by a ruthless small-town family.

In the small town of Martha's End, Kansas, trouble is brewing. Two feuding families, the McAlister's and the Morgan's, have been in conflict for generations, and Ben Shaw, a young and good looking man, soon finds himself caught in the middle.

With the Morgan family patriarch, Jim Morgan, ruling the town with his three sons, and dark and sinister things happening on the Morgan ranch, Daisy McAlister, the last of the McAlister family bloodline, is in need of help. But with his unique skillset and mysterious past, Ben Shaw may be the one to tip the balance in her favor.

Will justice be served in this town or will it take a higher power? Find out in this suspenseful thriller novel.

There is no justice in this town. But justice is coming...

No Justice is available through Amazon in Paperback and Kindle.

Ravenwood, from A Fall Kill, is my fictional small town in Maryland, USA. It's full of hidden secrets, heroes and villains, and dark deeds done at night. It's also where Haley Perez and the women of Mill Point Road live.

If you want to know more about Ravenwood and Haley Perez, then the next book you should read is **MILL POINT ROAD,** the first book in my RAVENWOOD SERIES. If you enjoy dark, domestic thrillers, evil neighbors, and small towns with hidden secrets, then I know you will love this series.

Turn the page for a sneak peek of
MILL POINT ROAD.

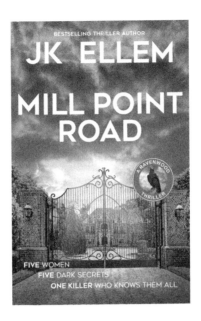

Thomas Harris moves into Wisteria Lane. Except these housewives aren't desperate. They're lethal...

Five women.
Five dark and sinister secrets.
One killer who knows them all.

When Rebecca Cartwright, young and recently widowed, moves into the exclusive gated community of Mill Point Road, in the town of Ravenwood, Maryland, she thought she had found her sanctuary.

Amongst the beautiful homes, manicured lawns, and high walls, she soon discovers that the other women on Mill Point Road are hiding dark secrets.

But no one knows Rebecca is hiding her own secret, and it's the darkest and most sinister of them all...

Synopsis

Detective Marvin Richards, a thirty-year veteran homicide cop from the tough streets of New York City moved to picturesque Ravenwood for peace and quiet. That was until a serial killer decided to dump their fourth victim near Mill Point Road.

Then there is Haley Perez, a rookie police officer who graduated top of her class, the only female in her entire cohort. And that can be a little tricky, especially when her fellow officers are now all male too. Some say she's abrupt, a little abrasive, and downright rude. Maybe it's just sour grapes from her work colleagues who have tried to hit on her with no success. But Detective Richards sees something else in this intense, young woman whose instincts and cold-focus are wasted as a patrol officer walking the streets downtown.

Richards enlists the help of Perez, and together they go on the hunt for the Eden Killer, a cunning, evasive serial killer whose victims are all young, male, and named Adam.

The trail of clues leads them to Mill Point Road, where they discover something dark and sinister is lurking in this seemingly tranquil and insulated Garden of Eden.

Mill Point Road is the Amazon US & UK #1 bestselling thriller from JK Ellem.

Mill Point Road is available through Amazon in Paperback, Kindle, Kindle Unlimited and Audible.

The Killing Seasons Universe

There are many characters and locations mentioned in the four books that make up The Killing Seasons, which are linked to other books I have written.

If you want a complete, immersive experience, then I recommend you also read the other books in the 'Universe' diagram. For example, Carolyn Ryder is the heroine in American Justice, Book #3 of my No Justice Series. If you want to know more about her back story, and Sam Pritchard, then you should read American Justice. You can read each book in my No Justice series as a standalone, and Ben Shaw is the main character in the series.

A Summer's Kill takes place in Erin's Bay, which is also the location of Hidden Justice, featuring Ben Shaw where he first encounters the villain, Dylan Cobb. There is a nice little story arc starting with Hidden Justice, then Raw Justice, and ending with Final Justice that you can follow. This arc will bring you back into the beginning of A Fall Kill if you wish to know more about Ben Shaw's journey and how he came to be in Ravenwood in this book.

Beatriz Vega, Carolyn's computer genius sidekick, also features heavily in my standalone crime thriller, Murder School.

Haley Perez, who is in A Fall Kill, is one of the main characters in my Ravenwood Series, set in Ravenwood, which you can also explore, starting with the first book, Mill Point Road.

Or, you can simply choose to just read the four books in The Killing Seasons and none of the other recommendations. However, if you are curious as to the origins of some of the other characters mentioned, their stories and past encounters with Sam Pritchard and other villains in The Killing Seasons, I have created this Killing Seasons Universe diagram for you to follow.

THE KILLING SEASONS UNIVERSE

Books also by JK Ellem

Ravenwood Series

Book 1 - Mill Point Road

Book 2 - Ravenwood

Book 3 - The Sisterhood

Book 4 - An Unkindness of Sinners

The Killing Seasons

Book 1 - A Winter's Kill

Book 2 - A Spring Kill

Book 3 - A Summer's Kill

Book 4 - A Fall Kill

Book 5 - A Wintry Kill

The Erin's Bay Thrillers

Book 6 - A Dark Kill

No Justice Series

Book 1 - No Justice

Book 2 - Cold Justice

Book 3 - American Justice

Book 3.1 Fast Justice –A Ben Shaw Road Trip Thriller #1

Book 3.2 Sinful Justice –A Ben Shaw Road Trip Thriller #2

Book 3.3 Dark Justice –A Ben Shaw Road Trip Thriller #3

Book 4 - Hidden Justice

Book 5 - Raw Justice

Book 6 - Final Justice

Stand Alone Novels

All Other Sins

Audrey Kills Again!

Taxi Man

Murder School

Also available by JK Ellem

Deadly Touch Series
Fast Read - Deadly Touch

Octagon Trilogy (DystopianThriller Series)
Prequel - Soldiers Field
Book 1 - Octagon
Book 2 - Infernum
Book 3 - Sky of Thorns - coming soon

Boxsets
No Justice Box Set 1
Deadly Touch, No Justice, Cold Justice

No Justice Box Set 2
American Justice, Hidden Justice, Raw Justice

Ben Shaw Road Trip Thriller Box Set 1
Fast Justice, Sinful Justice, Dark Justice

Octagon Box Set
Soldiers Field, Octagon, Infernum

JK Ellem was born in London and spent his formative years preferring to read books and comics rather than doing his homework.

He is the innovative author of short chapter, Hitchcock-style adult thrillers in the genres of crime, mystery, and psychological thrillers which have multiple plot lines that culminate in explosive, unpredictable endings that will leave you shocked.

In 2022 he was accepted into the Curtis Brown Creative, Writing Your Novel in Six Months course which he undertook in London while working on his manuscript for future submission.

He splits his time between the US, the UK and Australia.

Made in the USA
Middletown, DE
04 January 2025

68833500R00159